Also by Kevin J Garrity

Sparrow River

The Hatchery

UNCLAIMED PERSONS

By
Kevin J Garrity

UNCLAIMED PERSONS

Unclaimed Persons is a work of fiction. Names, characters, incidents and places are either the product of the author's imagination or are used fictitiously, and any resemblance to actual persons, living or dead, businesses, companies, or events is purely coincidental.

Cover Photo by Kurt Pankopf © 2014
Cover design and layout by Teemu J Garrity

Hammer Handle Press
6197 Quaker Hill Drive
West Bloomfield, Michigan 48322
(248) 757-2751
www.kevinjgarrity.com

Published by Hammer Handle Press

ISBN 978-0-9853310-4-7
ISBN 978-0-9853310-5-4   (eBook)

ACKNOWLEDGEMENT

For Cindy Lou Who, the strongest woman I've ever known.
You are the embodiment of true love.

And for my brother Michael. That your faith in all things good
might offset a few of my shortcomings.

CHAPTER ONE

Home

I am an immigrant in my own city. I was born to these streets, grids lined with the aluminum-sided two bedroom, one-bath bungalows of the postwar building boom. Aluminum-sided homes, not vinyl sided, not clapboard, not cedar shake. There was no glitz in their construction, just down-home honesty and utilitarian living for a generation that had too long been relegated to their parents' spare quarters and the refinished attics of their marginally better-off siblings. Aluminum siding. Plentiful, low-maintenance, easily washable aluminum exteriors. Asphalt shingled roofs. Plaster walls, not the cheap gypsum board they use today. Plaster over lathe, built by artisans, sweating, cursing Italian craftsmen in their sleeveless white undershirts, craftsmen that could lay an arched doorway or a coved ceiling without batting an eye. Any fool can throw a few screws into a sheet of gypsum board. Plaster walls require skill. Durable housing. Houses meant to be lived in, loved in, fought in. Children were to be raised here; ailing grandparents were moved in and eventually died in the "spare" bedrooms, that other bedroom that wasn't the parents' bedroom, while the kids slept two and three to a pallet in the sloped-wall confines of a recently finished attic. Children are small, after all, and do not require much space, and there was a time when taking care of one's parents in their old age was the right thing to do. It still *is* the right thing to do, but fewer and fewer are willing.

These wood-framed, one and a half story structures predate central air conditioning. Every house came originally equipped with a front porch, however small, so that summers could be spent relaxing in the cool evening air, watching the neighbors as they sat on their own tiny concrete fiefdoms. If you had money to burn, and some did but most did not, you added an aluminum awning as an afterthought. The awning would provide shade on the truly hot days, allow you to sit outside and watch storms as they rolled in from the North, and doubled the usefulness of your porch. Large wooden rear decks and patios, they didn't exist back then. Those arsenic-infused monstrosities with their carefully spaced baluster railings and permanent bench seating, they were a suburban construct, designed for a later time and a different sort of world. A world that in itself later spawned plastic decking and synthetic stone, for that more "uniform" and "pristine" look.. A world in which you didn't wish to see your neighbors, let alone know what sorts of things they might be up to, and where your tiny backyard parcel becomes a fortress sanctuary that keeps those that surround you at bay. Redwood fences, privacy fences, they didn't exist here either; at least not at first, not in those days. Back when these homes were built the goal was to be part of a new, shining community, not to bar the gate and arm the castle. Why would anyone in their right mind sit *behind* their house, where there was nothing to be seen? The street, now that was where all of the action took place. Porches should be constructed of concrete slabs resting over block foundations, and they should always face the road.

These cookie-cutter houses were of an era, that time of postwar enthusiasm and boundless horizons that eclipsed the forced frugality of the Big One and still predated the malaise and unrest brought on by the Next One. This neighborhood was like many on the outer rim of a once blossoming city, that Great Arsenal of Democracy and the home of Henry Ford. Close enough to the city core that one could work downtown, yet far enough to keep the "undesirables" from howling at the gates. "Undesirables," a catchall term that, on any given day, could include any and every ethnic or racial group that one might imagine. 'Not that there's anything wrong with them, mind you, you just don't want to *live* alongside of 'em.' The Poles had "their" neighborhoods, all of Hamtramck and many of the downriver communities. Italians dominated the working neighborhoods of the east side. Jews, well what could you really say about the Jews? With what happened to them during the war and all, you had to feel for them. And at the same time, they were different, too. Nobody wanted to let them get too close. They too were part of the "other."

This particular part of town was mostly Irish, 'undesirable' in their own right depending upon where you stood, but just as readily bolstered by false pride and xenophobia as any of the aforementioned groups. As long as you were able to perceive yourself as one rung higher up the social and economic ladder than the next group, well it was only natural that as someone grabbed beneath your heels, you'd keep kicking for the teeth. Yet the one thing that each of these subsets could all agree upon, the one inalienable truth that seem to be accepted across all boundaries and neighborhoods excepting but a few, was that they had to keep out the "Negroes," because indeed they were still "Negroes" in those days, before they became "blacks" and then later "African-Americans" and prayerfully, sometime in the future, maybe they

2

will just be "people." The one truth that these various groups all held was that they had to keep the Negroes out, or things would really go to hell.

I say "prayerfully," talking about that day when people might be viewed simply as people, and maybe this is a mistake: I am not, by nature, a prayerful man. I never have been. Don't get me wrong: in no way, shape, or form am I opposed to prayer. I envy those for whom prayer comes easily, although envy itself is yet another problem that occasionally plagues me. Yet for me prayer has never come easily. When I say things like "prayerfully," I can only wish that people somewhere are praying for good things to happen. Me, not so much. It's not that I lack faith. That I've got in spades. Unfortunately I have faith in all the wrong things. I could make a list, but I'm sure I'd leave something out. Maybe I should just say "hopefully," instead. It is a much less presumptive word, and takes God out of the equation. It suggests longing without expectation, and is much less likely to lead to disappointment. Mine or His. *Hopefully*, there will come a day when people are viewed simply as people. Much less chance of me being disappointed by an expected yet still undesirable outcome, excuse the pun, and less chance for God to find further failure with my life. He's got enough to do as it is.

So these were the dreamers. Laborers and insurance salesmen and schoolteachers and policemen and what have you, this mélange of people united almost exclusively by the twin facts that they had successfully convinced someone, somewhere, to lend them sixty-five hundred dollars to plunk down on a brand new home, and that their not-so-distant ancestors were incapable of growing potatoes back on the Emerald Isle. And the developers, those folks that designed and built this new neighborhood, most likely led by a group of accountants with slide rulers who laid it all out in tidy little rectangles that maximized company profit, were all too willing to package those dreams. The aluminum-sided, asphalt-roofed, two bedroom one-bath dream with a front porch included, conveniently located on the outer edge of the bustling city. Negroes not included.

I was not part of that postwar boom, at least not directly. I was a child, and in many ways I was a typical child, one of the many sleeping two or three to a bed in the refinished attics or cinderblock basements while Grandma rubbed ointment on her aching legs and slowly wheezed out her final days between the living room sofa and the second bedroom. Oversized families in undersized homes, thanks to the doctrine of the Catholic Church and the generally unreliable forms of birth control that were available to them. I was one of the later ones, born in the early sixties, and by the time I came along, my oldest siblings were off fighting their own wars, either with their spouses or with the North Vietnamese. In those days you moved out of your parents' house as quickly as you could and searched for a little room in which to spread your wings. You got a job, joined the army, did *something,* just so long as you didn't stay here much past your eighteenth birthday, because it was already crowded and the kids were all growing, and heaven knows there were enough mouths to feed as it was.

Mine was an uneventful childhood, and a majority of it I no longer recall. I'm unsure if this is by accident or design, my subconscious telling me not to bother, that the value of memories are no longer worth the effort of dredging them up. I was raised on the cusp of an era, just missing the innocence and unabridged hope of the fifties, and getting out slightly before the upheaval of the late seventies when things got really ugly. In retrospect, my youth was so benign that it failed to make an imprint on my own recollection. There are short snippets that still flicker to life, like the cuttings from a super eight film, swept from the editing room floor.

In the winter mornings we would put on stiff black dress shoes that were required by the Catholic school we attended. Our feet were then wrapped in empty Wonder Bread bags, which allowed the shoes to slide easily into our "rubbers," bulky, shin-high, waterproof boots with a series of clunky metal latches up the front. The metal latches on the boots would encrust with ice as soon as we encountered snow, rendering them nearly impossible to remove once we went back inside. I'm not sure why, but those god-awful boots stick in my imagination better than most things. Try telling a kid that you need to put your "rubbers" on nowadays, and wait for his response. A laugh, maybe, if you're lucky. Rubbers. Another word lost, or at least metamorphosed into something entirely different. In a world of neoprene, Gore-Tex and Velcro, it's often our language that dates us. We were behind the times even then, those post-boom kids. We just hadn't realized it yet.

We walked to school, rain, snow, or shine, because those were the days before busses. Well, not really *before* busses, but before school busses became a matter of fact for every child in America. We'd walk the mile to school, return home in the afternoon, quietly complete our homework, eat dinner, and try our damnedest to be seen and not heard. If one could devise a way to *not* be seen or heard, well, even better. You might squeeze in a game of street hockey or a snowball fight after dinner, and then off to bed.

In the summertime, we were shooed out the door shortly after breakfast and warned not to return until lunch time. After lunch we were told not to come back until supper time, and after supper told not to return until the street lights came on. These are the few recollections that I've retained of my childhood. They are broad-stroked, as if what remains of my youth has been painted by Impressionists. Bad Impressionists, Impressionists with day jobs, who only painted at night over a bottle of cheap merlot, split between friends. Occasionally one of my brothers or some other denizen of my past will remind me of a specific event in which I was a key participant, and that singular occasion becomes alive again. I will know instantly that the story is true, and wonder how I could have so easily lost the narrative of my own life.

The late kids, as I've come to think of myself and others like me, well I can't go into much detail there. We were fine, really, and to suggest otherwise might infer some self-bestowed sense of martyrdom. I think it has become fashionable to describe one's upbringing through revisionist history. But the upbringing of child number six, number eight, numbers eleven or thirteen by those aging Irish couples, well, let me just say that it was at best a benign style of parenting. There was nothing malicious there, no desire to shortchange us kids in any way. None of us were *hurt,* per se: we were fed and clothed and spoken to and properly educated and otherwise properly cared for. There just wasn't a lot of positive reinforcement. The adults, they were *tired*, is all, or maybe just preoccupied.

These tidy aluminum homes were never conducive to mass indoor living. They were places in which to sleep, to eat meals, to watch television quietly with adults seated on the sofa and kids sprawled across the floor. For most of those oversized Irish families, their version of the American Dream required additional space beyond the confines of their humble abodes, a little elbow room, so to speak. It demanded a porch and sometimes even an awning, a neighborhood park and a baseball field. It needed streets in which kids could safely run and play, and it relied heavily on faith. Faith that life would all somehow work out, faith that the kids would return home when the street lamps came on. Positive faith, that other kind of faith that I seldom have.

5

The aspirations, the fairy tales behind The Little House that Could, they were not my aspirations. They belonged to my parents, and a community of others just like them. It was a dream both generational and situational, a shining place for the displaced Gaels of southeastern Michigan; either that or a bunch of tin coated boxes for the drunken Micks, depending upon which side of the street you'd been born. I can't say exactly why they picked this particular neighborhood in which to settle, the Irish. Maybe they'd been kicked in the teeth a few too many times themselves, and sixty-five hundred dollars was the cheapest admission ticket they could find to a better world. It was possible they were merely naïve, thinking they were reaching for higher ground. It becomes hard to tell who is any higher on that life ladder, once you begin to look at things objectively. Maybe it isn't really a ladder after all, just a series of parallel step stools, set up for the amusement of the swags in the opera boxes. The rich get to watch as we clatter about, dragging others down with us whenever one falls. I knew this wasn't where I wanted to be growing up, but at the time, I couldn't put my finger on exactly *why*. Hell, I was just a kid.

To be fair, and not to disparage my upbringing or anything, by the time I came along the cracks in the mortar were already beginning to show. Not the *actual* mortar, mind you, because these damn houses were built to last. The materials used to build them might not have been the fanciest, but people still took pride in their craft back then. There was no poorly mixed concrete in those batches: you couldn't knock a hole in those basement walls even if you tried. No, I mean *figurative* cracks in the mortar were beginning to show. The bloom was off the rose, so to speak.

At some point the slide began. It was a subtle decline, those shiny new homes beginning to look just a tad the worse for wear, fifteen and twenty years after they were first constructed. All during this time, the time of my youth and the youth of others like me, the grass still got mowed on a weekly basis, the hedges were kept trimmed. Yet sometimes a roof cried out for new shingles, and that expense was postponed for an extra year or two. Fences were left unpainted; formerly snow-white wooden pickets bleached raw, eventually becoming rows of upright cattle bones in the desert sun. Examples of small neglect, sure, but neglect nevertheless. These were but symptoms, in fact, *precursors* to an unforeseen and accelerated collapse yet to come.

It could be, as I look back at that part of life from where I now stand, that maybe it wasn't the houses that were showing abuse as much as it was *the people* in those houses that were wearing out, because this was, remember, by and large a community of lower middle class Irish with limited resources. They were working stiffs, men with stay-at-home wives and too many mouths to feed. There were no Kennedys amongst the bunch, and few were likely to rise above the level of middle management. Their backs hurt from manual labor and too many hours spent on their feet. Their cars wore out long before the final payment came due. Expectations of what constituted "the American Way" continued climbing year after year, and all the while these self-styled dreamers were hanging on for dear life, hanging by their fingertips. Middle-aged men and women raising their six, their eight, eleven or thirteen children, each successive birth chipping away at rapidly diminishing reserves of stamina and joy. The body can only take so much before the mind becomes immune to enthusiasm.

I left this neighborhood long ago, shortly after my eighteenth birthday and the random freedom that coming-of-age implied. I say I am an immigrant, not because my parents were Irish, or second generation, hand-me-down Irish, however you wish to describe them. No, I stopped belonging to that clan of failed potato farmers one day after fifth grade recess, when Dominic Bonfiglio gave me a frozen face wash with ice crystals and snow, behind the playground of Our Lady of Sorrows Elementary. Dominic washed the Irish right out of me. That was but one step down a road, a road of attrition. Attrition of community, of belonging, of faith. Over time I became determined to no longer *be* anything: not Irish, not Catholic, not lower-middle class. I did not wish to be part of the great unwashed wearing rubber galoshes lined with empty bread bags. I would not be one damn thing you could put your finger on, no creed nor nationality nor faith that could be ground, face-down, into a snowbank. Just one hundred percent ready for the worst. I became a gypsy, a transient, waiting for my chance to flee, living in the moment. When that train arrived in the shape of graduation day, I didn't look back. Not for thirty years.

This isn't really about me, when you get right down to it, at least not directly. I don't believe that I've changed all that much, despite a lifetime of flight and denial. But then, how can one really tell? You can solicit outside opinion, sure, but even your friends, the ones who have known you the longest, well they're not the same people they were twenty or thirty years ago. So what are they really worth, those opinions you'd get? It is entirely possible that these others have changed, even your closest friends, and the world changed with them, and all the while you've been anchored in the same place, despite physically moving about. Tethered like those hot air balloons you see at carnivals that offer twenty-dollar rides. You might be hundreds of feet up in the air, getting bandied about by the wind, yet you're still connected to the very same ground whether you look down or not. It's just a thought. A theory, really, with no way to prove it or disprove it. This sounds a bit cynical, I know, but when you've seen some of the things I've seen, mistrust becomes second nature.

Now I find myself standing in the middle of a street. My street, if you'd believe it, a street both familiar and completely foreign to me. It is the street I grew up on. I stand here on a grey day in mid-November, with overcast skies and a cool breeze drifting in from the North. There is just a touch of winter's scent in the air. I should be wearing a jacket, but I'm not, standing here in jeans and a long-sleeved T-shirt. I can feel goose bumps erupting on my forearms, just enough of a chill in the air to get my attention.

I should recognize these houses, and in some respects they indeed seem familiar. I feel like some kind of amnesiac, recognition hiding somewhere in the back of my skull (if only I could locate it). There is something wrong with these houses. Their scale is off, the structures smaller than I remember. Trees seem taller than they once were or trees that I remember are missing altogether, and in rare cases, freshly planted trees exist in yards where once there were none. The cattle bone fences have vanished, ashes to ashes, replaced by the occasional chain-link compound and a "beware of dog" sign. This is a street full of houses in various stages of abandonment. I squint up and down the block, trying to bring things into tighter focus. The aluminum siding and screen doors have recently been stripped from most of these homes, raided for scrap in the middle of the night and sold for pennies on the dollar. Windows are gone, in most cases replaced by plywood and riddled with gang graffiti. Front porches, those premium seats to the theater that was this neighborhood, have been reduced to rubble. I am playing a game for one called "What Is Wrong With This Picture?"

There are still some stragglers living here, those that lack either the means or the inclination to move along. In each of the two houses that remain inhabited, a set of eyes peers out at me from behind cast iron security bars and bed sheet curtains. And glass: there is still glass in these few windows, between the iron bars and the dusty sheets. I am being watched. I cannot see their faces, but I know who they are. Clearly they know me. These are not the people that built this neighborhood, nor are they the kids that were raised alongside of me. They are the "others," latecomers to the city's dying dance. Low income renters that appeared long after the original denizens fled to the security of the suburbs. Long after the last of the Irish cut and ran. I have become the "other," the one who is out of place. If in some way I have remained tethered to this spot, nobody on the ground seems to have noticed. My connection to this place, while real to me, doesn't exist for them. As far as they are concerned, I was always up in the stratosphere: I am the past. I do not touch their lives, soaring in my balloon above, believing that I had left. I stare at my feet, shamed briefly by the realization that I am intruding in what is now their world. "I am not here to steal your window air conditioner," I whisper to myself. "I do not want to swipe your high-security screen door."

I look up, and it takes a moment to grasp that the house in front of me is the very same house that I slept in and ate in and watched television in for the first eighteen years of my life. It is unrecognizable. I reconstruct it from memory, placing skin back on the disfigured skeleton that stands before me. It is all there, the aluminum siding, the wooden framed windows, the hefty front door, even the painted wooden address numbers, but it is there only in memory. So here I stand an immigrant in my own city. Born to these streets, but not necessarily *of* these streets. A stranger in a strange land. Wondering how I got to this place, and where one might go from here.

CHAPTER TWO

Fallen

"Who the fuck are you?"

I am startled back to the present. The voice, a woman's voice, forceful and angry, bellows directly behind me. I turn slowly, trying to discern who is yelling at me, and wondering what I have done that warrants such vitriol. Is it because I turned my back on this city, moved away, that I somehow contributed to its demise? The voice is coming from an older woman, possibly in her sixties, though I can't be sure. "Black don't crack," someone once said to me. It is a generalism if ever there were one, but in this case it's true. The woman has beautiful skin. Perfect, smooth skin. If I only saw her face and not the rest of her, I might peg her for twenty. I see more than just her face. I take it all in, all the while failing to respond to her question. She is a solid woman. Grey hair pulled back tight, wearing a floral-print house dress and green, fuzzy bedroom slippers. Maybe sixty pounds overweight. She's making her way down the concrete front steps, their withered surface long ago laminated with one-by-six inch wolmanized deck planks. The steps are not easy for her, I see, her gait more of a waddle than a fluid stride. She must have problems with her hips or knees. Every step sends a wave of pain across her taut face. Restrained pain. She's coming anyway. There is anger in that waddle, a body stirred into motion against its very will. I still guess her age as easily sixty something, but she might only be forty-five. It is so hard to tell. Life can be hard around here.

"I said who the fuck are you, standing in front o' my house?"

She is now at the bottom of the steps, pausing long enough to grasp the railing and catch her breath after all that walking and yelling. This is not something she does every day, rushing outside to shoo away some vagabond standing on her side of her road. She is sweating profusely.

"That's a good question," I mumble, because I don't have any better answer. Who the fuck am I, really, and why did I come back here? Why, after twenty odd years, am I standing outside some stranger's home in a war-ravaged city, mining through a past that I once couldn't abandon quickly enough?

"What did you say," she asks, cautiously taking two steps along her front walkway in my direction? She must think I am crazy, a middle-aged white man standing alongside the street's curb with no obvious purpose. Her front walk is nearly as fractured as her porch steps, I notice, staring at the path beneath her feet. Miniature sprouts of green have infiltrated the cracks in the individual concrete slabs, further leveraging those fissures so that frost and snow can work their magic from below. It will all be gravel in another few years. She has stopped walking, no longer quite within reach of the porch railing. Her wide-legged stance is meant to say 'I'm not fooling around with you,' but it might just as easily mean that she has nothing left to lose. She is pitched and ready for battle.

"That's a good question. I'm sorry. I used to live here," I offer, still unsure just how much of an explanation this grey-haired woman wants. "Not in your house. I lived over there. That other one. Right across the street." It makes sense, somehow, seems logical, somewhere in my head. I am here because I want to examine my past. I realize my voice sounds weak, like I myself don't entirely believe that story, either. "I am really here with the power company; I came to shut off your gas." "I'm a scrapper, looking to see if there is anything left that hasn't been stolen from the abandoned homes up the way." "I'm a slumlord, thinking about buying every house on this block for less than two thousand dollars apiece. I'm going to raise your rent and make your life even more miserable than it already is." "I want to buy some crack, and I heard there was a place to score around here." Any of these would sound more sincere, more believable than the truth.

"Well, get the hell out from in front o' my house, whoever you are. Ain't you got more sense than to come around here scaring people in the middle of the day? Crazy fuckin' white boy."

I should apologize, I know. She's already turned her back to me and started up the steps, has reached the wrought iron bars of her high-security screen door and is entering the house. Much quicker in retreat than in attack, as if she's had plenty of practice. I am probably not the first "crazy fucking white boy" to be chased from in front of her home. She is a brave woman, a woman fighting the good fight. The steel inner door closes tight, and I hear the metallic thunk of a deadbolt lock cylinder. "I'm sorry," I yell out, having finally found my voice. It comes too late. She is gone, the bed sheet curtain pulled back across the grimy glass.

I turn my attention back to my childhood home, or what remains of it. How did it get this bad? Uninhabitable, beyond reclamation. I never knew, living in that house for all those years, that wood siding lay beneath the aluminum facade. It is for the most part bare, that wood siding. Here and there a dollop of mustard yellow paint clings tenuously to the weathered fibers. Mustard yellow, a hopeful color. Why was there paint beneath the siding? Was the aluminum exterior an afterthought, an expense that was financially out of reach during original construction? It wouldn't make sense to paint the wood if you knew you were going to cover it with aluminum. Yellow, joyful yellow paint. If my parents were still alive, I'd ask them, only they're not. What else have I failed to notice?

The swing set, *my* swing set, still stands in the yard behind the house, visible from the street. How did the scrappers miss *that*? This was one of the few homes that never had a garage, and the view to the back yard is unobstructed. The swing set is made of two-inch, galvanized steel plumbing pipe, fitted together by Uncle Walt and my father one hot summer afternoon long before I was born. The red paint, lead-based, last-for-a-lifetime fire-engine red paint, has weathered to a hue that more closely resembles dried blood and chalk. Chains supported by eye hooks and the two wooden seats are long gone. Even in my youth, a solid pine plank only lasted four or five years before it eventually rotted clean through. It is unlikely this swing set has been given new seat boards in a decade. The chains that supported the plank were inexpensive, and rusted out almost as readily. How did the scavengers, vultures picking the skeletal remains of a dying city, miss this load? The heavy pipe structure still stands. They'd already removed the chain link fence, posts and all, and the house's metal siding. Was their truck too full with copper plumbing and aluminum rain gutters to bother with low value steel pipe? Maybe the three feet of cement, into which each of the four corner posts had been sunk, was too much of an obstacle, although that seems unlikely. People around here are generally resourceful. Why wouldn't they have just hacked the legs free with a saw, a few inches above ground level? Why wouldn't they have tied a chain around a leg and yanked it from the earth with their truck? Another minor mystery in a world full of riddles.

I hear voices coming from somewhere up the street, a young couple fighting, I'm unclear about what. A car door slams, an engine starts. I look in that direction and see an older model Pontiac Bonneville tearing away like their house is on fire. Maybe it is. Maybe the fire was set deliberately. A few other cars are parked along the curb, most looking as if they've been deserted long ago. A battered Buick sits stripped of all four tires and rims, axles resting on the pavement. The license plate is missing, and the rust stains on the pavement around it suggest that this Buick has not moved in a very long time.

This is a dangerous place, even in daylight. I have heard the stories, I read the news. I've been told by those that stayed around longer than I did, but still managed to get out. Some never did; get out, that is. They are footnotes in a history that few bother to learn, a history I carry inside of me. Armed robberies of dollar stores, front doors kicked in and elderly people beaten and robbed for grocery money; most of it doesn't even make the paper. It has become the norm. While I have not lived in this city for a very long time, I still know its secrets.

One set of eyes is tracking me from across the way, a sliver of motion in the tiny exposed corner of a window. This neighbor is not so brave as that first woman, is unwilling to run outside on a crumbling porch to confront a stranger. He is watching, waiting, wondering what new scourge has arrived in his world.

There is a loud percussion a few blocks over, a reverberating "bang" that could have been caused by many different things. If I were elsewhere, in Seattle or Chicago or Boston or even in one of this city's wealthy generic suburbs, I would assume that the sound has emanated from a car accident, or was a minor disturbance created by ongoing commercial construction. For all I know, that is exactly what has occurred, a distant car crash, a bulldozer doing one of the things that bulldozers do. But I have heard the stories, I read the news. A loud percussion can also mean gunfire, or an explosion from an illegal natural gas hookup. It can be the start of a meth lab going up in flames or a myriad of other things, none of which do I want to bear witness upon. I am not frightened, not rushed to flee, but it is my cue to get moving. I have learned to play the odds, and the odds suggest that whatever has happened, not so far away and accompanied by a loud bang, will not bring good things to those who remain nearby. The grey haired woman was correct: I don't belong here.

13

My truck is parked up the street, three houses away. I turn casually and saunter toward it. I do not want to make any sudden motions, do not want to attract additional scrutiny from the four eyeballs in those two intact households. Anyone lurking in one of the many unsecured properties will see nothing other than a middle-aged man, walking with confidence in his stride. You cannot show fear on these streets. Fear is a pheromone that attracts predators.

The sky is slate grey, that cold color of polished steel that you only get in the low light of late autumn. No one ever believes me, but I swear you can smell the onset of winter on certain days, and this is one of those days. It is cool outside, sweatshirt weather. Winter is approaching sure as the dawn. A cold rain begins to fall as I reach the truck, heavy liquid beads as big as nickels exploding all around me.

I slip my key into the driver's side door lock and reflect that someday, somewhere, I will own a car that comes with a keyless remote. Most people have them, those little electronic key fobs. You push a button, the vehicle doors unlock. Presto! Magic! Someday I will own one, but not this day. My truck is still serviceable. The Ford is old but still manages to go where I need it to go. It is a little hard on gas. I've thought about trading it in on a newer vehicle, but I've done the math: the cost of upgrading isn't justified by the savings in fuel. And while the truck is not much to look at, the risk of theft is limited. There is no street cred in boosting a beat-up truck. I'll probably drive it until it dies. There are days when I wish the truck's death would come sooner rather than later, but not in this neighborhood, not on this date. Get me past the city line, dear truck, and then you may go peacefully to your grave. Better yet, die in your sleep, tucked nicely away in the comfort of your own garage. If only I had a garage.

I drive north, my hood pointing toward McNichols, or Six Mile Road, as it is better known. The Mile Roads run east and west, streets laid out like a giant grid composed of mile-wide squares. That makes it almost impossible to get lost in this town, as long as you stay away from a few confounding areas like the lower East Side. The grid doesn't cover the *entire* city, just most of it. The streets on the lower East Side were laid out on the French colonial lot system. You can get seriously lost over there, streets running cattywampus with hard-to-remember names like Cadieux and Vernier. French colonials must have done some heavy drinking in their day; I am glad I am here, and not there.

Sometimes these Mile Roads hide beneath an alias. Six Mile Road is identified as McNichols; Five Mile pretends to be Fenkell Street. It doesn't fool me. Only the ancients used those proper names. For most of this city, these streets are now and forever Mile Roads. Ignore the nameplates on the corners. I am driving on the far western edge of the city; I am still on the grid. Just one half mile and I will be out of this neighborhood, out of a past that is no more. The sudden downpour is already fading to a cold, steady trickle. The outside temperature drops ten degrees in less than five minutes. I dial the windshield wipers back slightly, matching the tempo of the wipers to the tempo of the rain.

More empty houses, more of the same. More squalor. I drive by the local elementary school, long ago deserted and windows shuttered. All the while I am dreaming, thinking about the old lady who came out of her home to yell at me, dreaming about the swing set still waiting to be stolen. I turn right instead of left because I am distracted. I'm driving by rote, deeper into the bowels of the city. In less than a mile I turn right again onto Grand River Avenue, one of the few major thoroughfares that run on the diagonal.

I pass other landmarks, unrecognizable from the world I once knew, metamorphosed into different waypoints for the present generation: storefront churches, payday loan joints, beauty salons. Bright colors and hand-painted signs compete for attention, gaudy placards screaming at one another. It all seems so strange. I glide past a once familiar haunt, but Walsh's Pub is no longer Walsh's Pub: it has become something other. The Irish that came to drink here have long ago emigrated to points north and west. What is the point of an Irish Pub without the Irishmen? No Micks, no money, and so things have changed. I reach the Southfield Freeway, a north-south gutter with sheer poured concrete walls, and realize that I should turn around. I've seen enough for one day. In the driveway of a gas station I perform an illegal U-turn. I'm not concerned about getting pulled over by the police; not for such a minor offense, not around here.

Now I'm driving west, out and away. I stay on Grand River Avenue, the big road that, if I had the time or the ambition, could carry me clear across the state to Lake Michigan. In most of the towns along that route, this road first laid on top of an old Indian pathway, Grand River is classic Main Street, America. It is populated by mom and pop stores with well-kept facades and hand swept sidewalks, five or six lanes of pure freedom. It is the kind of thoroughfare that evokes the soul of this country, or something like it. That's not what I see here: here there are but more wig stores, more cellular phone shops, more cast iron bars and steel grates defending vulnerable windows and doors. The rain has picked up again. I adjust the wipers to a faster pace.

The city limits beckon just a few miles further ahead. That used to mean something, twenty or thirty years ago. It used to mean safety, security. It used to mean regular police patrols, too, and home values twice that of the neighbors stranded on the wrong side of the invisible divide. It was the difference between East Berlin and West Berlin, even for the shoddier suburbs. Now, not so much. The markers are still there, "Welcome to Redford Township," and "Enjoy Beautiful Southfield." Clarions beckoning visitors to whichever bastion of white flight they are about to penetrate. While the road signs remain the same, the differences between city and suburb have merged and blurred, the once-obvious demarcation lines breached. I pass the city limit, in this case a few blocks the other side of Telegraph Road, and the improvements are negligible. There exist just as many boarded up storefronts here, with maybe a few more struggling businesses clinging desperately to life. It won't be long before they, too, get pushed to the next community west. Thus the core rots from within.

I suddenly realize that I'm hungry. It is late afternoon and I have yet to eat. I had two cups of coffee before I left the house this morning, but my stomach is beginning to rumble. Two miles further still and there is a hot dog stand where I used to work; I assume it still exists. I'll know in a minute or two. It is a vestige of another time, really, a throwback to the fifties with linoleum floors, chrome stools and red vinyl booths. The menu is made up of hot dogs with goofy names and unfathomable choices of toppings, homemade chili, loose meat sandwiches, Greek salads. I worked there briefly, back in high school, and was treated like family. In this case "family" meant underpaid and ordered about like a poorly trained dog, which has its charms, but gets old rather quickly. The entire time that I worked there I felt both loved and broken. Before too long I realized that there was more money to be made elsewhere, more love to be had with fewer insults. I decide I'll stop there (if the place still exists) and grab something to eat.

I see the sign up ahead, a giant rotating wiener rising high above the building. I swing into the parking lot and quickly realize that the original building has long been demolished, replaced with a more efficient, generic diner. It looks like every other diner built in the last twenty years. I admit the original building was a dump, long past the point of usefulness. I remember putting blue tarps on top of the roll roofing to prevent rain from leaking through, and old car tires to weigh down the blue tarps in the wind. The floors and the vinyl were both peeling (even then), and it was obvious the owners weren't making the kind of money necessary to replace or repair anything. It was a dump, but it was *my* dump. That *sign*, that fiberglass four-foot hot dog on a steel pole, is the only original fixture that remains. I hesitate, wondering if I should bother going in. Another piece of my past has fallen to the wrecking ball. Do I really want to eat here? My hesitation lasts only a moment. My gut gurgles loudly. Food is food after all, and we all have to eat somewhere. I step inside.

CHAPTER THREE

A Child in the Wilderness

"What's your name?"

Now it's my turn to ask the questions, as I sit at the last booth on the left and stare at the figure seated on the far side of the table. This girl is young, probably no more than fifteen or sixteen years old. Light complexion, brown eyes, a shiny metal stud stuck through her right nostril and a small gold hoop through her left eyebrow. Skinny. The girl is woefully skinny. She is dressed all in black; skinny black jeans that hug her not-very feminine legs. Black high-top tennis shoes. A black T-shirt with some sort of silver graphic logo peeking out from underneath a black, zip-up hooded sweatshirt. Black nail polish, chipped and obviously not a high priority in her world. Either black is the color of the day, or the girl is a ninja in training.

She looks at me, no discernible emotion on her face. "Buy me some lunch." Nothing more. She still hasn't offered me so much as her name. I flinch, noticeably. This is not at all what I expected. I'm not sure what I expected, to be honest. I guess that I expected to come into the restaurant, sit down at the booth farthest from the entrance with my back to the wall (the better to watch who comes in and who exits out the lone door), and order a middling lunch that would cost something less than ten dollars when all is said and done. I would eat that lunch. Quietly. Alone.

Instead, I sit in the booth farthest from the entrance, my back to the wall, and have yet to see so much as a glass of water before I'm joined by this sullen waif, silently planting herself across the table from me. She is a kid, really, maybe sixteen years old. A kid rapidly becoming a woman. I chew on that. On closer inspection, she may be older than fifteen or sixteen. She could be twenty years old. I'm bad at this, guessing someone's age. I finally decide that she's closer to twenty than she is to fifteen. Not a kid becoming a woman, but a woman disguised as a kid. I can't tell exactly. She is part of that broad class, a category I've grown to think of as "too young for me."

In high school, "too young for me" was the age of consent. The magic cutoff has risen over the years to include those who were below the legal drinking age, then those who hadn't completed college, those who had yet to find their first "real" job or have their own apartment. Nowadays, "too young" would include any woman up to age forty, any female who can rise from bed in the morning without sharing the same aches and pains that run through the knees and backs of people my vintage. If your life has been heartache-free until now, we probably don't have a lot in common. At this rate, "too young" will soon include all females premenopausal and eventually expand to those too young to collect Social Security.

"Buy me some lunch," she repeats. It is not an order, it is not a plea. It is a casual statement, as if we are friends who have previously agreed to meet for this informal get-together. I'm still trying to figure out where she came from, what gives her the audacity to arbitrarily join a strange man at his table and tell him to pay for her meal. Is she a prostitute? A beggar? She is wet, I now notice, soaked through from the rain. There is very little fat on those bones, and she tries to hide the fact that she is shivering. Just then the waitress arrives, sets two glasses of water and two sets of silverware rolled tightly in paper napkins on the table before us. The waitress then drops two plastic-laminated menus down and mumbles "Just the two of you?" as if we have disappointed her by not bringing others. I nod in agreement. "Back in a few minutes," she tells us.

"All right," I say, to the girl, not the waitress. I'll buy the girl something to eat. Because I'm not sure what else there is *to* say. If I decline, if I refuse to provide this girl in black some sustenance, what then? Do I really think she'll up and leave me alone? A girl with this much aplomb, this much *chutzpah,* as my Jewish friends would say, I do not think she will walk away quietly. She will make a scene, invent some lie, jump up waving her arms around while screaming "rape."

An eyebrow lifts on her side of the table, the one without the metal ring piercing through it. *"All right?"* she asks. She is surprised that I acquiesce so easily.

"All right," I answer. There is a momentary silence.

"Susan," she whispers.

19

It is a name; it is a start.

"Susan what?" I ask gently, fishing for more. I don't wish to scare her away. I am intrigued. Who is she, this strange beast?

"Just Susan," she replies, still concentrating on her menu. A meal will no longer buy you a last name, it would appear.

"Just Susan," I agree, and glance down at my own menu. The offerings have changed. The once glorious selection of delicacies - everything from a bacon-wrapped dog, deep fried and smothered in cheese, to a French Poodle Dog to an Italian Dog to a Beanie Weenie - the cornucopia of gastronomical joy that once was has been pared down to the very basics. Chili, onions, sauerkraut. Mustard, ketchup, relish. This is no longer a gourmet hot dog stand, despite the giant fiberglass wiener spinning somewhere in the rain above our heads. We are in a diner: a generic, run-of-the-mill diner. It is a "Coney Island," as they're called around here, offering a variety of soups and sandwiches, twenty-four hour breakfast service, and "petite filets" on the dinner menu. No more gourmet hot dogs, just meat in a tube with a handful of condiments, fiberglass wiener be damned. I'm not sure why I expected more.

Our waitress returns, an overweight and overworked woman who already knows that pleasantries are a waste of time, that regardless of whatever effort she puts into the service, my tip will not be adequate, not in a place like this. I guess things haven't changed that much after all. "What would you like?" she asks, matter of factly. No, things haven't changed much at all.

"The lady" speaks first, which frankly shocks the hell out of me. For a moment I forgot she was sitting there, this silent waif. I was distracted by Miss Personality in the blue jumper with the dirty half apron. "Just Susan" orders two coneys with everything, a large order of chili cheese fries, and a gyro sandwich. With a chocolate shake, thank you. A rather expensive lunch date. You'd never guess it by looking at her. Where is she going to put it all? She looks like a wet, possibly underage rat. Apparently she hasn't eaten in a while. I order two coney dogs, hold the onions, and a Coke. I won't be getting out of here for under ten bucks, that's for certain. Miss Personality takes our order and heads back behind the counter. She pours some Coke into a glass with ice, brings it over and sets it in front of me while casually giving me the snide eye, then walks away again. She must think I'm on a date, or something like a date. Silence. I look at "Just Susan" again, and don't even know where to begin. She's looking at me, but in a disinterested sort of way. We are in a showdown of sorts, similar to a schoolyard staring contest.

"Do I know you?" I finally ask. I just can't take it anymore, wondering who this person is and why she invited herself to my table, on my dime. "Have we met?"

"No," Just Susan answers shyly. She diverts her eyes. She's fidgety, restless. She's taken a handful of paper napkins out of the stainless steel dispenser on the Formica tabletop and is nervously shredding them into tiny pieces. She stacks them neatly in the form of a tower along the windowsill. *Is she an addict?* Probably not, her skin is too smooth, her eyes too bright, her speech too concise.

"Why?"

"Why what?" she responds.

"Why any of it? Why my table? Why me?"

"I think I might know you," she answers back.

I pause, not sure what to make of this. Thus far our conversation, such that it is, has been perfunctory, if not circuitous. We have used our inside voices, spoken in even tones, with no significant content to our conversation. We have been in a polite social setting, invited to high tea with a friend of a great aunt. I realize that perfunctory isn't really working for me. The rain falls steadily outside the window, the hood of my truck glistening with sweat. I gaze through the glass, watching the beads of water rolling off the hood. Finally I speak. "I thought you said we haven't met."

"We haven't."

Now I'm truly confused. Maybe this is like the game show Jeopardy; I must voice my answers as a question. "We haven't met?" I echo, my voice trailing up at the end of the sentence.

21

"No, we haven't met, but I might know you." The waitress sets our plates on the table before us without another word. She is going back behind the counter for the chocolate shake. Susan digs in without waiting.

I think about this. There are many ways a person can know another person. Maybe she knows my *type,* although I prefer to think that I don't really have *a type.* Nobody does, really, like to think that they are so readily categorized into a *type.* Old dude? Easy mark? Hippie do-gooder? What is my *type?* Everyone likes to think that they are unique, singular. Maybe she knows who I am, has somehow heard mention of me. That, too, is unlikely. I didn't come in the door and announce my name to the world at large. I've not led a consequential life, and I'm no celebrity. I'm rapidly running out of ideas. Maybe it is time to shift topics.

"How's your food?" I ask.

"About what you'd expect," she rejoins. It's hard to argue with that. Mediocre fare hasn't prevented her from inhaling most of her meal, however. She's down to half the shake and a fraction of the chili cheese fries. I'm still working on my second coney, too consumed by thought to match her culinary intake. I devote my attention back to my plate and finish the meal in silence. We sit there for a few moments, stealing glances until our eyes finally lock: we quickly look away.

Miss Personality reappears and asks if we want coffee, but I decline for the both of us. "Just the check, please," which she promptly whips out of her dirty half apron and slips face down on the glossy surface in front of me like she already knew the answer. I must not look like the coffee drinking *type.* The waitress strides away and I rise slowly, ready to pay the tab. It comes to twenty-one eighty-two. "It was great dining with you. We'll have to do this again sometime," I facetiously tell Just Susan. I drop a five dollar bill on the table for the tip and head to the front of the diner.

The cash register sits atop a glass counter by the door. A stocky bald man is working double duty, taking customers' money while manning the grill. He grunts as I approach, reaches for the chit without asking how I liked my meal. He, too, already knows the answer. He takes my money, wordlessly making change from the till. Twenty-one dollars and eighty-two cents. My hope that I could get in and out for under ten bucks shot to hell. I look back over my shoulder, and the girl is now slipping out from her seat at the booth, slowly walking toward me. She is eighteen, tops, I've decided. I lift my hand to her in a casual wave of farewell. She fails to acknowledge the gesture, just keeps walking toward me in silence. No word of thanks, no explanation of why she chose *me* to hit up for a meal; she is an odd girl in a city full of oddities.

Outside the rain is falling at an ever-steadier rate. It is coming down hard, little steel pellets bouncing off of everything and everyone in sight. The clock over the doorway claims that it is only five p.m., but the sky outside looks like it may as well be nightfall. The slate sky has become one continuous sheet of angry molten metal. I open the diner's door and sprint to my truck with keys in hand. I turn the lock and quickly dive inside the driver's side door, slipping behind the steering wheel. I am jiggling the key in the ignition when a gentle thumping on the passenger-side window startles me. The girl is standing there, rapping on the glass with her closed fist. She is already drenched. I pause, wondering what she wants this time. She raps even harder. I make a decision, one I may soon regret, and hit the little button that unlocks her door. I wonder if I have just opened Pandora's Box.

"Give me a ride?" she asks, her head and torso leaning inside the truck but her lower half still rooted to the ground, sucking up rainwater like a sponge.

I pause for an instant. What is her game? Remember, I tell myself, you were born to these streets. You might not be *from* these streets, but you know the games, have seen the charades and the sleight of hand tricks and the strong-arm tactics of the scammers and the thugs and the hookers and the junkies. Tell her no. It is that simple. "No," a two-letter word that will make her go away. She will leave, flag down some other passing driver, tell him her sob story, inflict whatever hell she has in store on his life in lieu of mine. "No. Just say it," my inner dialogue implores.

"Hop in," my disembodied voice finally croaks out. *"What the hell?"* I silently curse myself. *"What the hell am I thinking? What am I doing?"* Instead, my calm, other-self, the one that currently controls my vocal chords, gently warns her "But no funny stuff."

"No funny stuff," she agrees. She relaxes a little bit. Maybe she was worried that *I* was the one that would try some "funny stuff" on a girl less than half my age. There is relief in the air now that the ground rules have been established: assuming that those rules are honored.

23

"Where are you going?" I ask. I'm still uncertain why I let her in my vehicle. I could ask her to leave, tell her I've changed my mind, that I have somewhere I urgently need to be. I still have time. The truck is idling, the blower motor trying to summon enough heat from the engine to erase the fog that collects on the inside of the windshield. *Throw her out now*, I think, *before it's too late.*

"Wayne State," she replies: the University, Midtown, the heart of the city. Not in the direction I was heading, not whatsoever, but I say nothing. I pull out of the parking lot, make a Michigan left, one of those complicated maneuvers indigenous to this state whereupon you must first turn right, merge to the far left lane of the multilane divided roadway, and wait for an opportunity to turn back around in one of the little paved pullouts which bisect the median. Allegedly they reduce traffic congestion, Michigan lefts. I doubt that. For sure they frustrate out-of-towners. They are dangerous for the uninitiated, but not so for me. Another right turn onto Telegraph Road, southbound three more miles and I pull onto the Jeffries Freeway eastbound, yet another of those concrete ditches that serve as arteries to the Motor City. Thirty minutes and we'll be in Midtown. We ride in silence.

"Aren't you wondering why I asked you for a ride?" It's the first thing she's said since we left the restaurant. We've already passed Greenfield Road, been in the car for over ten minutes.

"Not really." It's all I've got. I'm still wondering why I bought her a meal: I haven't gotten around to the part about unlocking the passenger side door and agreeing to play taxi driver to a girl who can only spell trouble.

"Not really?" The other eyebrow, the one with the gold hoop dangling from it, arches upward. It's good to see that both sides of her face are equally lissome.

"Not really. I figure you didn't want to walk in this downpour."

"Humph." Susan knows this is a load of crap. She turns her head away, gazing out the passenger side window at the parade of ugly that passes by. I steal a peek at her, this feral animal that has come to me for a handout. She might seem tame, but I know she can bite in an instant. *Little steps*, I think, *take tiny little steps.*

24

More miles, and we come to where the Jeffries meets the Edsel Ford Freeway. I still call it the by its original name, the Edsel Ford. To nearly everyone else it is known as I-94. The state decided sometime in the eighties to deemphasize proper names on the interstate freeway system. Signs were changed, history was erased, families were forgotten. Numbers are easier to memorize than deceased dignitaries, perhaps. I may have given up on families that settled the Mile Roads, but the Ford Freeway is still the Ford Freeway in my mind. It's another concrete ditch, no matter what else you call it. Warren Avenue is coming up quickly, our exit to Midtown, and to Wayne State University. I get over to the right lane, preparing to exit the freeway.

"Are you a student at Wayne?" I query, because it seems like the logical thing to ask, and I want to break the ice with *something*. It might give me a clue as to her true age, her true intentions.

"No." One word, terse. "Well, on and off," she eventually embellishes.

"Live in the area?" I'm fishing again, but she's not biting. Still driving, now on surface streets, dodging potholes high above the express gutter system, hoping to learn something from this thing that sits next to me before she vanishes.

"I have friends in the area." At least she doesn't mince words. "Here," she says, pointing to the curb. "Pull over here," as if I might not have heard her the first time.

We're still on Warren Avenue, just past the light at Cass Avenue. Marwil's Bookstore squats low by the corner. The University's main campus is across the way, a jumble of students and staff scurrying to and fro in the rain. A variety of buildings, architectural hodgepodge from different eras, dot the campus. The Main Public Library sits hidden around the corner, the Institute of Arts across the street from it. University apartments, bistros, coffee shops: she could be going anywhere. I want to ask her who she is meeting, will she be safe, and is someone expecting her at home (wherever "home" might be). Thoughts race through my head, yet I remain silent. I don't have a right to ask, or to care. *Tiny steps*.

"Thanks. I'll see you later," she says, slamming the truck door shut and striding briskly away. She hurries back towards Cass, where she merges into the pulsating mass of souls at the corner. They wait for a light to change, and when it does the mass rumbles across the road as one herd. She is gone before I can ask. Just Susan.

CHAPTER FOUR

The Relics

You're probably wondering how it is that I happened to be back in this city. "The D," as they are currently calling it, as if by shortening Detroit's name you can somehow make urban blight seem both fresh and vibrant. Come ye hipsters, one and all, for a limited time only we are providing an opportunity for you, *you personally*, to participate in a one-of-a-kind Urban Renaissance! Faith, young techies, upwardly mobile twenty-somethings without kids, ye rising professionals, you have to have faith. Believe in yourselves, believe that you can *create* where, for forty or more years, there has been only destruction! Get in on the ground floor, the Initial Public Offering of the New Millennium lies before you. Buy a loft apartment, start a business, kick start the future, because no one else is going to do it on your behalf. Unlike previous generations that have tried and failed, communities that have died and bailed, you are savvy, you are fresh, you are edgy. That is the sales pitch of "The D," and a few reckless souls have even gone so far as to answer the call. I'm not one of them. No, I'm here for much more mundane reasons.

It was after college, after Muskegon and then Columbus, after South Bend and Des Moines and Sioux Falls and Boise and a couple of other whistle stops in between, while I was living and working in Portland (Oregon, that is, not the other one). I had a small apartment in Portland, a third-floor walk-up studio that was more than adequate for housing myself and my meager possessions. It wasn't a fancy neighborhood, but it wasn't a dump, either. It was close to reliable public transportation, night life, good food, and the smell of the ocean when the wind blew just right. I had an income, what most people would refer to as a job, but which I preferred to think of purely as a source of revenue. I focus on the end, not the means. I was legally employed and paying my bills. The nature of my employment, while not particularly stimulating nor rewarding, was irrelevant: waiting tables, keeping books, selling retail clothing, in the end they're all the same. Income. That Thing You Do that permits you to do the things you *want to do*, or at least *some* of the things you want to do, *in your real life.*

One night my brother Patrick phoned me at my Portland place, well after midnight. I remember that I was alone in my apartment, sitting in my one overstuffed chair that I'd picked up from a local resale shop. It was a Thursday night in February, and I was watching the Marx Brothers while having a small glass of scotch (not *too* small). I recall thinking, like I generally do when the phone rings late at night, "Somebody had better be dead." It is not a pleasant thought, I know, but what is the alternative? Usually such a call is nothing but a wrong number, or some distant friend who has had too much to drink, a friend who has run out of local shoulders on which to cry. It's not as if I was thinking 'I hope somebody is dead,' a different thing altogether, because it is not the same thing, not at all. I don't *wish* death upon anyone. I just don't like people calling me in the middle of the night unless they have a *damn good reason*, and there are fewer and fewer circumstances in life that constitute a *damn good reason*.

So I answered the phone thinking it was probably some drunken friend from back East pestering me (as I sit alone in my tiny apartment on the West Coast) since I was the only one that he "knew would still be up" at three-something Eastern Standard Time: that or some idiot searching for "Rhonda" or "Shaniqua" or some other stranger I've never met. It never ceases to amaze me how few people can dial a phone number without error. "Shaniqua does not live here," I might tell them, and then the person will proceed to grill me as to what I'm doing with his woman. Idiots. So I answered the phone with anger cocked and loaded, finger on the trigger. I was surprised to get Patrick with the news (not totally unexpected or earth-shattering) that my father had just passed away from a heart attack. He'd been sick on and off for a while, hadn't been taking care of himself ever since mom died. Refused to move out of that rat hole of a neighborhood, even after everyone he knew had moved on years before. At least he went quickly. Patrick was being the responsible kid, letting everyone know, making the calls. "Sorry to bother you, brother, I thought you'd want to know. It would be great if you could make it back for the funeral, we understand if you can't. Gotta go, still have calls to make. Let us know if you're coming in for the service." And then he hung up.

I muted the sound on the Marx Brothers, although at that particular moment the screen was full of Harpo, so what was the point, really? I was muting a mute. Later I digested Patrick's call, sipping scotch alone in my third-floor walkup, and realized that this death had even less to do with me than you might expect. I hadn't been back in years, had disconnected physically if not entirely. It was hard to get overly emotional about the loss of someone that quit living long ago. Still I knew that I should return for the funeral, put in an appearance, and so I did: in and out, three days of mourning in the western suburbs without so much as setting foot near the old homestead. That was a little more than seven years ago.

I'm not saying that was a turning point or anything, more suggesting that a seed was planted. It wasn't long after this that two friends of mine, a couple I'd met while I resided in Portland, and with whom I'd been hanging around with for a little over a year, decided to move back to Virginia in order to take over the family business (something to do with real estate investment). Two weeks later a woman whom I'd been dating (on-and-off for the entirety of two months) repatriated to San Diego to care for her ailing grandmother. The seed sprouted and took root.

Others left. I gradually came to the realization that Portland was but a way station in the lives of those whom I considered friends, a brief respite before they each moved along to where they were *really* going or inevitably returned from whence they'd come. Moving forward, I could continually replace my current crop of Portland friends with a new, fresh crop of recent arrivals, or I could join the hordes in choosing a less transitional stop along the railway of life. When the day inevitably came that I should die, hobbled and disheveled, keeling over from a heart attack on my way up three creaking flights of stairs to my sparse Portland apartment, well who was going to stick around to "make some calls?" It took me a few years to come to grips with the idea, but Detroit, for all its flaws, was slowly beckoning me home.

Patrick long ago emptied Dad's house, my childhood home, splitting the sentimental pieces with our sister and discarding the rest by the curb (one Wednesday at a time) over the course of the summer. By the fall of that first year he sold the house for thirty-eight thousand nine-hundred dollars, a sum so paltry it would make you laugh if you lived in New York or Boston or Los Angeles. In reality it wasn't a bad return on a place that cost so little to begin with, and that provided safety and shelter and security to a large family for a good portion of those years. It is not even a bad return when measured against the values today, just seven years later, with similar homes selling at auction for as little as five hundred dollars apiece. Seriously, five-hundred bucks. That should tell you something.

29

There was a brief spat, during that time in which the house was first being purged, over "the relics" as they have come to be known. My mother, the official keeper of all things familial and esoteric, had (for most of our lives) a glass-front shadow box hanging on her bedroom wall. The shadow box contained what looked like a few chicken bones and a folded piece of paper. At some point, and forgive me that I do not remember this with more precision, my mother had explained to us kids that the bones were partial remains of some departed saint or other, brought over from the "family cathedral" back in Ireland. They were extremely valuable, Mom said, smuggled out of the country when my ancestors fled the Emerald Island. Like I said, I do not remember the details very clearly and I probably shrugged the story off even then because who in the hell was truly going to believe that this family, this rabble of potato-eating hellions wearing hand-me-down clothes, had any significant connection whatsoever to a "cathedral," in Ireland or anywhere else?

In any event, my sister Mary got it into her head that Patrick, while emptying the old homestead of Dad's crap and clutter, had decided to keep the priceless "relics" for himself. Mary claimed rightful ownership of the shadow box and all that it contained. She was not going to speak to Patrick, not now nor ever again, unless he produced the relics and handed them over. The relics were promised to her vociferously and repeatedly by our mother (or so she argued), despite the absence of any witnesses to these claims. The result was that my brother and my sister were no longer talking to one another, and Mary was no longer talking to *me*, either. I'd refused to side with her in this dispute, refused to cut off all contact with Patrick, and that was enough to cast my lot with the dark side.

Patrick and I are not particularly close; we haven't been in a long time. I'm not siding with him, not exactly. It's not as if we had much contact with one another to begin with. He is older than me, for one thing, and even when we were young we ran with different crowds. Patrick was one year younger than our brother Bobby, who died in a tragic car accident at the ripe old age of nineteen. Our eldest sister, Margaret, passed away from liver disease while I was just a tyke. This probably explains why the Church encouraged large families: spare parts. It's now just the three of us. I can only speculate as to the truth of the matter regarding the relics. It didn't help that when Mary called me to plead her case, asking me to get involved in retrieving her supposed inheritance, it was well after two in the morning my time. I answered the phone with "Who the hell died?" and that invariably set the tone for the remainder of our conversation.

For what it's worth, I don't think Pat currently has or ever did have this mysterious shadow box and its chicken bones. It is possible the box got thrown to the curb with the rest of the crap my father owned, its contents mistaken for the remnants of last month's KFC dinner. Maybe one of the other relatives took it right after Mom died, and nobody noticed until Dad, too, was dead and buried. There are great mysteries and small mysteries: this I categorize as one of the latter. The one thing I *am* certain of (without any trace of doubt) is that the "relics" were indeed priceless artifacts smuggled over from the old country: they were part of the world's largest cache of pure blarney, Irish fertilizer, that gift that keeps on giving.

So, despite the family war raging over the relics (which has carried on for these seven years and counting), I heeded the call and returned to the city in which I was born. There is no hipster inside me, no "cool factor" beneath the surface. I don't go "clubbing," or attend raves, or whatever it is the next crop of "in" kids do in the city with their spare time. I long ago abandoned any illusions of upward mobility. Don't get me wrong, I am not a recluse, not by any means, but I live a solitary existence. I have friends, or at least I did have friends until I moved back here. Nevertheless I do what I want, when I want, excepting those hours when it is necessary to earn a living. It's a lifestyle that doesn't lend itself to lasting attachments. I am not a mover, not a shaker: I don't aspire to be. I am a survivor, a cat whose most enduring quality is the ability to somehow land on his feet. So far.

The first order of the day, once I'd committed to returning, was to pare down my meager belongings to the extent that everything (and I mean *everything* that I owned) could be fit into a standard pickup truck pulling a five-by-eight U-Haul trailer. It wasn't that hard to do, really. Once you discard sentiment, nearly everything in life is disposable. I quit my job. Again, not a difficult thing to do when you've nothing vested. I gave two weeks' notice, but I don't think they'd have cared if I just walked out the door at the end of my shift, never to return. The apartment took a little more effort, as I still had four months remaining on a one-year lease. I've learned that even the toughest landlord inevitably understands that there is no wringing blood from a turnip. A man whose life fits comfortably in one truck and a trailer, a man who surreptitiously ups and leaves his job, well you might as well just let him be on his way. It took a few days of idle threats back and forth before they finally agreed to retain my security deposit and call things even.

I didn't come directly back home: it is not in my nature. I took a swing through Provo and Salt Lake, if you can believe it, just to see how the other half lives (it turns out they don't live, at least not in Provo and Salt Lake City). They go to great lengths to avoid living, hiding their liquor low behind the bar and chastising pedestrians who dare to smoke and drink coffee in public. Every day is Judgment Day in those two towns. Less than a week there and I'd had enough, hot-tailing it to Albuquerque. I spent a month exploring the Southwest, one of the few parts of this country I'd so far neglected to examine. I probably could have stayed in New Mexico, forever wandering through that beautiful desert, but I recognized the dangers that would present. Again, should I decide to stay there, who would "make some calls" on my behalf, when all is said and done? I could not stay in Albuquerque.

So here I am. The rental trailer is parked alongside Patrick's garage where it won't offend his neighbors, at least not for a few days. They've got rules, you know, *standards* (and a homeowner's association that is more than willing to let you know if you step across the line). I should probably unload the thing and return it to the rental agency, but this is my first day back, my first *full* day back, anyhow, and I'm not even sure where to begin. Maybe I should find a place to live. Let me get my bearings, figure out what's what. The swing past the old homestead, that certainly put to rest any ideas I might have entertained of city living. *It will all work out*, I tell myself. *I am a cat. I will land on my feet*.

CHAPTER FIVE

Midtown

Bells ring as I walk through the door, that jarring little alarm that tells the person working behind the counter or sorting inventory somewhere in the back of the store that he has a new customer. He either has a new customer or a new threat.

"Can I help you?" The clerk is young, thin. Skintight jeans, a long-sleeve T-shirt with the logo of some band I've never heard of on the front. He is probably a student at the University when he's not working here. I do not recognize him, but then, why would I? Most likely he wasn't even born the last time I set foot in this store.

The store was christened Antique Cool, back when I myself was a skinny student with the logo of some obscure band emblazoned across my chest. It was where you went when you needed something cool to wear, something no one else would have. I worked there for a few brief months, long, long ago. It was another whistle stop on the wagon train of life. As long as I was in Midtown, it made sense to stop by.

The store sits just north of the big university, an unassuming block building strategically chosen for its proximity to 40,000 plus students with some discretionary income, and sporadic pockets of successful entrepreneurs and business owners sprinkled throughout Midtown and downtown. There is also a tight-knit enclave of artists, community activists, and martyrs close by, most residing in what is commonly referred to as the Cass Corridor, south of campus. The store has easy freeway access from all directions, a critical feature when appealing to people who don't necessarily *live* in the city. The downside to this location is that the Corridor also comes with a historic inheritance of a nearly equal if not larger population of junkies, hookers, and street people drifting through the neighborhood, each trying to get a leg up on anyone and everyone they meet.

The owner, a gruff Armenian who knows his trade, made a business of purchasing clothing in five-hundred pound bulk bales that he had shipped in from New York or Los Angeles. We'd pop the wire on those giant bricks of compressed garments, sorting through them as quickly as possible to separate the wheat from the chaff. The "good stuff," stain-free shawl-collared suits from the sixties, rayon dresses, poodle skirts and gabardine sweaters or the like, we'd steam and put out on the rack (with a hefty markup, of course). Most of what remained was packaged back up and sold to a rag picker for pennies on the pound. Most of the initial investment was made back from the rag picker. The rest was all gravy, at least the way I remember it. We'd fill out the remainder of the sales floor with things found at estate sales, auctions, and from one particularly resourceful insider volunteering at the St. Joseph's Thrift Store. The good stuff that people donated to charity never quite made it to the sales floor at St. Joe's.

I didn't last long at Antique Cool. I was far too restless, and there was a bigger world calling.

"CAN I HELP YOU?" the clerk repeats, louder this time, as if I might be hard of hearing or slow of mind. I can't argue with the assumption. I might be slow of mind.

"Just looking," I respond. That seems to satisfy him, at least for now. He steps behind the counter. I remember that this is where the owner used to keep his big .44 caliber magnum pistol. The kid is reading a book, possibly required material for some class. Then again, it might only be pulp fiction. That is all I ever read when I worked here: cheap mysteries, popcorn for the mind.

The clerk glances up occasionally, long enough to make sure that I am not stuffing merchandise down my pants. I never had to pull that big cannon on anyone, but the owner did, more than a few times. Eat or Be Eaten, one of the credos of the inner city. That's one of the many reasons I got restless working here; I wasn't willing to die for five bucks an hour. It occurs to me that this kid might be silently thinking the same thing. He is reading, but one hand rests on a shelf, barely out of view. I wander down the farthest aisle, appraising the inventory and hoping Skinny Clerk Guy isn't trigger-happy.

Antique Cool would be a misnomer nowadays. Nothing on this sales floor is truly "antique," as in, "old inventory." The old stuff, the "cool" one-of-a-kind find that everyone was seeking back in the early eighties, well that pipeline dried up a long time ago. It was inevitable. Even as we picked and sorted our way through the discarded fashions of the fifties and sixties, a tide of mass-produced crap from the seventies (think leisure suits and wide disco collars on polyester prints) was rapidly flooding and clogging the system. That stuff, that ugly, useless, synthetic blight, it is still waiting its turn to be "retro," waiting for blind nostalgia to kick in. Good luck with that one. Davros changed the name of the place to "The Emporium" a decade or so back. It sounds more current.

No, I'm not sure what to call the inventory in the store now. I'm certain it sells well. "Reproduction Retro," maybe. New stuff made to look *kind of* like old stuff, only with cheaper materials and less attention to detail. Nothing wrong with that, but if you have an eye for the original stuff, the *good stuff,* you notice the minor differences. If they did it the old-fashioned way, hand sewn piping and cashmere, no one would be able to afford a single shirt. That accounts for some of the merchandise. "Rock Star Wardrobe" makes up another significant chunk of the store's offerings. There are things you'd want if you were the lead singer in a band, or wanted to look like you were in a band and didn't happen to be shopping in London or Paris or New York this year. Leather jackets, racks and racks of leather. Then there is a smattering of urban hip hop stuff and a few tilts at bondage-light. There are two other customers currently in the store, both young women of about college age, kicking tires in the "Rock Star" section towards the back.

"Is Davros in?" I finally ask the skinny clerk, because if I tell him I'm looking for "The Big Man" (my nickname for Dav) he'll probably figure I have a bone to pick with management. Sensitivities run deep around here, and many people have bones to pick with Davros. More often than not, the bone picking is justified.

"Just went to get something to eat," he answers, not bothering to look up from his paperback (a Walter Mosley novel, it turns out). At least he has good taste in literature.

"You expecting him back?"

"Sooner or later," still not looking me in the eye. His attention is now focused on the two young ladies giggling in the back of the store, who look as if they *might* be planning on stuffing merchandise down their pants. He sets down his book, decides he *might* just get up off his seat and see if he can help the two ladies in the back. On the other hand, he obviously doesn't want to leave me standing there alone, lurking so close to the register. It is possible that the women and I are working together, that they are merely acting as decoys. Maybe I'm the decoy. The kid has been trained well.

Just then another bell rings. The employee door behind the counter opens, and Davros bursts in. He has always entered every room with gusto, as if he expects to receive a round of applause whenever he makes an entrance. I fail to clap. The kid immediately hops up and rounds the counter to go check on the two women in the back. The choice has been made for him.

"Davros, how are you?"

"Great," he says, looking me over. "How about yourself?" He is putting up a front, a generic smile plastered across his face. The twinkle in his eye, that mischievous gleam of awareness that indicates he and he alone knows your secrets, is missing. He is scanning the files in his head, seeking a match: one more person in this world thinking 'Who the fuck are you?'

I realize immediately that he doesn't recognize me, this man who once prided himself on knowing each and every customer by name. He is frantically processing the thousands of faces stored in his memory, trying desperately to recall. Was I once in a band? Did I work in the deli down the street? Did he meet me at some shindig, meet me in a bar? Employee, customer, thief? Friend or foe? I am frankly disappointed, not that I have a right to expect better. He hasn't seen me in forever. I am about to cave, reintroduce myself like some wide-eyed freshman, when the twinkle reappears. In Davros' eye the switch of recognition has been thrown.

"When did you leave, nineteen eighty-eight?" This man is good, I'll grant him that. Not perfect, not as sharp as he might have been when he was thirty, but still, damn good. My spirits rise.

"You got it," I lie, figuring plus or minus a year or two is no big deal. "How's business?"

"Good. You know how it is, up and down. Are you looking for something in particular?" No small talk, always the salesman. Most people mistake it for greed, this back-to-business demeanor. I was once told by a friend that Davros is always sniffing for that last dollar, hidden in the lining of your shoe. I don't think that is true, not at all. Trade and currency are the official language of his life. He has invested all of himself, not just his money and

36

his time but his heart and his passion, into this store and the community that surrounds it. He couldn't *exist* outside of The Emporium. The money is just a bonus.

He has other interests, sure. But it all comes back to this place. I'll admit he's a mercenary, or at least he was a mercenary. I recall when he used to transact occasional business outside of the store, always legal (if only just), and he always demanded a significant piece of the pie. Sometimes he demanded most of the pie. He stepped on toes. Everything came with a price because cash was the common denominator in his world of competing interests: it's how he used to measure success. I wonder if that is still true, or has he, too, changed? Yet as ruthless as he sometimes seems, Davros is at heart nothing but a big kid. He is fearlessly loyal to his friends. He wants to be loved. He'll do anything for you, if he likes you. Just don't screw him over, and don't expect too much of a discount.

"Not really, I just came in to say hello." I can see the momentary disappointment sweep over his face. The smile fades ever so slightly, the wattage feeding that eye twinkle is cut back by half. It is only for a moment, and then the power is restored. Maybe the disappointment is imagined. "I haven't been in here for a while," I tell him.

"No shit. You should check out these jackets over here. What are you now, a forty-four long?" He is right, of course. His eye for sizing has become more precise over the years. The jackets are fresh, they are stylish, they are only slightly overpriced, and they are decidedly not vintage. I haven't bought anything "new" in over a decade, and I'm not about to start now. Who cares how I dress, anyway, a man my age? Most of his inventory is meant for a younger audience, but I humor him anyway.

"These are interesting, what are they going for?" I ask politely.

"Two and a quarter, but for *you,* " with a pause for suspense, emphasis firmly on the *you* as if he and I are the very best of friends and this is a deal he is only willing to offer to me and his mother, God rest her soul, "for *you,* one ninety-five." The gleam in his eye is back in full force.

I am impressed. Not just that he can say this with a straight face and appear to mean it, but I am impressed that he legitimately *believes* his own sales pitch. I am fairly certain that if Davros' mother were to rise from her grave and walk through that front door, he would willingly offer her the exact same deal. "But for *you,* Mom, only one ninety-five."

"It *is* beautiful, but a little steep for me." I know he couldn't have paid more than one and a quarter wholesale for the piece. He knows that I know. Besides, the jacket is not really my style, hasn't been for many years. As they say, you can't kid a kidder. The twinkle is again losing intensity, but only slightly.

Skinny Clerk Guy is busy in the back of the store, showing sexy little cocktail dresses to the two young ladies. Either the clerk has decided the two girls are potential customers and not just lookie loos, or he is putting on a dog and pony show for Davros' benefit. "Every customer should be personally engaged. Every single person that walks through that door is a potential customer." I remember The Big Man's spiel like it was yesterday. This kid must have heard the speech as well, and for him it probably *was* yesterday, and yet again this morning.

"Come and have a seat with me," my long lost friend suggests, and pulls a pair of padded stools around to the front of the counter. "What brings you back to the neighborhood?" He is serious now. He sits, and I place myself on the stool next to him. He's gained weight, I notice, at least twenty pounds. He was a bull of a man back in the eighties: not much older than me, but seemingly more mature and imposing. Davros was muscular, a man to be feared, with a fuse and temper to match his size. Now he is slightly soft around the middle. There are wrinkles beneath his eyes, and where there are no wrinkles, there is puffiness. Still powerful, but it's obvious he's spending more time at the deli than at the gym. He must be in his mid-fifties, I realize. That alone should be excuse for him having found a little pleasure in life, having cut back on his workouts. I still wouldn't test him.

"I figured it was time to come home," I tell him. I'm not sure what else to say.

"Why now?"

"That's a good question," I chuckle, and Davros laughs along with me. We sit and watch the kid for a few moments; he's still trying to make a sale to the ladies in the back. They're lookie loos after all, and it's obvious that he's not going to get them to bite on the matching mini dresses that will "have every guy in the club drooling, trust me, I know." No way is he going to close that deal, but the kid gets an "A" for effort in my book: he learned at the feet of a master.

"You're just in time."

In time for what? I wonder, but I let him keep talking.

"Many things have changed in twenty plus years," The Big Man muses. "It's not the same city that you left." (As if I might not have noticed). "Where are you staying?" Davros finally asks, one eyebrow raised slightly as if he is holding some kernel of knowledge, some significant trinket that I haven't yet discerned. The eyebrow gesture seems somehow familiar, but I can't quite place it.

"My brother's house, out in the suburbs. For now. Until I find a place."

He sighs, the weary sigh of a man who has seen it a thousand times, could have foretold this ending twenty years ago. He doesn't think highly of suburbanites (although he is more than willing to take their money). "You working?" God, I hope he's not about to offer me a job. That would be too much, life coming full circle and then some, working the same job I started with back in college. He must smell the fear, read it on my face. Fortunately that is not what he has in mind. "You should talk to Janey," he finishes. The two ladies have finally broken free of the young salesman-in-training and scurried out the door. Davros turns and gets up slowly, ambling toward the mini skirt section to have a talk with the kid.

I'd forgotten about Janey. Not really forgotten, I guess, as much as I'd blocked that part of my life out, wrapped it in butcher's paper, and shoved it in a box on the back corner shelf of my mind. Sometimes memories can be so pungent they're painful. Thinking about Janey hurt.

She and I dated for a little over three years, my senior year of high school and the two just following. Janey was a year younger than I, so for her it was two years of high school, one year of college. That final year is what did us in. Our youth did us in, really. Naiveté did us in. Jealousy, my jealousy, certainly helped grease the skids. The world was a big place, full of temptation (hers) and opportunity (hers again), and we were pulling in opposite directions. Neither she nor I were very focused, when you get right down to it, and we were young, young in our passion and young in our

39

surety. Compromise was not in her lexicon, nor was it in mine. After too many nights waging the same argument, we found ourselves riding a carousel of mutually assured destruction: fight, make up, and fight again, round and round she goes. Janey was prescient enough to get off first, and I never quite forgave her for being smarter than me.

I'd heard bits and pieces about her life from various friends, not that I've ever asked. Personally, I'd rather not know too much. Even when things are going well, it doesn't help to be continually reminded of your previous failures. In summary, her life is good. Her life is more than good. It is great. It is damn great. She's married, has kids, owns a fancy home. She and her husband, who is wildly successful in his own right, are actively building a small empire of retail, dining, and real estate holdings throughout the heart of the city. Her tenacity and unshakeable conviction in herself, traits that didn't necessarily further our particular relationship, appear to have benefitted Janey greatly in her post-me life. I'm happy for her, I truly am, but I'd still rather not know any more, old wounds and all. I have no intention of tracking her down now, hat in hand, asking for a handout. In this instance, I decide it is best to ignore Davros' advice. I should *not* talk to Janey.

"Seriously, give her a call." He is back sitting on his stool, the kid having gone into the back room to sort inventory or something.

"Thanks, but I'll pass."

"You need to let it go."

I hate to admit it, but truer words were never spoken. I *do* need to let it go, need to let many things go. Because, for all my running and relocating and dating and leaving and devil-may-care attitude about relationships and commitment, I still carry minuscule pieces with me, tiny vestiges of each and every person and place and thing that has somehow crept into my world, as I move through life. All those tiny pieces eventually add up. The weight gets heavy. You try carrying a mosaic on your back everywhere you go, and see if you don't get tired. Yet I'm failing to see how calling up one more ghost from my past constitutes "letting it go."

"I'll think about it," I tell him. I silently think that having a chat with Janey is the worst suggestion I've ever received, *that* is what I think about it, but I don't need to mention this to my friend. It'll only make him more adamant.

"You should spend more of your time doing and less of your time thinking," the sage warns (as if he still knows me well).

"I'll give her a call," I acquiesce. Or lie, I'm not yet sure which. And that is that, as they say.

Just then the bells on the front door jingle. Another young woman walks in, one stark silhouette framed by the doorway behind her. The rain outside has finally subsided. An eerie, pre-dusk mist, backlit by the sun trying to celebrate one last hurrah before dipping beneath the horizon, has engulfed Woodward Avenue. A yellow cab cruises slowly past, a ten-year-old Ford Taurus, and I momentarily ponder the loss of the old Checker cabs. They had style, those Checkers, a dedicated purpose. They were made here in Michigan, somewhere around Kalamazoo, I think. Now the only thing left of the Checkers is their paint scheme. Another tile from the mosaic of having once been. Davros is already at the door, greeting this new customer and turning on his charm.

"How's it going?" His vibrant younger self reemerges. "Turn on the smile and don't blow the sale," Davros always taught me, and he follows his own advice to this day. His enthusiasm is both genuine and infectious. He would be successful selling anything: real estate, used cars, life insurance, or goat cheese. In the days of the Wild West, Davros would have made a great horse trader.

"Great, how about you, Dav?" I recognize the voice and I freeze, if only for an instant. For it is the same waif, the same Susan who, just an hour before, was riding alongside in the front seat of my truck. I am momentarily struck with fear. Has she followed me here, finally prepared to spring whatever nasty surprise she has in store? Is she launching a shakedown, some kind of blackmail, a plea for more, more, more? Everyone in this town has a racket. What is hers?

"Always working," Davros replies, because in his mind, nothing equates to happiness like "always working." They murmur quick pleasantries to one another, and then she and Davros are striding toward me lockstep, longtime buddies and comrades in arms.

It is coincidence, I soothe myself. This girl did not follow me here, did not know where to find me. How could she, unless she noticed my truck parked behind the building? Why would she even care? I owe her nothing. Not everyone is out to get something for nothing. She has no hold on me, no tools with which to leverage imaginary assets from my grasp. What assets do I have that anyone would want? I can't think of a thing. These two obviously know each other, Davros and Susan. She is a customer. They are friends, and my fear is therefore irrational.

"Have you met Susan?" Davros asks me, as if that would be the natural thing, she and I having met. Why the hell not? I've been in town all of twenty-three hours. Of course I would know Susan. Because Davros knows Susan and I know Davros, and in his private solar system that rotates exclusively around himself and The Emporium, well of course I should know Susan.

"As a matter of fact, I have," the dormant salesman from twenty years ago speaks up. My voice resounds smooth and calm. I wonder where I find the courage. It hasn't been around in a long time, this confidence and bravado. Inside I am still anxious, feeling like prey, exposed, out in the open. Davros shows no surprise at my bold pronouncement, though I wonder how that is possible. Maybe he believes I'm bluffing. The man is not dumb, after all. For all his bluster and selective myopia, Davros must know how unlikely such a meeting, me and Susan, Susan and me, should be. Or has he seen so much, lived here for so long, that there is no longer anything that can faze him?

"Good. Hey, I've something you've *got* to see," he says to the girl, ushering her down the aisle that straddles urban hip hop and Victorian bondage-light. Although the more I think about it, "steam punk" is the current buzzword to describe such fare: not really whips and chains, but not far from it. I pretend to look interested in the costume jewelry that adorns the glass shelves in the counter display case. I can't hear a word the two are saying, as much as I try. They are chattering away, heads close together. The skinny student clerk is still in the back room, unless he raced out the rear exit and is gone for Muskegon, South Bend, and points west. What am I still doing here? I could slip out the front without notice, disappear for another twenty years, no excuse necessary. The only sign I'd ever existed would be the ringing of bells, another angel getting his wings. Instead I squint at a silver and marcasite art deco pendant, feigning interest. Eventually Davros and Susan make their way back to the counter with no evidence of a sale pending.

"You need to give Susan here a ride home," he tells me. Davros is my boss once again, at least in his own mind. This is not a request: He thinks he knows what is good for me. All of this is implied in his tone of voice. I'm not sure if this ordinance is for my benefit, Susan's benefit, or his own. I only know that this decree, this *commandment,* The Big Man expects that I will obey.

"What the hell," I reply. It is only one ride.

CHAPTER SIX

A Gypsy

"So how do you know Dav?" she asks. She is back in the front seat of my truck, safety belt secured and ready to roll.

"I used to work for him, a long time ago. We're friends, sort of."

"I bet. He's a good guy." It is a statement, not an invitation for discussion.

"He has his qualities," I add, a little irony in my voice, and she smirks ever so slightly, the twisted smile of a co-conspirator. Davros *is* a good guy, but anyone who knows him well also knows that Davros is a complex guy with more than his share of annoying tendencies. Susan obviously knows him well, or she wouldn't have smirked. "So where are we going?"

Susan gives me an address on Selden Avenue, no more than a mile from here and just south of the campus: still in the Corridor. It would be walking distance on almost any other college campus, but not down here, not in Detroit with dusk settling in. There are too many predators, though I suspect this girl can handle herself just fine in most situations. She has that certain look about her. Again, I question Davros' intent. Is the chauffeur service for her benefit, his benefit, or mine?

"How do *you* know Davros?" I ask right back at her, not expecting much by way of an answer. I'm sure it will be your basic "I came into the store one day...." tale. She throws me a curve, instead.

"He and my mother go way back. They're friends, sort of. Both fixtures in the area. It's complicated."

My interest is now piqued. Complicated is one of my specialties. And we've finally reached common ground: Davros' past is, to some extent, my past.

"Try me," I push her. We are driving south on Cass Avenue, almost to Alexandrine, and I know I've got less than three minutes before she hops out via the passenger-side door and runs off into the night.

"Mom was pregnant with me, not married yet, and she had a lot going on. Davros helped her a lot, at least in the beginning. Now they don't get along, don't even really like each other. They've hardly spoken to one another in years."

This I can understand. Davros has always had a soft spot for orphans and strays. It doesn't shock me in the least that he'd end up helping some wayward, knocked-up school girl. He can be generous to a fault. It also doesn't shock me in the least that a woman couldn't stand him after any prolonged period of exposure: the man is too used to getting his own way, for one thing, and gets frustrated when folks don't act in the manner which he tends to expect. To the best of my knowledge, pregnant women tend to be unpredictable.

"He has his qualities," I repeat dryly. She offers no smirk this time.

"This is it, the white one," she points at a freestanding, three-story walkup apartment with a light stone facade. Three-and-a-half stories, really, since the basement is only half below grade. Cast iron burglar bars protect all the windows on the first two floors. A locked foyer with an intercom buzzer is supposed to help keep the riffraff out, at least the riffraff that doesn't live here, but there are many ways to beat that system. She slides out of her seat, standing at the curb. "Are you coming up?"

I hesitate. Are we now friends? Is it part of some great scheme? Or did Davros say something to her, suggest some peculiar arrangement that I cannot foresee? I pause, and she senses my indecision.

"Just for coffee," she adds, "Dav says you're safe."

"Well, that's good to know, that I'm *safe*," I mutter as I slide out from behind the wheel. *God, I hope my truck is still where I park it when I come back down. Fifteen minutes, max*, I tell myself, *then I'll come back out and be on my merry way.* "Coffee sounds great." Maybe I can discover what makes this girl tick. She might be "too young for me," or the newly developing category, "*way* too young for me," but it still hurts when a young woman

45

calls you "safe" (like I've been neutered or something). I'll have to say something to Davros the next time I see him.

She's got her keys in hand, with a sweeping motion so smooth I never even saw her reach into the pocket. She has had plenty of practice, I guess. "Always have something handy in case you need to defend yourself." "A key is as good as a knife, in a pinch." These are lessons every urban dweller knows all too well. Susan effortlessly turns the lock cylinder, and we are inside the building. Up ten stairs, turn at the top, up ten more, turn, another ten and ten. Foot-worn and faded, red brocade carpet adorns the hallway. The paint on the walls is a tobacco-stained yellow. Three doors to the left, three to the right. We reach the last door on the left, apartment 305, and she turns the deadbolt.

"You live alone?" I ask.

"Yeah," she answers back, ever the conversationalist. She heads directly over to the gas stove, a small four-burner, and starts boiling some water while I take a seat on the couch. Her movements are concise, efficient. She reminds me of someone I've met before, but I can't lay a time or face to it.

Hers is a small apartment, a great room maybe fifteen feet by fifteen feet that includes both living space and the kitchen. Two doors on the back wall lead to what I presume are a bedroom and a bathroom. A contemporary couch and two chairs, worn but not shabby. A pair of mission end tables, clean and uncluttered. A few framed paintings in all the right spots, nothing I'd recognize, maybe a friend of hers or some other local artist. A potted fern sits in one corner, real, not plastic. She must have some skill with plants, keeping it alive in a room with so little natural light. One window faces out on the brownstone next door. The kitchen has a tall, espresso-tinted table with two matching chairs for dining. This place is tidy, *homey*, and not remotely what I expected. I'm not sure what I expected, truth be told, but it definitely wasn't this. I guess I thought it would look more like the girl's stark exoskeleton, that minimalist armor she wears for battle with the world outside.

She disappears beyond door number two, which I presume is the bathroom, my suspicions confirmed when I hear the loud "whoosh" of water running through the ancient pipes followed by the squeaking of faucet handles. By the time she returns to the great room her tea kettle is whistling violently on the stove top.

"How do you like it?" I assume she means the coffee, not the apartment.

"Black, thanks." I'll probably regret that, I realize immediately. I do like my coffee black, but instant coffee can use all the masking agents one can find. I quickly revise my original request: "Sugar, if you've got it."

"Here you go," she says, handing me a mug full of brown tar. She is drinking tea herself. "Cheers."

"So what do you do?" I ask.

"Many things," she replies vaguely, taking another sip of her beverage.

"Yeah, I can understand that," I answer, and she nods in silent agreement.

"I'm taking classes at Wayne State, when I can afford to, and I wait tables nights at Union Street," she finally proffers.

"Studying anything in particular?"

"Life," she responds.

"Me too, and you can see where that's got me." That gets a small laugh out of her.

She takes a sip from the cup, stares up at the ceiling, then continues. This is not as uncomfortable as one might guess. Almost cozy, in a way.

"Dav says you need a place to live. The guy in 205 is moving out next week."

"Thanks for the information." I don't want to hurt her feelings, assuming she *has* feelings, but I'm not sure I'm ready to move back to the city proper. The images from visiting the old neighborhood are still fresh in my head. Midtown is better than the far west side, but only in bits and spots. Rebirth has been a long time coming, and it's not fully arrived yet. You can still find yourself a lifetime supply of blight without having to stray far from Midtown.

"It's clean. No roaches," she adds. This girl really knows how to sell a property. She should go into realty.

"I should probably think about finding employment, first."

"Yeah, but you've still got to sleep somewhere. It's only month-to-month, if that makes you feel any better. No lease required." She is a smart girl. Studies in Life have already given her a jump start on most kids twice her age.

"Who do I talk to?" I ask, taking another drink of the bitter brew. I'm not committing to the idea, I'm just asking. Making conversation. A one-month deal I can probably live with.

"Andy, the property manager. Stays in 102."

"Thanks." Another sip of the sweetened sludge.

"No problem." And that is settled. I look around the apartment. I hadn't noticed the little alcove, set off towards the end of the wall behind me. Not much bigger than a closet really, with an open arched doorway. It probably *is* a closet, I realize, but then, it also contains two wall shelves mounted on l-brackets. Framed photos are neatly arranged on the twin pine planks.

"Do you have family in the area?" I query, as I get up to take a closer look in the alcove.

"A brother, he lives out on the coast. My mom and dad."

"Are you and your mother close?" I'm merely being polite. Rarely am I all that concerned about other people's entanglements. I have enough trouble avoiding my own. Why should I care if she has mommy issues?

"Not really," she responds. I haven't met too many college students who are (close to their mothers, that is). "We talk once in a while. We're not fighting or anything."

These are the usual framed photos and keepsakes, I realize, squinting in the dimly lit alcove. There's a brother, or a boyfriend, a good looking guy in his mid-twenties with tousled hair, the picture taken shore side at a beach. A little girl maybe six years old in a canary yellow dress, holding hands with another little girl about the same age at the Belle Isle Conservatory. It is a brilliant thirteen-acre glass-domed building, housing a botanical garden that was once unrivaled in the Midwest. The girl in the yellow dress is Susan, I surmise, her much younger self. I recognize the cute chin.

"I hate to say it, but family is overrated," I opine, still checking out her mementos. An old man in military uniform, probably a grandfather or great-grandfather, World War II. Two fat women sitting on the tailgate of a Model-T pickup in front of a clapboard sided farmhouse. Great Aunts, maybe?

"The picture to your left, the one taken at the beach, that's my brother," she tells me, still cozy in her seat.

"I thought it might be a boyfriend or something."

"Nope, a brother. Half-brother, really, but to me he's just my brother."

"People are just people," I answer mindlessly, that little wisp of utopian dream seeping from my subconscious. Let's get rid of the half- and step- and ex-prefixes in our relationships, while we're at it. The world would be a much better place. "The little girl in the yellow dress is you?"

"Yes, with the other little girl? That was my best friend, Annie. We took that picture on Belle Isle when I was seven."

"Stunning. I recognized the building. Albert Kahn designed that, back around the turn of the century. When I was a kid, I always thought the drainage troughs in-between the planted areas were stocked with alligators."

"I used to think that too! But then I got older and wiser. Another urban legend bites the dust."

"Well, you never know. The theory has yet to be officially disproven."

"Maybe we can recruit a team of urban archeologists to investigate on our behalf," her one eyebrow again arching ever so slightly in sly mockery.

"I prefer the mystery of it all," I tell her, meandering back to the couch and gently placing my empty mug on the wooden table beside it. "Let there be alligators, if only in our imaginations. Thanks for the coffee. I really should get going." I set my cup down, start to make for the door, the one leading to the dimly lit hallway and the hope that my truck hasn't been stripped by the time I get downstairs.

"Davros says you're lost," she opines to the nape of my neck.

"He says *what?*" It stops me in my tracks. I'm slightly taken aback, drawn once more back into the room.

"He says you're lost. Says you don't know where you belong, don't know what you're searching for." She tells me this grudgingly, like she might have already said too much. I don't think she means to hurt my feelings, though.

I hadn't realized Davros was such an expert on my life: it's not like I've been seeing him for weekly therapy. "I don't know where he got that idea. Did he tell you how long it's been since he's seen me? Not including today, of course."

"Something like twenty or twenty-five years, but he claims that doesn't matter. Says he knew you were a gypsy back then, and nothing has changed. He said you could use a friend." That's a lot of information for him to have disseminated in one brief conversation. At this I can't help but chortle. "I probably shouldn't have told you this. I didn't mean to freak you out," she apologizes.

"That's all right. It's good to know where I stand." *A gypsy,* I think. He is not far off the mark. It is a term I've used to describe myself. *Lost,* well that is something else altogether. I have never once believed that I am lost, at least not before today. Today I feel lost, disjointed, *something* new. Who wouldn't be thrown akimbo, when everything you once recognized about a landscape has morphed and shifted? It's disorienting. I ease my way back over to the alcove, pretend to study the photographs on the shelves once again, try to gather my thoughts.

"Are you going to talk to him?" After a quiet moment.

"Who?" I answer, thinking she means Davros.

"Andy. About the apartment. Two-zero-five is vacant: he's in one-zero-two," she reminds me. It is hard for me to keep up.

"Yeah, sure. I'll talk to him," distracted. "What's the rent?"

"He'll tell you six hundred dollars, but he'll give it to you for five-fifty."

"Thanks for the tip." The last photo on the bottom right has caught my attention. It is turned slightly to one side, facing the wall, having probably been bumped when Susan or someone else was reaching for an item from the pile of clothing in the back corner. I extend my arm to straighten the frame, align it with the others on the shelf, and then I recoil as if it were a cobra. The hunter green frame contains a portrait, a portrait taken of a beautiful vixen in her mid-thirties. "Who's this in the photo to the right?" I ask, already knowing the answer.

"Which one?" because she can't see the far edge of the shelf from the chair in which she sits, can't tell which image has caught my eye.

"The one in the green wooden frame," I say, the blood draining from my face with every word. "A portrait of a woman."

"That one? That's my mom."

I don't know what else to say to the girl. I greet the portrait instead. My voice is a whisper. "Good to see you again, Janey."

CHAPTER SEVEN

A Game of Twenty-One

We're bouncing along Mack Avenue, Davros and I. He's driving his big Cadillac and I'm half snoozing in the passenger's seat. The sun is low on the horizon but it's radiating warmth through the glass. It is nearly eight in the morning. The heat is comforting.

When I left the girl's apartment last evening, "Just Susan" as I now like to think of her, I'd headed straight for the bar. I wasn't particular about *which* bar, just so long as it was close by and open for business. I settled for a place over on Third Street, a hole in the wall with all the atmosphere of a damp basement. The waiter was surly, letting it be known to all that he was doing me a favor by letting me sit at his table. A watering hole, nothing more, nothing less. It suited me just fine, as I had some thinking to do. *Hard Thinking*, as they like to say.

Janey: it's not like I hadn't thought of her in all these years, hadn't heard her name come up in casual conversation with mutual friends. That portrait, though, sitting there on Just Susan's shelf, well it was a bit of a shock. *Out of context*, you might say. It immediately brought to mind some questions that I have long avoided. Most of the evening's considering was done over tumblers of Jameson's Irish Whiskey. By the time I'd polished off my sixth one, I recognized that driving back to my brother's house was no longer a good idea, so I meandered over to Davros' apartment and he let me find a spot on his couch.

"You don't look so good," he tells me from behind the wheel of the Cadillac.

"Thank you for stating the obvious," I respond, my head pounding. *God bless that sun streaming through the window*, thought the man who rarely prays, the reflected light embracing my skin.

"You drink like that every night?" concern creeping into his voice.

"I don't drink like that every *decade*," I let him know. There is silence, other than the sound of the big Cadillac groaning as it finds new potholes every twenty or so feet. It's the truth. Yes, I like a little snort now and again, but I can't remember the last time I actually got tipsy, let alone snotty-boogered. Last night was an exception.

"You drove Susan home yesterday?" he changes the subject, or maybe this is a roundabout way of coming back to the subject.

"You asked me to." An indirect admission that I had driven her home. "*Before* the bar."

"Good."

The driver's side front tire finds yet another crater, this one deeper than most, and the Cad bounces like one of those Fiberglass horses mounted on steel springs that used to dot the city's playgrounds. "Christ, Dav, you might want to put a set of shocks on this thing."

"What are you talking about? This car is a classic."

"That doesn't mean you shouldn't maintain it. The car needs shocks."

"Humph." This is his way of pretending that he values my opinion, and that he will carefully weigh my recommendation before soundly and quickly rejecting it.

"So where are we going again?"

"Over by Eastern Market. I bought some things a while ago at an estate auction. A friend let me stash them in his storage unit until I had time to pick them up. Now I have time."

That is fine by me. I've got nothing better to do, other than maybe talk to Andy, the "property manager" or "superintendent" of whatever title slumlords are going by nowadays. At some point I need to find a place slightly more permanent than Davros' sofa. Susan's building might do. What do I have to lose? I haven't been to the Eastern Market in forever, a little enclave of farmers and meat cutters and importers and merchants that refuse to fold up the tent and flee. It has been a constant in this city for generations. The Market is fairly quiet during the week, but still draws big crowds from the surrounding areas on Saturday mornings. Today, being a weekday, should be low key.

"You sleep with her?" He's talking about Susan.

"What are you, some kind of asshole? She's just a kid. No, I didn't sleep with her."

"Good. Just checking. I know you didn't sleep with her. I was just trying to wake you up. It worked. You look better, getting some blood back in your face." I'd forgotten what a wise-ass Davros could be, stirring the pot for his own entertainment. It led to more than a few back alley fights when he was younger.

"So why'd you ask me?"

"To come along for the ride? You were sleeping on my couch."

"No. Why'd you ask me to give her a ride home? She can walk."

"I know she can walk. I thought you two should get to know each other."

"She's not really my type." I catch myself staring out the window again. Some new construction is going on; they're still framing in the buildings. I try to guess. *What are they building now*? Possibly low-income apartments, but for every new building going up thirty more are dissolving into the earth. A hooker tries to flag us down, steps off the curb and lifts her skirt, flashing her cooch like that might close the deal. *Subtle.* Davros tweaks the steering wheel to the right, catches a well-placed puddle with the front passenger-side tire and sends the girl scurrying back to the sidewalk in a cascade of muddy water. We keep on driving. She's flipping us off with both hands raised high in the side-view mirror: I can't say I blame her.

"I think you two should talk. Get to know one another." He doesn't mean the hooker. We turn right onto Russell Avenue, and we're almost to the Market. Another brief silence.

I finally decide to cut to the chase. "Why didn't you tell me she's Janey's daughter?"

"Would it have mattered?"

"Of course it would have mattered."

"Would you have still given her a ride home, talked to her?"

"How should I know? I don't like hypotheticals. Sure, why not? Probably. Yeah, I would have still given her a ride home."

"Humph." This is his way of saying he will carefully weigh my answer before rejecting it as a complete load of bullshit. He chews on my answer for a minute more. "Then why would it have mattered if I told you or not?"

"It just would have, alright?" With that Davros pulls the big boat over to the curb. We have arrived at our destination, a nondescript brick warehouse in the Market district. There are dozens of similar buildings, some still being used and more than a few sitting vacant. There is nothing to differentiate this building from the many others just like it, no sign to suggest that it is open for business, or that it *ever* operated as a business. It is a silent red brick building. We wait. Davros taps the fingernails of his left hand against the big padded dashboard. Eventually a figure steps out of one of the doorways down the block, walking hurriedly in our direction.

"That's him," Dav says, opening his car door to get out. I slowly follow suit. The man approaching us is in his early thirties, Hispanic, muscular. He is wearing jeans, work boots, a Detroit Tigers hoodie and a matching knit cap: the universal uniform of a street hustler. "This is Salvador," The Big Man tells me by way of introduction. He doesn't bother explaining my existence to Salvador, and Salvador doesn't seem to care.

"You ready to pick up your stuff?" Salvador asks, and Davros nods yes. The man produces a ring full of keys from his pants pocket and begins to open a series of padlocks on the steel roll-up door.

I am personally wondering what the benefit is to having four locks, because if you can cut through one lock, why couldn't you just as easily cut through all four?

Salvador reads my mind. "Slows 'em down. You can chop through all the locks, but it'll take a lot longer to cut four than it does one. In the meantime maybe someone will drive by and see you. Crooks will move on to easier pickings. It eliminates the lazy ones. Here you go," shoving the spring-loaded barrier upward toward the massive header that spans the gap. The big steel door shoots up on its rails, clatters above our heads and recedes into the building. It is dark inside the warehouse, and it has an ambiance strikingly similar to that bar on Third Street.

"No lights?" I ask.

"No lights, no power," from our host.

Davros pulls a small LED flashlight from his back pocket, hands it to me, and finds another flashlight for himself in the same pocket. He has been here before and has come prepared. "Turn it on," he tells me, as if I am a child in need of instruction.

We go to the far back of the warehouse, make our way through ravines between mountains of unmarked boxes and castaway furniture collecting mildew and mouse turds. At the back wall we turn left, weaving our way through more treasures before finally reaching a small pallet of shrink-wrapped boxes in the far corner. "This is it," Davros states with authority. He is beaming with pride, an explorer who has just discovered the lost city of gold. "Start loading." He means me.

I look over my shoulder, shining the meager light towards the entrance. I'm hoping there is a more efficient path back to the trunk of the car, but for the life of me I'm not seeing it. "Have you got a hand truck?" I ask, but Salvador is shaking his head "no" before I even get the words out of my mouth. He is resting, feet up, perched on a crate ten yards away. His posture tells me that physical labor was not part of the deal; at least not part of the deal for *him*. He is just the gatekeeper.

"You helping or what?" Davros bellows, a large box in each hand and already half-way to the car.

"Yeah, I'm coming." I grab the topmost package, a cardboard cube sealed with clear packing tape, and wonder if Davros did indeed swing some special deal on a pallet full of gold ingots. I don't know what else could weigh this much. "Damn this thing is heavy," I curse. Reluctantly I heft the package to one shoulder and follow the maze out. An hour later we are again seated in his Cadillac, the rear seat and trunk loaded with The Big Man's mysterious auction booty, floating back to the store.

"So why didn't you tell me she's Janey's daughter?" Maybe if I ask often enough, he'll eventually give me a straight answer.

"I thought you should hear it from Susan herself."

"I don't see where I should have to hear it directly from her. I didn't hear it from her, now that you bring it up. I discovered it myself. I saw a picture of Janey. I had to *ask* Susan. I don't even know what any of this has to do with me. Is having me give Susan a ride some sort of backdoor way to get me to talk to Janey? And why should you even care who I am and am not friends with?" My diatribe falls on deaf ears. He is ignoring me. Fine. If he is going to ignore me, I'll ignore him right back.

I look out the window and realize that we are not heading back to The Emporium after all. We are on Fort Street, whizzing south past the main post office and the crumbling facade of the old Salvation Army retail store. An entire city block, burned to the ground, floats by. More post-apocalyptic decline, more razor wire. If I hadn't seen it with my own eyes, hadn't driven these streets, I'd find it hard to believe. *The product of an overactive imagination*, one might say, *it can't really be that bad*. Trust me, it is. Fourteen shot and eight dead in the city, just this past weekend. We are a third world country in the making. Losing the war. It should make me angry, should make *anyone* angry, but instead I feel beaten down. I am too weary to stay pissed off, a new recruit already suffering shell shock. It isn't even lunch time yet. "Where are we going, Dav?" I ask, out of resignation more than anything else. I'm hoping it's for a pulled pork sandwich at Hog Heaven. Does Hog Heaven still exist?

"I've got to make one more stop, down near the bridge. It'll only take a minute." I can see it looming in the distance: the bridge, a big, aging beauty spanning the abyss that is the Detroit River. It links Detroit to the smaller, gentler, kinder city of Windsor, Ontario. Night and day, the differences between the two. Windsor still maintains most of the civility and charm of a small college town. Sure, it's got a floating casino, and it's got more than its share of topless bars, where every dancer is a French-speaking native just arrived from Montreal. Montreal somehow *sounds* sexier, far more exotic a locale than Brampton or Moose River or Hawk Junction. The hucksters understand human nature. As the old adage goes: sell the sizzle, not the steak. Despite all of that, Windsor is a significantly healthier city. It is a town that remains largely unscathed by her unruly neighbor to the North. It must be comforting to have a moat around your world, if you're the Canadians: the river keeps the barbarians outside the gate.

"What do you need to do down there?"

"Pick up something." He is not in a chatty mood. "It'll only take a minute," he adds, as if I didn't believe him the first time he said it. Surprisingly, he is correct (not correct in that I didn't believe him the first time, but correct in how quickly the errand is completed). Five minutes later we pull up outside a different warehouse, hunkering in the shadows of the bridge's mammoth twin suspension towers. A heavyset bearded man waits for us in the outer office. He hands Davros an envelope, nothing more. A quick "Thanks, Billy" and we're on our way, in and out in less than two minutes. I don't bother asking what's inside the envelope; I don't want to know. Just as quickly, we're back in the Cadillac cruising up Fort Street.

I make the long reach to my left and turn on the car radio, seeking distraction. I scan the dial. The ancient beast picks up only a handful of stations, most of which broadcast the same right-wing buffoon spewing vitriol about how the liberal media is ruining our country. There's irony for you. Davros reaches over to his right and clicks the volume off. He's not willing to listen to that crap, either.

"She's a good kid." Davros is once again speaking to me.

"Who are we discussing, Susan?"

"Susan."

I pause. "I wouldn't really know."

"You *should* know."

The hell if I can figure out what he's getting at. Since when did this inner city clothing store operator decide he is Confucius? Screw him, I think to myself. I'm tired of playing his little games. He should try his riddles on somebody else. Maybe he can test this routine on the next freshman art student to wander through his shop's door.

"Again, Davros, what are we talking about? What's the topic of this conversation? My need to make new friends in the city? Because I really don't have the faintest idea. What's your point?"

"I'm saying you should get to know her is all, she's a good kid."

"And I should get to know her why? You said it yourself, she's just a kid."

"You have more in common than you think."

"Like what, for instance?"

"Like Janey, for instance."

"Janey has many friends in this city, Dav. She has a husband. She has kids. She has a couple of thousand regular customers. It doesn't mean I need to be best buddies with every one of them."

"You're not as smart as you think you are," he tells me.

Now *that* is funny. I've lived my life racked with self-doubt. I don't believe I've ever been one to overestimate my own intelligence. If anything my life choices have been driven by fear - fear bordering on paranoia. That ever-looming threat that the paralysis gripping so many of my friends' lives will hold me, too, fast to the ground. "Always keep moving," my motto. The shadows aren't far behind you, and they're gaining every minute. Keep running.

"I've never claimed to be smart," I tell him.

"You might not have *claimed* to be smart, but you certainly think you are. You always think you're the smartest guy in the room, you and your smug shit. You went to school here, right, smart guy? Wayne State? How'd you do in math?"

"I did alright." I'm reticent, not sure where he's going with this. Math wasn't my best subject, and I don't much feel like entering into a debate with Davros. I'm playing defense in a bad police drama.

"You did *alright* in math. Good. That's a start. When did you leave the city? What year was it that you first moved away? How long ago? Do you remember?" He is grilling me now, a full-blown interrogation. It's a bad cop show, and I'm the defendant.

"It's been twenty-two years. About that. Maybe a little less." Give or take a few months. I'm not in the mood for splitting hairs.

"Now we're getting somewhere. Twenty-two years, more or less, since you moved out of Detroit. How long since you last saw Janey? Again, twenty-two years, maybe a tick less?"

He's hit the nail on the head. Janey and I split up eight weeks before I left the city, before I left Detroit 'for good.' It was too painful being around her, too painful being reminded of all the good times and places and quirky moments we'd shared while we were still a couple. Every place I went reminded me of her. Brother's BBQ and their Seven-Up cake, a favorite destination with Janey for dinner. Orchestra Hall, my first taste of strings and culture was with Janey in a black mini dress. Clutch Cargos, not the current incarnation, the original one, where the stain of disco music was washed away for good, her again. We were punks, riding a new musical tide that brought the bands X, Black Flag, and the Dead Kennedys to a frustrated city, all sequestered in the mouldering remains of the former Detroit Women's Club on Elizabeth Street: Janey written on every decaying wall. She wasn't the only reason I left, she wasn't even the *primary* reason I left. I'd forever longed to get away from here, pined to see The Great Big World. I'd been waiting for any excuse to come along. Our break up was a catalyst, and a quick way to quench the desires living inside my head. Leaving town wasn't a byproduct of our schism insomuch as getting the hell out of here at the time was *just plain convenient.*

"Twenty-two years." I reiterate. "Again, when are you going to get to the point?" Here is where the defendant in the movie would start to sweat, maybe twitch his hand a little bit and ask for a cigarette or a soda.

"How old is Susan?" Davros asks, and that is when it sinks in.

"Twenty-one?" I answer meekly, as the blood rushes from my head and my stomach slowly churns.

CHAPTER EIGHT

Return to Ground Zero

So, I think, *I've got a twenty-one year old daughter in a city that I and the rest of the world have pretty much given up on. Not the welcome home surprise I was anticipating.* What do you do with that kind of information? Normally I'd say go out and get a drink, or better yet, go out and get multiple drinks: but then, that's not exactly how a new father is supposed to behave, is it? I'm a new father, despite being two decades late to the baptism.

I decide that the first thing I need to do is to visit Andy, the superintendent of the apartment building over on Selden. I'll have to stick around town until I get the answers to some questions. An hour later I find myself five hundred and fifty dollars lighter and equipped with the knowledge of where I'll be sleeping for the next thirty days: on a cockroach-free, badly scuffed hardwood floor, unless I arrange for something more comfortable. A quick stop by The Emporium and Davros donates a battered couch that he's kept squirreled away in one of his various storage areas, along with a box of miscellaneous cooking utensils and a cast iron floor lamp minus one lampshade. One more hour, twenty bucks lighter, and Andy has helped me get the entire lot up the winding stairs to my proud new home, exactly one floor beneath the apartment of my newfound daughter. Home sweet home, better late than never.

That was the easy part. No thought required on my part, no soul searching or confrontations with the ex or the kid or the past or the future. I've never been good at confrontation. I shouldn't say never; I used to be up for the battle, and Janey and I had our share of brouhahas, but I've since changed. I know some guys live for it, thirst for the fight. Davros is a prime example. They thrive on that stuff, yelling and posturing and exploding and finally making up or breaking up. Others get silent and brood. Some just cut and run. After my "fling" with Janey I became gun-shy. I got to be a mix of the latter two categories: hunkering down until a storm blew over, prepared to move along if the tempest looked as if it might do any permanent damage. Increasingly in life I find myself watching the early forecast, moving out before a cold front ever arrives. I have become an Avoider. That is no longer an option, having learned what I've just learned: this time I need to stick around to see the show.

The restaurant is only a few blocks over from my apartment. Its exterior siding is painted simple black, a cinderblock affair with strategically placed brick veneer to make the structure look nicer than it really is. Ivy climbs the front facade. The name is there in simple script, "City Fusion," and if you forget where you are for a moment, you might be tricked into believing you've stumbled across a hidden bistro on the edge of an upscale resort community. You might be in SoHo, or some other trendy place in a real city where people fearlessly walk around outside at night. You might have found an undiscovered gem in a little stretch of wild country. Don't fall for it. One look across the street to the parking lot, where a lone security guard holds watch on an asphalt island surrounded by six foot fencing with high powered security lights and cameras, and you'll know it isn't the country. You might find it hard to believe that it can be *this* country.

I park in the lot across the street, the one protected by barbed wire over cyclone fencing. I give the attendant (an older black man who, in a better day and age would be retired by now) a buck. I hope the truck will still be there when I come out. If it is, I'll give him a couple more dollars. That is how it's done around here: a small down payment on faith, but never pay in full until services have been rendered.

I cross the street and enter through the front door. She's done a tremendous amount of work since I was here last. They've added a bakery in what used to be an old warehouse next door, and the sickly sweet smell of yeast hovers over the entire street. The scent reminds me of my first apartment, the left side of a duplex not far from here. It was within a block of where the Hostess Bakery stood sentry over the Lodge Freeway and the city itself. Hostess sprinkled us all with the magic fumes of Wonder Bread, Cupcakes, Twinkies, and Ding Dongs, those sweet things from which children's dreams are made. I remember speeding down the Lodge at sixty miles per hour, always looking up just in time to catch the red neon blinking lights that advertised "Hos_e _s," four stories high in the blackened sky. No one was willing to fix the *t* or that first *s,* even back then. That assembly line of confectionary delight has long been shuttered. It was converted for use as a casino, which will probably exist until the money boys that run this town find a better neighborhood to exploit. Less than a mile away from that sits a former Internal Revenue Service Center, which itself was used as a temporary casino for the better part of a decade. Currently *that* building is being repurposed as a state-of-the-art city police headquarters, to be completed just as soon as the bankrupt city government finishes feuding with the corrupt unions. At least these two structures won't join the legions of empty lots and gutted treasures that currently dot the city's landscape. Will the cops get free Twinkies, when it's all said and done?

My eyes take a moment to adjust to the dim restaurant lighting. Inside the door is an antique wooden podium with fake vines climbing the side, and a young lady standing behind it. "Sarah," her name tag reads, a perky brunette collegian serving as the greeter and seater at City Fusion. She writes my name in a ledger with an elegant onyx pen. I can only guess what it says: "ex-boyfriend, party of one." This girl doesn't know me, but I still expect to be identified. There is probably a secret list behind the station, a brief tally of those who are no longer welcome in these parts, like those wanted posters you used to see at the post office. Sarah says she'll be right back and goes to check on which tables might be available.

I came to visit here briefly, twelve years ago, and was silently relieved that Janey wasn't working that night my friends and I stopped by for dinner. It all filters quickly back to me: Janey working here throughout college, paying her own way. Now she owns the place, and I must say, has done well by it. In a city where most things get hacked down at the knees and parted out by thieves in the night, she and her husband took a quaint little university hangout and forced it to grow and thrive. Business might not be booming, but the joint is three-quarters full, even in the late afternoon. Not too shabby by any standard. One or both of them have the Midas touch, and this is but one tiny slice of their inner city empire.

Sarah is back, and motions for me to follow. I'm paraded through the dining area, beyond the first narrow room and the stairs to a balcony that holds but a handful of tables. We keep walking. A second large room accommodates seating for sixty or so, and then a half dividing-wall with six tables set behind it in semi-privacy. I'm seated in this far back section, at an intimate table for two. Sarah smiles and hands me the leather covered menu: real leather, not that cheap vinyl stuff they give you in the fake coney islands on the outskirts of town. Then she begins the long trek back to her station. With the exception of one other couple I'll be dining alone in this cloister, which is fine by me. The young lovers are almost through with their meal anyway.

I catch a glimpse of Janey in the kitchen, speaking to the chef. Their conversation is very one-sided. It amazes me how quickly my eyes are drawn to her, how I sense her presence before I even see her. I watch a mini-drama from the shoulders up as I peer beyond the pass-through window. Janey is taking the chef to task for one thing or another. She is focused on the issue at hand, and so I stare with impunity. Janey doesn't notice me. The chef doesn't look happy, but he is smart enough to keep his mouth closed while the boss is taking him to task. The woman is more beautiful now than when I first fell in love with her: raven-haired still, mature but not yet old. Her face is thin, what you'd describe as slender bordering on gaunt. Somehow it enhances her allure, as if all the pretense of youth has been whitewashed by the dignity that comes with maturity. She is a rose *not quite* on the cusp of fading.

Her mannerisms suggest that this is all business, her conversation with the man in the kitchen. Janey is a woman who knows who she is and knows how she got there. She is still forceful. As I watch, I am struck by the thought that I'm glad I don't work for her; there is a hardness about her. I don't have the faintest idea what has taken place in Janey's life these twenty-some years. Whatever has occurred, it is apparent she's been forged in fire.

My waitress arrives and so I have to quit gawking. This one, another in the seemingly endless line of early twenty-something or slightly older kids looking to earn their living while attending school at Wayne State, takes my order. Her name is "Kristi" and she has far too much energy as far as I'm concerned. I'm not against energy, per se; I actually *like* energy, in its proper place and time. What annoys me is that this girl exudes "happy" like a large dog coming out of the lake, shaking it all over you. I'm in no mood to be showered with happy. She takes my order. A moment later the girl returns with a glass of extra bitter India Pale Ale. My Carolina Crab Cakes will be ready shortly. Kristi departs for the kitchen, and I distract myself with the wine list. It doesn't take long before my train of thought again gets derailed.

"I'm surprised to see you here."

I'd recognize that voice anywhere, a sound as smooth as melted butter. One look up and there she stands, not three feet from my table. I could reach out and touch her, but something tells me the gesture wouldn't be welcome. "That makes two of us," I respond.

"You're surprised to see me working, or surprised to find yourself sitting in my restaurant?" The question hangs unanswered, a time bomb hovering between us before being reformulated in a more civil tone. She is reminding me that I have invaded her sanctum.

For the most part I'm surprised she recognized me. I'm not the kid I used to be. The years haven't always been kind. "Both, I guess," I finally reply.

She mulls this over for a second before following up with another question. "So what brings you to town?" Janey was always direct, I'll give her that.

"That's a loaded question."

"You must have some reason. Are you just passing through, or are you visiting someone?" That's Janey, always straight to the point if not straight to the jugular.

"I'm thinking about moving back, in fact." Heaven knows why I say this. It sounds strange, uttered words I don't expect to come out of my mouth. I find myself scrambling for cover, deflecting the inquisition that I know will be forthcoming. *Stupid.* Ever since we split up she has had that effect on me: I either get tongue-tied or I get stupid in her presence. Today I opt for stupid. "I just rented a place not far from here," I spout with childlike enthusiasm.

"Really!" her enthusiasm comes across as both contrived and transparent: the transparency is intentional, meant to put me in my place. Hers is a cry of feigned disbelief. "You should have let me know. I've got quite a few rental units in the area. I could have helped you out." She is a good actress, but then, in her business one has to be.

"Thanks, but it's just short term, until I decide what I'm going to do next." I can see the relief on her face. She doesn't want me for a neighbor.

"And where will you be working?"

Ah, another bullet from the gun. I'm not about to tell her that I'm not working, that I haven't even given thought to the *concept* of working thus far. I should probably put that on my to-do list. In the meantime, I stall for time. Why give Janey further reason to look down on me? I'm flying by the seat of my pants here. *Why do even I care what she thinks?* "I'll be helping

Davros with a couple of side projects, nothing major, just until I sort things out." It sounds like a load of crap. Even I don't believe me.

She wrinkles her nose reflexively, showing her regard for the both of us, Davros and me. I'm damn sure she knows I'm lying. "That's *nice*," she says, in such a way as to suggest it is anything *but* nice. "Don't let him rub off on you." You can tell she really loves that man.

"He hasn't rubbed off on me yet."

A server comes from the kitchen and sets my meal down in front of me. "Here you are sir. Could I get you anything else?" He's putting on his best face, but he appears nervous. He can tell this is not the normal Jane-customer chit chat, and he doesn't want to say a single word that can get him in Dutch with the boss. The crab cakes look great, although I usually wince at the idea of ordering fresh seafood while dining in the middle of the country. As a rule I don't like to tempt fate. Today I felt reckless, though Janey is quickly sucking the reckless right out of me.

"No, I'm good, thank you." The young man scurries off to the kitchen, wise enough to clear out when Janey is involved in a semi-personal conversation. I look up into her eyes. "Care to join me?" I know she won't. She's got a business to run, for one thing. She doesn't particularly like me, for another. I was being polite.

"Sorry, I've got a million things to do. I wish I could." As expected. She, too, is being generous.

I'm sure *she* is lying now, though maybe not about the million things to do. However, I came *here*, chose to meet the woman on her own turf; I can't expect her to be happy about it. I might as well get things out in the open and speak my peace before she fades away for another decade or two. "I met your daughter today," I let slip through a mouth full of crab cake. This food is good, even *better* than good.

"You met Susan?" There's a trace of disbelief in her voice; I've struck a nerve. This is real disbelief, not that fake syrup she was pouring over me moments earlier.

"Just Susan," I affirm. I'm trying to be funny, but the joke is lost on her. I should realize the joke would be lost on anyone. That's one of the problems that comes from spending too much time alone: you begin living in your own head, forgetting that you're the only one *in* on those inside jokes. "Yes, I met her," I correct myself.

"Really?" This time it is neither contrived nor transparent. Janey is legitimately stunned by my little morsel of information. She eases herself effortlessly into the seat across from me. So much for those million things to do. "And how did this come about?"

I take another bite of crab cake and decide to skip the part of the story about Susan bumming a ride from me from the far West Side. It would take a while to tell, and I'm still not sure what to make of it myself. I go with the short version. "I ran into her at The Emporium. Davros introduced us."

"I see." Her nose wrinkles again. She'd be horrible at poker with a tell like that. Is it the mention of Davros that annoys her most, or the fact that her daughter dared set foot in his store? They used to be friends after all, Janey and Davros. I wonder what happened between them. Maybe it's the mention of the three of us, me, Dav and Susan, in such close proximity that's getting to her. Janey looks a little flustered. I can't say I'm not enjoying this.

"She seems like a good kid." I'm quoting Davros now. "What is she, like nineteen?" I know quite well how old Susan is, but a man has got to strike while the iron is hot. Janey is visibly uncomfortable with the direction our conversation has taken. I take another bite.

"Twenty-one," she answers, her steely composure gradually returning. Her guard is up, though her cheeks remain red.

"Cute kid."

"Thanks. I like to think so."

"These crab cakes are delicious, by the way. Are you sure you don't want to join me?" I'm enjoying myself.

"No, thank you. I've got to get back to the office in a minute. Did you two have much opportunity to chat?"

I find that humorous, her use of the word "chat." Like I'm some Englishman, out for afternoon tea and crumpets. I guess I find many things humorous that are wasted on others. I'd forgotten how prim Jane can be when it suits her. "A little bit. I didn't realize she was your daughter, at first."

"Well, how *would* you? It's not like you've exactly *been around* for the last twenty years or so."

"Touché. I guess you're right." Talk about hitting a nerve. Score one for her team. I'm not sure how to respond without sounding defensive. I could point out that I wasn't exactly *wanted* around here for the last twenty years, but what would that accomplish? She's got enough reasons to dislike me as it is. I decide to quit while I'm behind: I keep my mouth shut.

"So how'd you figure it out, if you don't mind me asking? That Susan's my daughter?" She floats this out there like it is the most natural question in the world, but I can tell she's got her hackles up. She's trying to figure out exactly how much I know. "Did she tell you to come here? She wouldn't exactly be wearing a name tag."

It's time for another white lie; I can't see the benefit of telling her I was in Susan's apartment. Try explaining *that one* to an overprotective mother and former lover. Try telling her that her daughter bumped into you on the far side of town, a man she didn't know but thought she recognized. She jumped in your truck, rode with you (a stranger) through this war-torn city, and later invited you up to her apartment. Try telling her you know Susan is your own kid, and you deserve better than this. Any one of these issues could blow up in your face. Drop them all on a woman I haven't seen in decades? I might as well be poking an angry bear. White lies exist for good reason. "Davros mentioned it in passing. He says you've got another kid, too, a son?"

That seems to calm her down, at least a little bit. It distracts her if nothing else. Janey stands up tentatively, smoothing her A-line skirt. Always the proper lady, at least that's what people like to think. I remember back when she wasn't a proper lady. I suspect she was a lot more fun back in those days.

"You know, Davros has always been a fountain of information." It is not intended as a compliment.

"He's definitely a fountain of something, I'm not sure what." It is a good quip, intended to lighten the mood, but she's still not smiling. Again, I'm the only one who thinks I'm funny. She *used* to think I was funny, a long time ago. I realize I should probably get out more often. "He says you should stop by the store and see him sometime." I'm not sure why I throw this into the mix. I'm thinking it might help to ease the tone of our conversation. It seems like a fairly harmless remark.

"You can tell him thanks for the offer, but no thanks. I really do need to get back to work. It was good seeing you again. Enjoy your lunch." Janey is done with me. I have been officially dismissed.

"You bet. The same here. It was great talking with you. I'll see you around." It appears as though I've learned all I'm going to learn from her on this day. I wonder though: have I learned enough? Have I gotten the answers I wanted about Susan, about Janey, about us? Not by a long shot. She is already walking away from the table. I make one parting attempt before she escapes: "Jane, in all seriousness, what happened between you and Dav? You two used to be friends."

She pivots on one heel and answers sharply: "We were *never* friends." The emphasis is clearly on "never." I have officially poked the bear, and I can tell that she is angry.

"My mistake," I put my hands up in mock surrender.

"It wouldn't be your first one," she scolds, before trotting away to her office.

CHAPTER NINE

With Janey, Down By the Bridge

There is more than one bridge in the City of Detroit. When people say 'down by the bridge,' they generally mean the Ambassador Bridge, a twin suspension behemoth rising three-hundred and eighty-six feet into the air and connecting the Motor City to Windsor, Ontario. Built in 1929, the Ambassador at the time of construction held the record for the longest suspended span in the world. Two years later the title of longest span was lost, abdicated to the George Washington Bridge hovering over New York's Hudson River. Still, it's the biggest thing going in these parts. The Ambassador supports twenty-five percent of all trade between the United States and Canada, more than ten-thousand commercial vehicles on a daily basis. Freighters migrate freely along the river beneath her. No picture of the Detroit skyline is complete without a shot of the bridge in the background. Yet, for me, "the bridge" has an entirely different connotation.

We were young and in love, or at least *I* was in love. Now that I'm looking back on it, I can't really say *what* she was: possibly just an illusion, a *symbol*, if you will. She was a conduit, my imagined channel to a better life. There's an expression that is often bandied about: "the world is your oyster." Let me point out that if you are young and in love, and not particularly well off financially in a decaying city like Detroit, the world most certainly is *not* your oyster. There's no pearl waiting for you once you figure it out, no tasty treat inside the shell when you finally get it open. The world is anything *but* your oyster. The world is your zebra mussel: a nasty, invasive little thing, sharp and intrusive, insidiously choking off your intake pipes and slowly collapsing entire ecosystems all around you. We were just too naïve to have figured it out.

There were clubs, sure. In the historically Polish enclave of Hamtramck lay sordid little dumps and cinderblock bars, the best of which hosted alternative local bands on Friday and Saturday night. A five-dollar cover and a one-dollar bottle of Cinci Cream Ale would allow you to sweat, nuts to butts, with the rest of the lost rebels. For the larger crowds there were those stately old theaters of the previous generation: gilded motion picture palaces from a bygone era, stripped bare and gutted by the decadence of the brave new world. The Madison and Michigan Theaters, crown jewels from the city's heydays of previous wealth and opulence, replete with lush orchestra pits, red velvet upholstery, stone cherubs and granite surfaces, both were shredded and defaced by the angry youth of our day. The city's abandoned tiki lounges too, became our playgrounds, full of leather and spike adorned punks, anarchists, addicts and the merely curious, slowly stealing the buildings' icons and fixtures while gyrating to the imported sounds of hope lost. Sometimes we went to those places, but not often. Clubs were for people with money. Most of the time, Janey and I were not people with money.

Thus we created our own diversions. We'd hopscotch across the deserted campus of Wayne State University at night, drunk on youth and enthusiasm and once in a while, on other stuff. Statues became mountains, fountains begat dares. Dares begat falls, and falls brought about laughter and memories and kisses and more challenges. We snuck in to lousy movies at the local drive-in movie theaters, in that age just before VCRs and live streaming video. Parks were often our hangout, because parks were free. We'd linger well into the wee hours of the night at the foot of Southfield Road, where the pavement meets its end by the big river. Standing there alongside the iron railing with copper bells attached to the tips of our fishing rods, we'd watch the blast furnaces from Great Lakes Steel in the distance. Janey and I would ooh and ahh as the titans of industry showered volcanic eruptions of molten metal high into the night sky, all the while sipping cheap malt liquor and waiting for the sheepshead to bite. Then there was the island.

Like I said, there is more than one bridge in the City of Detroit. For most people, the big one comes to mind. Others might think of the I-75 overpass that arches high over the Rouge River when approaching the city from the South. Some would mention either of the two little links that connect the mainland to that tiny bedroom community of Grosse Isle, although technically those two are not *in* the city itself. For me "down by the bridge" will always bring to mind the Douglas MacArthur Bridge, a relatively flat concrete span that connects the near East Side to what was once the greatest of all Detroit's playgrounds, Belle Isle. The MacArthur Bridge is not nearly as long as the Ambassador Bridge, at a little less than half a mile in total length. It doesn't tower majestically above the water: at its highest point, it rides a mere thirty feet from the river's surface. Yet for two kids with little money and too much time on their hands, the Douglas MacArthur Bridge was a ticket to freedom.

"Hog Island," or Île Aux Cochons, that is what the French called it when they first settled this area. They used the place to house their swine and poultry, a haven from mainland coyotes. Somewhere along the line the name got changed to Belle Isle, which sounds a hell of a lot prettier. Either way, it's a nearly one-thousand acre playground in the middle of the Detroit River, an oasis in a city ravaged by her own. At one time it contained a world-class aquarium, a small zoo, and of course the botanical gardens and glass-walled conservatory that appears in that picture which I spotted in Susan's apartment. There's a casino, which turns out is not the gambling kind of casino, but rather, a turn-of-the-century Spanish Renaissance gathering place where you could meet with friends for a special occasion. There was more, too: a museum, a yacht club, hiking trails and a large beach. The Isle contained a riding stable, a golf course and a canoe livery. Most of this, I would say at least eighty percent of it, maybe ninety-percent of it, was permanently closed or fallen to *complete shit* by the time I was a teenager. The island was one more reflection of what Detroit *used to be,* back when it used to be something.

What Belle Isle did offer, in a way so very few people were wise enough to appreciate at that time, was *opportunity.* It offered miles and miles of open space, winding roads with hidden canals and quiet lagoons, private vistas of both downtown Detroit and the Windsor shoreline to boot. There were fishing piers along the back side of the island where we could sit and talk all night, with nary a soul to disturb us. Janey and I discovered cul-de-sacs and empty parking lots, places where you could conceal a car and spend hours necking with impunity. The island contained a free-roaming herd of fallow deer. Those little white beasts, seeming so out of place in a major rust belt metropolis, had survived generations. When we managed to track down the herd somewhere along the back side of the island, we could entice them to our car and they'd eat right from our hands. It was ours, all ours.

This was all in the late seventies and early eighties, before the gang bangers took over the island. They came not long after with their loud music, never-ending traffic jams, roadside drug deals and weekend shootings that made the island yet another dangerous place. We didn't need a dangerous place, we already had enough of those. I resented those criminals, hated them for having stolen and destroyed the one place that was my respite from the world as it really existed.

In our time, Janey and I, we'd roll across the MacArthur Bridge into the sanctity of Belle Isle and we'd play. Back then the island was largely deserted, at least during the work week. It was there that we could be young and carefree. We'd take long walks on the shore and watch the freighters lumber past. The Hiram Walker Distillery winked red lights at us from Canada; a deserted Uniroyal tire factory sucked up a large portion of the shoreline on our side of the border. We'd talk about anything and everything, and then talk some more. Summer days we'd spread out a Navajo blanket and picnic on the grass, playing and napping and drinking and dreaming. No subject was taboo, no idea off-limits. In the evening hours, long after the sun went down and we were once again nothing but two desperate kids with nowhere else to go and nothing better to do, we'd crawl into the rear seat of my car and make crazy, stupid love.

She and I would go at each other with unfettered desperation, all the longing and desire for a better existence packed into a few short hours of carnal bliss. We meant it, every single word whispered, every tender caress and every bite mark to the chest. In the steaming confines of a cramped back seat we swore to love one another forever, promising with our words and with our bodies. I knew so few people that had managed to escape the *emptiness* of that city. Where were our role models? We had none. So we clung to each other with reckless passion and ferocity, crafting for ourselves an unattainable ideal that would never survive inspection by the light of day. It was our only hope, this unbreakable pact of two who didn't know any better.

It turned out to be a stupid plan, a naïve plan. We'd created a conspiracy of the uninformed to say the least: but then what conspiracy isn't? In every well-designed strategy there is always some detail that the relevant parties can't foresee, some minute problem that unravels an otherwise entirely feasible plot. It's how spy thrillers are made, after all. "Us against the world," well it wasn't nearly as original an idea as we'd first believed. Love conquers all? That is probably the most unoriginal concept *ever,* when you get right down to it. What makes *you* so special? We've all been asked the question. *Nothing.* Nothing makes you so special, and life is a lot simpler if you can remember that. Romeo and Juliet weren't all that special, either; they just had a better publicist. So in some ways it was inevitable that Janey and I, as far as being a *couple,* were bound to self-destruct. Life itself would intrude on our island paradise; we just didn't know any better.

Most people don't know it, but there was an amusement park on Belle Isle at one time. That was back around the turn of the century, not this century but the previous one: nineteen-hundred and six, I believe was the year in which it opened. It was called "Electric Park," and by all accounts it was a thrilling and exciting hub of this city: a Coney Island of the Midwest, if you will. People came from all around to soak in the fun and excitement. After the novelty wore off and a glorious fire or two, Electric Park went belly up. What remained of the park was quickly deemed an "eyesore." It may well have been. By the roaring twenties the entire thing was gone, bankrupt and razed.

Yet I wonder how that's any different from what you see happening today? Hope, joy, neglect and destruction: they're all part of a seemingly endless cycle. Every day is laundry day in Detroit: wash, rinse, and repeat, until the offending stain is removed or the fabric itself is destroyed. One man's eyesore becomes another man's reclamation project, right until the point where people quit hoping and there is nothing left to reclaim. There were race riots here in nineteen forty-three, and there aren't too many people who choose to remember that, either. The old folks who lived through those times continue to die off, their memories getting swept under the carpet of the city's collective conscience. The sixty-seven riots are well-remembered, but eventually those too will fade into the history books. Maybe that's what "progress" really means; a convenient denial and shedding of our unrealized aspirations and grandiose failures. Maybe the corrosive disassembly of our past is in actuality a good thing, though I doubt it.

I'm standing on a breakwater comprised of fractured concrete blocks. Those blocks might possibly be concrete from the foundation of the old tire factory across the water. It's gone now, that factory. Everything is repurposed here, one way or another. It's been a long time since I've set foot on this island. After lunch at City Fusion I needed some place to think. I couldn't think of any better place. The gang bangers from the eighties' drug wars are long gone, at least on this day. I wonder if the police finally got around to patrolling the area, or if the resident vermin have just run out of other vermin to shoot. In any event it's peaceful here and I've got the parking lot to myself.

Granite slabs of water force their way slowly toward Lake Erie, Lake Ontario, the St. Lawrence Seaway and beyond. There is a dirty froth to the river's surface. Winds from the South and West whip hard against the current. I'm gazing across the main channel, Windsor hiding safely in the distance. The breeze is fighting a losing battle, the river current far too powerful. I'm still not sure what brought me here; the desire for space, I guess. I frequently require space in which to think, and space is an ever-dwindling commodity. You can never find enough of it, particularly in a big city. That is such an odd thought, considering there is so much of Detroit that is both vacant and abandoned, but true nonetheless.

The sun is shining brightly, though the stiff wind renders the sun's rays impotent. There is a sharp, bitter taste in the air, the flavor of winter hovering just around the corner. That feeling is even more pronounced standing here, exposed on the rubble, so I walk back to the truck and get inside. Ten minutes on the rocks was ten minutes too long. If I smoked, I'd light a cigarette about now. Maybe I should take up smoking.

The main road is a five-mile long, one-way loop around the island's perimeter. The outer road exists under various names: it's actually a combination of connected streets. Most folks just call it "The Strand," even though Riverbank Road and Lakeshore Drive comprise large chunks of the loop. There are two parallel paths, Loiter Way and Central Avenue, that run the length of Belle Isle's interior, and a handful of shorter, perpendicular streets slicing from shore to shore. It is a long, narrow island. Unless someone is in a hurry to reach a particular destination, they follow the outside loop counterclockwise around the shoreline, so that's what I do now.

I pass the "fountain," but it's no longer really a fountain: the Scott Memorial Fountain doesn't pump water. The structure itself is an incredible sight though, liquid or no liquid. It was designed as a series of marble basins some five-hundred feet in circumference. These basins are guarded by statuary lions, dolphins and turtles: I can't quite discern if those particular sculptures are made of marble or not, as they might be bronze. A couple of the turtles are missing. The basins themselves are adorned in hand-crafted tile. Tucked behind the fountain rests a life-sized statue of James Scott, the city's long-dead benefactor. The whole thing sits at the far western end of the island, surrounded by a small sea of asphalt.

The Scott Fountain was a gift to the city, paid for by a large bequest upon the death of the playboy millionaire Scott in 1910. Back then, people pissed and moaned about whether to accept the man's money. He was derided as a playboy, a scoundrel, a "misanthrope" (a term just as archaic as "rubbers"). He was rumored to have consorted with women of loose morals. At the time it didn't seem right accepting his gift, didn't seem right paying tribute to a man of such low character. Eleven years later the city finally took his cash and began construction. The monument was completed in 1925. In 2005 copper components were stolen from beneath the Scott Memorial Fountain and it has remained inoperable ever since. Low moral character is apparently making a comeback.

On any other day I'd stop and take a closer look at the fountain, but I'm not in sightseeing mode so instead I keep moving. Windsor is across the water, and from here Windsor seems like any other modest, Midwestern city, only cleaner. A handful of high-rise apartments crowd her shoreline, though "high-rise" on the Canadian side is significantly less imposing than the skyscrapers that populate the American side of the river. I pass the Dossin Great Lakes Museum on my right, athletic fields on my left, and then the Model Yacht Basin (which looks a lot like any other small frog pond). A few moments later I spy the South Fishing Pier jutting out from the island's bank. The pier reaches deep into the water, and for an instant I consider stopping. Then I decide against it. If it was too cold for me standing on the breakwater, it has got to be downright miserable out on that pier.

A tiny inland lake is further up the road to my left. I continue driving past the Coast Guard station, the Blue Heron Lagoon, the Nature Center. I'm already beyond the midpoint of my journey. I round a bend and then the road angles once more, pointing back toward the city and the Douglas MacArthur Bridge. The Detroit Yacht Club appears on the right before fading away in the rearview mirror, her stubby, gated gangplank designed to keep out the riffraff. The beach and the giant waterslide float past my window. In fifteen minutes of painstakingly slow driving, I've nearly completed the circuit. I pull over to the curb, park and lock the truck. The North Fishing Pier lies before me, and while it will be cold standing out there, at least I'll be partially sheltered from the wind.

I stroll out onto the jetty and immediately know that I've made the right choice: I'm the only person here and I've finally found some solitude. The wind from the West is still doing a number against the river's current, but the island at my back helps deflect the southerly breeze and minimizes the effect of the wind. Canada geese, hundreds of them, waddle around the shoreline and swim in the slack water around me. They are huge, cumbersome birds, fun to watch, but they are rapidly transforming Belle Isle into Goose Shit Island. The pier is rife with slick, greenish gobs of bird excrement. I carefully pick my way through their minefield of crap to the end of the pier. Thankfully there is a place at the end of the structure where the metal railing is not covered with goose residue; I can lean against the iron bars and watch the city from afar.

The problem now is that the onus is on me. All of that driving around, reflecting on the past history of the island and my relationship *to* the island, it was nothing but a stalling tactic. The drive merely served to postpone dealing with the real issues: thinking about Susan, about Janey, and about how I should fit as the long-lost piece to a puzzle that I never knew existed. Do I want to be a father, and am I even remotely equipped to do so? Do I even have a choice? Hasn't that ship already sailed? I guess you always have a choice. Flight has been a hallmark of this city for generations, and I'm no exception. I have a healthy track record for getting out while the getting is good; I've practically made a career of it. Would running away this time really be any different?

Yet I know that running away *would* be different, for one good reason, and that reason has a name. My past indiscretions (and there have been many) were all relatively *minor* in the damage that they caused to others. Most of the pain, it turns out, was self-inflicted. I could sleep soundly at night knowing that while my previous flights from responsibility might have left an occasional wake of hurt feelings or broken hearts, even that rare tragedy of a restaurant being forced to operate without a busboy for one evening, the wreckage was always temporal. Those were fleeting injustices that readily heal. Susan, *my daughter* (and it amazes me now to hear myself say those words) is anything *but* temporal. She might be the only lasting proof that I've even existed.

I can see the MacArthur Bridge from here, the city's skyline beyond that, and the Ambassador Bridge even further in the distance. I'm trying to remember how I arrived at this place; not how I got to Belle Isle, that's not at all what I mean (I took Woodward to Jefferson Avenue). I'm trying to remember how I got to this point in my life. I'm standing here alone, on a finger of concrete extending out into what is formally known as the Scott Middle Ground, with no job, no home, no significant relationships or entanglements whatsoever. How is it possible that I've had a child for over twenty years without even knowing? What else have I missed? What other permanent waves have been created by the ripples I've left behind? What can I do now to rectify the situation? The sun is quietly setting in the distance, and the windows of the city absorb and reflect the warm orange glow of the fading light.

My truck beckons as the daylight fades. I've come to one conclusion at least: I've decided that I will be a father if Susan will allow me to be a father. There is nothing in my history to suggest that I will be any good at it. My opportunity to do any good in this world may well have come and gone. I lack skill, patience, practice, or any true frame of reference for parenting. I know little about raising kids and even less about guiding young women. How much guiding does a girl her age really need? I believe, however, that I'm somehow bound by a moral imperative. I'll *try* to do what is right and see if I'm any good at it, take my chances. There is no other option: walking away now would amount to a permanent exile in shadows, and I've been a shadow for too long. I can't say where Janey fits into this scenario. I'm pretty sure that Janey *won't* want me to be a co-parent, or an ex-something, or any other classification of quasi-partner that comes to mind. She would prefer I remain what I have been all along: a nonentity, a rumor. That will have to remain her problem, hers and hers alone.

The geese start honking and fighting behind me, capturing my attention. I look back toward the island where a dozen or more of the birds are gathering along the water's edge preparing for flight. It's a chaotic scene. One goose tries to take charge and there is a goose debate; a different goose argues briefly before backing down. Others follow, challenging the leader and then backing down, before order eventually forms. Most people don't know this, but a group of geese are only called a "gaggle" when they're on the ground. Once in the air they are called something else: a *skein,* a *team,* or a *wedge.* When flying close together the geese become a *plump.* It's almost as if by the very act of leaving one place for another, they are transformed from what they were to something else entirely. The past, the "gaggle" as it were, ceases to be. They are no longer one thing, but one of *many* things - skein, team, wedge or plump - a subtle change of location opening up an entire range of possibilities that only seconds before didn't exist.

Wings flap with violence. There is more honking and squawking, then the thunder of feet charging violently across the turf before these giant birds gradually gain lift, taking to the air and circling back over the island. The geese, no longer a gaggle, gain height as they loop over the police mini-station and once more circle above the water's surface. I watch them disappear into the distance, one mass in an imbalanced V-formation following the flow of the river past the bridge, the city skyline, and beyond. If only life were that simple.

CHAPTER TEN

Fire in the Hole

At first I think that the beeping sound must be coming from the alarm clock, and in my sleep-induced stupor I reach over to where the nightstand should be while swatting at an imaginary snooze button. It takes me a few swipes before I realize that I don't own a nightstand, I have yet to unpack (let alone set) an alarm clock and I'm not in Portland anymore. My eyes open to total darkness and my mind zeroes in on an incessant beeping sound that is still going full tilt. Is it coming from the microwave, an oven timer, or something else? Then my nose detects the faintest whiff of smoke coming from beneath the door, and I realize that it's the smoke alarm making all the racket.

In my imagination I've always assumed that an apartment fire would be total chaos, people running willy-nilly through smoke-filled corridors in a total panic. There should be wailing and gnashing of teeth, lost babies and frantic mothers. That's what it looks like in the movies, and how should this be any different? Yet it is. I step out into the hall, where a slight haze is gradually thickening and building, carcinogenic storm clouds of disaster. My neighbor from 201 is standing in the hallway wearing nothing but his boxer shorts and a T-shirt, untied army boots on his feet and no socks. He looks slightly stoned or disoriented, but certainly not panicked. An elderly woman dressed in a floral bathrobe casually rounds the corner and begins making her way down the stairs, miniature poodle in arms. A twenty-something girl I've never met, probably a student at the University, is close behind her. There is an overriding sense of calm, like this is just a drill and we've all done it many times before.

"Hey man, you alright? You should probably head downstairs." It is stoner dude from apartment 201 talking to me, while simultaneously pounding on the door to 206, another neighbor I have yet to meet. "I'm Mike, by the way. Keep an eye on things. The neighbors call me Watchdog."

"Good to meet you, Watchdog Mike. Do you need to grab a pair of jeans or anything?" Getting burned out of your home is one thing. Being homeless and without pants sounds even less appealing. It's still hazy in the hall, but I get the sense that there is no immediate danger, that whatever has gone up in smoke is at the very least temporarily contained or at worst smoldering. There are no raging flames licking at the staircase in any event.

"No, I'm good. You might want to get outside, though."

"Sure. But first I'm going to shoot upstairs and check on a friend."

"She's already down there, man."

"Who is?" I've never met Mike before. I have no idea how he might know who my friend is.

"All of them. Susan. And Pete and Mark, Katie and Leo. They're all there. Everybody on three is already downstairs, I checked. You and Booker are the last ones to get out, and I don't think Booker is even home tonight. I'm just being super cautious."

"Booker?"

"Second floor, apartment six," he answers, as if it should be obvious. "Across the hall."

On the sidewalk out front everybody is milling about. It's pitch dark, and I'm not wearing a wristwatch. Who wears a watch nowadays? I ask if anybody has the time, and the old lady with the poodle (it turns out her name is Eliza, but I can call her "Betty," and the poodle is Bruce) informs me that it is exactly two forty-three in the morning and "too goddamned early for these kind of shenanigans." I humbly agree.

I try to count heads, but everybody keeps moving and shuffling. It's a bit like trying to herd cats, and I don't know how many are supposed to live here, anyhow, so I quickly give up. I see Susan speaking to someone that I can only assume to be Mark, Leo, or one of the other residents I haven't yet met. There's still no sign of a fire truck, though I can hear sirens far off in the distance. This city is not known for rapid response. Mike finally steps out from the front entry, miraculously wearing pants but still sans Booker. I walk over and try to make small talk.

"Booker's not home?"

"Probably spent the night at his old lady's. It's hit and miss with him."

I'm not sure whether or not I should be grateful for this insight into my heretofore unknown neighbor's romantic entanglements. "But everyone else got out?" I ask, beginning to feel like maybe we need to verify, maybe there is more I ought to do. I hate to admit it, but I'm worried he missed someone and it's somehow my fault.

"I'm pretty sure," Mike responds, and I realize that the disoriented, stoner thing that he has going is just a facade. It is a "look" that allows him to pass unnoticed, dismissed as harmless and irrelevant by the worst of the neighborhood when in fact he is a guardian, silently monitoring the comings and goings of our little three-and-a-half story society. "We're good," he tells me after quickly surveying the ever-shifting crowd. I believe him.

"How'd you know it was a girl?" I ask.

"What do you mean?" Mike checks back.

"My friend, on three. When I said I intended to check on a friend, how'd you know it was a girl?

"It's always about a girl, man." He's right.

Twenty minutes later the fire trucks finally arrive. I'm pretty certain that whatever tripped the alarm is now out, or the building would have been burned to a crisp. The firefighters are still required to go inside and perform a thorough search. Another twenty minutes pass before Booker from 206 shows up and the firemen are still inside. Mike introduces me to my new neighbor. It turns out that Booker was indeed at his "old lady's place," but for some reason that Booker can't quite explain, they had a fight and she kicked him out for the rest of the evening and possibly even longer. He is two sheets to the wind and particularly upset because he wants nothing more than to fall asleep, but he's not allowed back in the building until after the firemen give the all-clear signal. Going back to the girlfriend's would likely result in physical injury (hers or his, I'm not quite clear). I get the feeling it's not easy being Booker, or maybe it's too easy.

Susan comes over, asks how we're doing and if anyone knows where the fire originated or how it started. So far we've come up with nothing, although it looked as if there was less smoke on one, so more than likely it started somewhere on the second floor. I know it didn't come from my place. Mike swears it wasn't him. My new friend Betty is down toward the end of the block talking to someone from one of the other buildings, so we can't ask her, and Booker wasn't even home. At the moment he's sitting on the stoop, rocking back and forth to keep himself awake while quietly humming "Whiskey in the Jar." There are two other apartments unaccounted for on the second floor, but I don't know the tenants. A small crowd had formed earlier on the street, tenants from the other buildings ready to enjoy a show, but the lack of activity sent most of them quickly back to the warmth of their own beds.

When the firemen finally do come outside and give the all clear signal it's well past four in the morning. The fire *did* start on my floor: in apartment 206, as a matter of fact. It turns out that somebody left a saucepan full of SpaghettiO's simmering on the stove, and that particular somebody is approaching his two-hundredth round of singing "I take delights in the juice of the barley, courting pretty maids in the morning oh so early." The majority of the building is fine, but Booker's apartment is toast and off limits due to smoke and water damage.

"Booker, are you Irish?" Watchdog Mike asks, trying to get his attention.

"Hell no, I'm not Irish!" He shouts back, with an indignation suggesting that whatever boat *his* ancestors first abandoned must have set sail from the Royal Yacht Club. "I'm Italian," he tells us, truly offended.

"Then why do you keep singing that Irish drinking song?" Mike asks.

"The song's not Irish. It's just a song. I'm singing it, and I'm Italian. That makes it an *Italian* drinking song," he says with certainty. It would be hard to argue with that logic.

"Why don't you head inside for the night?" I ask him. I can see that he's freezing. The alcohol he'd ingested earlier is beginning to wear off, but not quickly enough. His hands are quivering: telltale tremors of the long-term drinker in need of a fresh infusion. Most of the other residents have gone back inside, Susan, Betty and Bruce included. It's just the three of us standing out here in the dark.

"Off limits!" Our friendly fireman shouts as if he's been eavesdropping.

"You heard the man. I'm not allowed. My place is all burned up. Where am I gonna go?"

"Could you head back over to your girlfriend's place, you know, just for one night?" Mike suggests.

"Ain't gonna happen."

"It could happen, maybe. If you ask her real nicely."

"Ain't gonna happen. You weren't there. It was bad, and no way is she gonna let me back in tonight. Maybe in a few days she'll settle down," he finally suggests.

"How about if you tell her what happened, you know, your place being all burned up and everything?" Mike's working him like a schoolteacher, hoping to lead Booker to the answer without providing the answer outright. Let him think it was his idea.

"You weren't there," as if that is the final word.

"No, I wasn't," Mike agrees, and shrugs his shoulders at me.

We're standing there in silence, or, at least in relative silence. Even in the middle of the night this city is never truly quiet. Sirens can be heard wailing in the distance, the slam of a car door, the bark of a dog: despite the early hour and the vast tracts of abandoned land nearby, the city rarely sleeps. When it does sleep, it does so with one eye open and a loaded gun behind the door.

For the second time in the last twelve hours I'm thinking a cigarette would be welcome. I also know that's a habit I don't need. I'm tired, would like to get inside and get back to sleep, yet all of a sudden I've inherited a shared responsibility for this frozen, shaky drunk sitting on the concrete porch. It is Mike that finally slices the dead air between us.

"Why don't you come inside, Booker? You can crash with our friend here." I wasn't expecting that. Sucker punched. *Who told him that was acceptable?*

"I can?" My new buddy pipes up with optimism. I see the hope in his eyes, a hope I'd like to extinguish right here and now, before it takes me down with it. I decide a consultation is in order.

"Mike, could I have a word with you, please?" I suggest in my less-than-friendly tone. We step to the side, leaving Booker alone on his stoop. I follow up with Mike. "I don't think that's such a good idea."

"Look, he's got to sleep someplace. It's just for one night. I'd take him, but my place is trashed right now. He's got nowhere else to go."

"I don't have any furniture," I point out. It's a flimsy excuse, and I can tell I'm already losing the argument. I'm trying to remember how I got drawn into this mess to begin with. I should just walk inside, lock the door behind me, and go back to sleep.

"He can crash on your floor. I've got a sleeping bag I'll let him use. It's got to be better than leaving him out here: the wolves will tear him apart." I know there aren't any *actual* wolves in the city, but I also know that he speaks the truth. Don't let anyone tell you differently, there are certainly wolves about.

"I don't know the man," I plead. "I've just met him." The argument sounds weak, even to my own ears, and I am *definitely* losing the battle. Where's the humanity? How can I turn my back on a neighbor in need? At the same time, Booker looks like a guy I'd like to keep at arm's reach. Trouble is bound to follow wherever he goes.

"I'll vouch for him," Mike intones, as if that's supposed to bring me comfort. I've known Mike for what, forty minutes now? "Take him in. It's just for a few hours." It's well past four a.m. already. He's right, morning is just around the bend.

"One night, and one night only," I reluctantly agree. "You'll help me get him out of my place if he won't leave in the morning."

"Scout's honor."

"Seriously," I tell him, more a question than a statement. I'd like to make him double-pinky swear, too, but that might be asking a bit much.

85

"Seriously," he agrees.

"You were a Boy Scout?" I ask suspiciously. He doesn't look like a guy who used to be a Boy Scout. He looks more like the guy that your local shopkeepers chased away for stealing penny candy.

"Just as sure as that was an Italian drinking song," Mike responds with a hearty laugh.

Then the three of us are inside the building, Watchdog Mike and I to either side of Booker, who is wobbly but at is least moving under his own power. We climb up ten stairs, turn and pivot at the landing, go up ten more, then traverse the foot-worn and faded red brocade carpet of the hallway. Mike's apartment is the first on the left. He slips inside, finds a weary, army-issued sleeping bag which he hands over, and then thanks me for being such a sucker. Booker and I stagger the last few feet to my apartment door.

"I really appreciate you doing this," Booker tells me.

"No problem," I reply, even though it is in fact a problem.

"Is it all right if I take the couch?" he asks once inside.

"The couch is mine. I don't have a bed yet." I tell him. I see the disappointment on his face, but he gets over it quickly. Booker's not asking for much: he's a man just grateful to be indoors.

"No sweat. I'll lay out over here, against the wall. This is really cool of you." His hands are still vibrating, but not as much as they were earlier.

"Don't worry about it. Get some sleep."

"Yeah, it's been a long night."

"No doubt," I tell him as he crawls into his army bag. I lie down on the couch, grab my blanket from the back, and drape it across my body. "Is it all right if I turn out the light?" I'm not used to having a roommate and I'm unclear about the proper protocol for entertaining overnight guests on one's living room floor.

"Yeah, I'll be fine. The layout here is the exact opposite of my place. I'll be able to find the bathroom if I need it."

"Good. See you in the morning, then," I tell him as I pull the lamp switch. A minuscule beam of light continues to leak in from beneath the door, and the pungent smell of smoke satiates the air. The only sound is the gentle rattle of ancient plumbing, shuddering behind the plaster walls. All is still and I'm alone in my thoughts. It doesn't last long. Five minutes later the quietude is broken by a single whisper.

"Hey, can I ask you something?" Booker is but a phantom lodger, one disembodied voice wafting through the night.

"I guess so. What is it?"

"I'm feeling kind of hungry. You got any SpaghettiO's?"

CHAPTER ELEVEN

The Accidental Adoption

I'm amazed to wake up in the (very late) morning and find that Booker is gone. I sit up slowly, rubbing my head with both hands in the hope that increased blood flow will revive my foggy mind. I scan the room, checking back to see that the bathroom is vacant and the bathroom door is wide open. The only residue of my recent houseguest is a carefully rolled sleeping bag in the far corner behind the door. It's indeed a miracle. Outside my window the sun rides high across the sky and I realize that it's closer to noon than it is to daybreak. The room still smells faintly of smoke, so I get up and open the window.

The city has reawakened. Cars rumble down the street, dodging potholes as they race back and forth. Horns are honking, people are yelling, and pedestrians are making their way to wherever it is that pedestrians go. A nearly deserted city bus flashes by on its way downtown. On the corner I can see two men talking, one carrying a brown paper bag and the other with both hands in his jacket pockets. It takes me a minute to realize that the two men on the corner are my new neighbors, Booker and Mike. Their conversation ends, and Mike heads off down the street while Booker starts strolling toward our building. It's too late for me to make an undetected escape so I sit, knowing that his knock on my door is only seconds away.

"Come in, Booker."

He opens the door slowly, paper bag still in hand. "How'd you know it was me?"

"I saw you coming down the street," I answer, nodding back toward the open window.

"I've brought us lunch," he tells me, hoisting the brown bag in the air as evidence. "Pierogies and Mountain Dews. We need to heat the pierogies," he adds.

"Where'd you get the pierogies?"

"Betty made 'em for us. She said we could probably use a good meal, on account of us being awake half the night and my place being uninhabitable and everything. Kielbasa and kraut, potatoes and cheese, we've got both kinds."

"That's really sweet of her, but I haven't even eaten breakfast yet."

"Nothing says breakfast like pierogies and Dew, roomie," he spouts with enthusiasm.

"Yeah, about that. You do understand this was a one-night deal, right? That we're not technically roommates?"

Booker gets that look on his face like a puppy that's been kicked, but can't understand what he's done to deserve the abuse. He recovers quickly, or at least pretends to. "No, yeah, really, I get it. I appreciate you putting me up for the night and everything. It was really cool of you. Not your fault I got no place to live. We can still have lunch together though, right? 'Cause we're friends?"

"Friends?" He's stretching things here, but I keep my mouth shut. I don't think I'm up to taking a second kick at the puppy, and so I reluctantly agree. "Sure, but I'll do the cooking." No one wants a replay of the fire across the hall.

"Betty says they're best if you pan-fry them in butter."

"I don't have any butter." Or any other food, for that matter.

"Betty sent butter, and some sour cream, too" Booker offers cheerfully. I'm beginning to like having Betty for a neighbor more by the minute. "You want a Dew?" he offers, a full bottle of soda in one hand.

"Why not," I answer, accepting his humble token.

Thirty minutes later I'm pitching our paper plates in the trash can beneath the sink and washing the pan with soap and hot water. He's telling me about his apartment, how nearly everything inside is trashed from the smoke but he managed to get inside this morning and salvage his laptop.

"So Booker, what do you do?"

"Network solutions," he answers.

"You are frickin' kidding me." I thought he'd tell me he was collecting disability, or "used to" do x or y. There are a lot of people in this city who "used to" do something or other. Booker doesn't look like a guy that can hold an actual job doing actual work. "Where at?" I ask.

"Don't look so surprised. Downtown, the First National Building. In the financial district," he adds, in case I have no clue about the layout of the city. He's overstating things a bit: this isn't New York. What we have is more of a financial "block" than a financial "district," a handful of buildings owned by a handful of wealthy individuals all concentrated in an area one-quarter mile from the riverfront. But why should I split hairs with the man who brought me pierogies and Mountain Dew for breakfast?

"I wouldn't have guessed it. Full-time?"

"Full-time, afternoons." He confirms. "No benefits, though, contract work."

"Do you like it?"

"It pays the bills," he shrugs.

"And this girlfriend of yours?"

"I think she's more of an 'ex-' after last night. Definitely not full-time."

"No chance you two might reconcile?"

"Not for a while, anyway. Monica's got a temper. Once she gets hot she's in no hurry to cool back down. I need to stay away from her for at least a week or two."

"That's a bummer."

"Yeah, but most of the time she's worth it." He has a look on his face that tells me love can be complicated.

I'm about to ask him where he'll be sleeping tonight, but our little tête-á-tête is interrupted by a rap on the hallway door. The door opens slowly before I even have the chance to answer, and Susan pops her head through the gap.

"Good, you're here. How are you two doing?" She's full of enthusiasm as she steps into the room.

"Fine," I answer, although I'm not sure that's true. I'm not fine, actually. I'm barely muddling through. I like to go about my business uninterrupted, and ever since I arrived in the city life keeps intruding on my personal space.

"It still stinks down here, but there's not much smoke left up on three. I just wanted to tell you how sweet I think it is that you're letting Booker crash here until they get his apartment back together. It's really kind of you." She's two steps away now, and Booker is smart enough to stay seated on the couch, keep his mouth shut, and see where this conversation leads. Maybe he'll hit the jackpot and win a free home.

"Uh, we were just discussing that. Booker was talking about finding other accommodations for a bit." I glance over at him to see if he'll play along with the charade, but the wounded puppy has reappeared. If I want to bullshit Susan, it's all on me: there's no help coming from his corner. "We're still working out the details."

"No, honestly, I think it's great, neighbors helping neighbors and all that. You're a good man. I just ran into Andy down the hall. He says the repairs are going to take about six to eight weeks, maybe longer."

"Six to eight weeks?" Booker has finally found his voice, though he sounds a bit suspicious. I don't think he was expecting to be locked out of his apartment for that long.

"You two will be fine," Susan waves off his concern, and in the blink of an eye she's gone, the door closing slowly behind her.

"Six to eight weeks," Booker bemoans.

"It'll go by quicker than you think," I assure him.

"Easy for you to say. You've got a place to sleep."

91

"You don't have any family in the area?"

"Nope."

So much for that suggestion. "Close friends?"

"Not really."

"You sure Monica won't take you back, given the situation?"

"Don't worry about it man. I'll figure something out. Maybe I can grab a cot at the mission." Booker's not necessarily making me feel any better.

"The mission?"

"Yeah, you know, one of the shelters."

As of now I am officially a jerk. What will Susan say if she finds out I've banished my neighbor to living on a cot at the mission? Will I still be a "good man"? Is this the first step in being a parent, subjugating one's own needs and desires to the projected guilt induced by your offspring? I suppose it's as good a place to start as any.

We sit there in silence before I finally give in. "You can stay," I reluctantly inform Booker. It can't hurt. What do I have that the man can harm or steal, other than my solitude? Even solitude can be overrated. "But no cooking," I warn.

"Fine."

"No coming in loaded every night. Do you have a drinking problem?"

"Working on it."

"Getting one or losing one?"

"Whichever you prefer," he smiles.

I let that slide. "And no overnight girls," I add, almost as an afterthought. "Nothing illegal."

"No problem," my new roommate smiles. "You got Wi-Fi?"

"Hell no."

"That's not a problem," he backs off a bit. "Thanks."

Our pact has been sealed. I round up a second key to my apartment and officially bestow temporary resident status upon Booker, one more entanglement I'd just as soon not experience. "Don't burn the place down," I warn him.

"No problem," Booker rejoins, and a few minutes later he's off to work.

His departure exposes a new conundrum: where do I go from here? I can't just *exist* in this newly created universe, a universe composed of both the new and the familiar. I'll have to *do* something. I just don't happen to know what that something will be. Do I look for work? Try once more to speak with Janey? Attempt a heart-to-heart talk with Susan? Do I drive out to my brother's place, get the trailer and what few possessions of mine have survived the trip from out West, and bring them to my new digs? The choices are frustratingly plentiful and universally unappealing. Thus I do none of the above. I get in my truck and drive over to The Emporium to see Davros.

The bells chime as I walk through the door, and Dav's standing behind the counter as if the man has been expecting me all morning, wondering when I was going to show up.

"Good. You're here. Where've you been? I've been waiting half the morning." My friend is full of piss and vinegar, even though I don't remember promising I'd show up at his store, today or any other day.

"What are you talking about? Was I supposed to be here for something in particular? I don't work for you, Dav." He's managed to tick me off in less than thirty seconds, a new personal best.

"Never mind that. Hey, I need a favor. What are you doing today? You want to earn a little money?"

It's not a bad idea, earning a little money, but I've learned to view any offer from my old boss with a jaundiced eye. I don't mean to say that I don't entirely trust him, but I don't entirely trust him. "What do you have in mind?" I ask suspiciously.

"I've got a load of shirts up in Marysville I need you to pick up. It's nothing heavy, and everything's already paid for. I just need you to drive up there, get them, and bring them back."

"Why aren't *you* going to get them?"

"I've got a store to run. Besides, I don't think they'll fit in my car. Four big boxes," he clarifies. He's obviously forgotten our previous trip to the Eastern Market and the mountain of crap we'd managed to cram into the back of the Cadillac.

I'm thinking about it. I could probably use the money. Moving isn't cheap, and I've been watching my cash reserves slowly trickle away with a lunch here and a dinner there. I'm not broke, but it wouldn't hurt to see some cash heading inbound instead of outbound for a while.

"Marysville: that's up by Port Huron, right?"

"Yeah. One hour north, approximately. Pretty much a straight shot up I-94. I'll give you seventy-five bucks. You drive up there, pick up four big boxes, and bring them back. I've got some other stuff around here you can help with if you want something to do when you get back. What else have you got going on today?"

As usual, he's right. I don't have anything else going on, and seventy-five bucks is seventy-five bucks, although I'll probably burn fifteen of that in gasoline alone. I look around the store: not a single customer in the place and it appears as if it's been dead all day. Where does Dav get the cash to pay me for anything when the store's not making any money? He's got rent, utilities, and a quarter million dollars tied up in inventory on the floor. It's possible his cash is coming from alternative sources. I know he owns other properties, a parking lot and a couple of rental houses. Maybe it doesn't matter if the store turns a profit. From a business standpoint it doesn't make much sense, and I'm beginning to wonder if I've become Dav's latest charity case. All of this races through my mind before I finally decide to accept his offer. What does it matter whether his money is coming from the sale of a shiny leather jacket or five parked cars in a lot downtown? It's his life and his money. Twenty minutes later I find myself tooling north on I-94 (the Edsel Ford Freeway for us old-timers) past newer subdivisions full of fake colonial homes and miles of recently harvested farmland, preparing to pick up a load of western shirts from some guy named Julio.

One of the downsides to my truck (and there aren't too many) is that it only came equipped with an AM radio. There's not much to choose from as I drive to Marysville, certainly not much by way of music. I start at the left side of the dial and work my way up: Canadian news, Baptist preacher, middle eastern music and talk, national right wing talk show, local news and weather repeated every ten minutes. I keep working my way up the dial, finding stations that identify themselves with words like "Patriot," "Faith" and "Glory." I find oldies (too old), more Faith (different denomination) and America's Best Talk (which is not) before giving up and working the dial back to local news on a never-ending carousel. It's the lesser of available evils.

The city is in bankruptcy court, or is trying to get into bankruptcy court: I'm a little confused with all the talk of pending and possible lawsuits. There is brief discussion about selling off the art from the Detroit Institute of Arts, but that presents a new set of problems (something to do with regional taxes and determining who actually owns the individual art works). The City Water Department, Belle Isle, it's all up for grabs and no one can predict what will happen when all the dust settles. Such is the nature of a city in collapse. There's a car crash on the Lodge which is screwing up traffic big time, but won't affect me whatsoever. The roads are clear to the North. A cold front will be moving in Thursday night, but no snow or precipitation is expected. Most of this is just static, something buzzing to distract me from the suffocating silence of my ride. I do take notice when they mention the Heidelberg Project.

Heidelberg, for those of you that don't know, is something of a cultural touchstone in Detroit: a stretch of art installations that began in the nineteen eighties in one of the long-neglected neighborhoods of the city's lower east side (not very far from downtown or Belle Isle, when you get right down to it). It has grown significantly, and at times has been credited with attracting over three-hundred thousand visitors a year to a neighborhood that otherwise resembles a rundown Mogadishu. Depending on your point of view, Heidelberg is either a world-class and epic display of open-air art intended to create discourse, inspire action, and foster community, or it's a bunch of discarded rubbish nailed to the exteriors of a floundering array of abandoned houses. Love it or hate it, benign is the one thing that Heidelberg is not.

I mention this because the carousel of radio news is commenting on a series of arsons on Heidelberg Street. There have been six such fires since May. Six fires in six months: even here, in the pyro capital of America, that's a lot of fires for one or two city blocks. Someone is on a mission. The Obstruction of Justice house has been torched (twice) as well as the House of Soul, which apparently featured a bunch of vinyl records affixed as exterior siding. I'm not even going to begin to describe these displays as they once stood: like I said, love them or hate them, they were virtually impossible to ignore (at least if you have the misfortune of living in this part of the world). There is now debate about the bankrupt city providing adequate protection for these derelict homes. Not that there's any shortage of abandoned homes to affix things to, but the world renowned artist in charge would have a hell of a time keeping up with whoever is doing this. Years of his work, love it or hate it, gone in an instant. I wonder what's wrong with this picture, but then I realize how far off the mark that questions lies. The real question should be "is there anything *right* with this picture?"

By the time I get back to the city it's late afternoon. Then there are other tasks awaiting: helping to reorganize the back room, moving floor racks, a brief trip to the post office. Before I know it the light outside is growing dim and I'm leaving The Emporium in the twilight, suddenly hungry for supper. It's a quick drive to my apartment. At some point I should get to my brother's house, collect the detritus of my previous life, one that lays sequestered in a trailer alongside his garage. That won't be tonight, though. First I need to eat.

I make my way up the stairs. I hear the rumblings of other residents behind their doors; television sets with their volumes turned all-too-high, an argument between two lovers, and somewhere a small child screaming that he does not *want* to go to bed. Odors drift and mingle, completely mitigating the effects of the smoke that choked the building just this morning. I believe the scent is Thai or Vietnamese, some kind of purple anchovy paste (of which I once knew the name) meeting peanut oil, before kissing the air with exotic hints of ginger, coriander, and cayenne.

On the second floor the aroma shifts again, the smells of Southeast Asia giving way to a world more familiar: onion and garlic, for sure, but beneath that a second layer of roots and traditional spices. I detect potatoes, carrots, cabbage, thyme and vinegar. It's a deep, earthy bouquet that fills the hallway. Yet there is something else I haven't identified, a subtle sweetness about it all. For a moment I can't quite put my finger on it, but then the missing ingredient finally comes to mind: beets. Someone in this building is making borscht. I'm halfway down the hall when I realize that the smell is coming from my own apartment.

"Booker, what are you doing? I thought I said no cooking!" I'm barking at him before the door is even open. I've told him no cooking, and I'll be damned if he's going to burn my place down, too. I'm taken aback as soon as I cross the threshold.

"I'm not, man." Booker is standing by the stove, wanting to be clear that he hasn't officially broken protocol. He isn't *cooking* anything; he's just an observer to the actual borscht preparation. The old lady from across the hall, Betty, is positioned next to him, carefully stirring a large aluminum pot with a tall wooden spoon. The place smells great. I'm trying to figure out what's going on here, why these people are in my apartment. Did all their apartments get smoked out, every one excepting mine? Susan is leaning against the kitchen table, a glass of wine in one hand and a half empty bottle resting behind her. A young man and woman I've never met wave at me sheepishly from the far side of the room. Mike is sprawled across my couch/bed with a rat-sized poodle named Bruce tightly pressed against his right leg. "You said *I* couldn't cook. Don't mean a man can't eat."

"Shut up and grab a bowl," Betty tells me. "You're having a housewarming party."

CHAPTER TWELVE

The Wine and Blessings

"I was head over heels in love with your mother," I tell her. All the guests but Susan have gone, and between us sits an empty wine bottle (which by my count is our third this evening). It's well past one in the morning. Even Booker has departed, fortified with enough whiskey to endeavor a reconciliation with the legendary Monica. I expect to see my roommate back any moment, tail between his legs. Still, this time with Susan is golden. "When she was younger, your mom, she was something special."

"I didn't realize you two are friends."

"Were. Past tense."

"Were. Any particular reason for that?"

I think hard on her question, taking another sip from my ceramic mug of wine and letting the taste linger in my mouth. "There's always a reason," I finally respond, "but there isn't always a *good* one."

She mulls that over for a second. "So you two were, like ... a couple?"

"For a few years, anyway." I'm guessing there are parts of Janey's history that she never wished to share with her offspring. No doubt she'd like to leave me dead and buried in her past. It's no wonder she was so cold toward me when I saw her at City Fusion: Janey must have believed that this particular Lazarus was permanently out of her life, only to find out that here I am, ready for an encore performance.

"How come I never heard about this, you and Mom?"

"Have you told your mother about every individual thing *you've* done in the last three or four years?"

"Point taken."

"Anyhow, that's ancient history." *At least to Janey,* I'm thinking. My opportunity to come clean, let Susan know what I know, is gradually slipping away. This would be the time. *Tell her,* my instincts shout, and at the same time I wonder what the point would be. Tell her what exactly? If I tell Susan that I'm her father, do I expect her to jump up, call me "Daddy" and throw her arms around me? Will we suddenly change everything we've become, making up for lost time? Confessing the truth, would it really *accomplish* anything? Or would it only serve to alienate and divide the family she's always known?

"Whose idea was it? I mean, who dumped who?" She's excited by this nugget of hidden history. I'd expect her to be tipsy, but the girl holds her alcohol far better than most. Neither one of us is drunk by any means, but Susan seems more energized by the moment while I'm growing increasingly contemplative and tired. A friend once told me, long, long ago, that there are two types of drinkers: those that grow exuberant and friendlier with the addition of alcohol, and those that merely gravitate toward melancholy. My friend pointed out that I have always been (decidedly) in that latter category, the King of Melancholy. Susan, on the other hand, seems to be getting sharper by the minute.

"She dumped me," I tell her plainly.

"Really? I mean, most men would claim it was a mutual decision at the very least. You know, try to save face."

The girl is right on the mark. Most men would try to save a little face, but I've never been overly concerned with what other people think. "You're right. The decision was mutual. We both decided that she was dumping me," I reply, and she and I both burst out laughing.

"You're not even going to try to spin the story? I'm giving you a chance to plead your case here."

"I was guilty as charged." I try to sum it up as best I can. "We weren't right for each other. At least that's what I was told at the time. We had our issues. If I'd have looked hard enough I might have seen the train coming, but your mom was the first to pull the switch. In the end, she was doing us both a favor."

"Did you believe her?"

"Did I believe that she was breaking up with me?"

"No, did you believe that you two weren't right for each other? Did you believe her at the time?"

"No one in love ever wants to believe that a relationship can't work. People always like to think that they can fix those things that are fractured. I guess I thought that over time she'd see the light, and we'd get back together."

"So were you heartbroken?"

"A little," I admit. More than a little. I was *plenty* heartbroken, but Susan doesn't need to know that. "But I got over it."

"It's crazy that I never heard about any of this. How old were you?"

"We were in college," I mumble, trying not to get too specific.

"No shit," she sighs, and I can see her doing the math in her head. "This must have been, what, twenty-three years ago?"

"Something like that."

"Because I'm twenty-one, so this must have been before she met my father. That's just amazing." And then I see her reworking the math, making a small adjustment for historical markers here and there. She sips the dregs of her wine, and the moment when everything clicks is broadcast clearly across her face. "Twenty-two," she tells me, a rising note of alarm in her voice. "Twenty-two" is not a number so much as it is an accusation. "Twenty-two, right? You left twenty-two years ago?" She's getting more adamant now.

"That's probably a bit more accurate." I'm feeling suddenly uncomfortable. The room is too warm. This is a moment I've been both anticipating and dreading. I didn't expect it to take place in quite this manner, at one a.m. over three bottles of cheap chardonnay, but here it is no less, the moment when Susan learns I am her father.

"You left, and you knew. You knew that she was pregnant." It *is* an accusation. She has gone from congenial to disbelief to anger to a state of shock, all in the span of about two minutes. Disbelief is waning while anger is in full ascension. "And then you left."

"I didn't know," I try to diffuse the ire. "She never told me." I'm not sure what else I can say. How can you explain something like that? What kind of a man would walk out on a pregnant girlfriend? I *didn't* know, and that is the god's honest truth. I was a different person at the time, and Jane was too. It wasn't just due to our youth, and it wasn't just our precarious seat on the precipice of adulthood. It was *all of it*, our *lives,* and I don't know how to accurately characterize the situation in this one brief conversation. I can't. All a person can do is try to make amends and ask for forgiveness, forgiveness for both the real and the perceived sins of my past. "Honestly, I didn't know." I hold out my arms and show her my palms in a gesture of surrender.

"But she let you leave." The shock appears to be wearing off. "Why would she let you leave without even telling you?" Disbelief again.

"We were broken up by that time," I remind her. "She didn't owe me anything."

"That's no excuse. She cheated you. She cheated me."

"It's not an excuse," I agree. Although it might well have been a reason, or at least a *factor* in Janey's mind at the time. I'd like to give her the benefit of the doubt. Who's to say? Did she think life would be easier without me? Was she trying to spare me the pain of being a father with a woman that didn't want me involved in her world? Was it for my benefit that she let me walk away, or was it for hers? Maybe she was trying to spare me from commitment, or maybe she wanted one less complication in a suddenly complicated life. Only Janey can answer those questions. In any event, I find it hard to believe that Susan was *cheated* out of anything. "Spared" might be a better word. "I don't think you can fault her." That's my job.

"And just like that, she let you go."

"Just like that. She let me go."

"Well, *shit.*" Susan belts out, and takes another swallow from her mug.

"You've got that right." I agree. Then we sit in silence, finishing our wine.

It's fifteen minutes later when Booker comes through the door with a bag of sliders in hand. "I thought you guys might like something to eat."

"Thanks, Booker." I'm not sure where he found hamburgers at nearly two in the morning, but he's right, man can't live on borscht alone.

"I brought fries, too."

"You're a good man," I tell him, and I mean it. I am gradually warming to the idea of Booker staying here for a few weeks, staying here and feeding me.

Susan opens the bag and prods suspiciously at the grease-soaked wax paper that surrounds each burger. "Are you sure these are safe?"

"Of course they're safe. They're the best burgers in the Corridor," he assures us. "I brought fries, too."

"Beef?" She asks, and I wonder what other kind of meat people might be disguising as beef. I hope she's not vegan.

"Of course it's beef," he answers, slightly offended.

"I'll try one." She gives up her resistance. "Midtown," she corrects him.

"Excuse me?" Booker looks confused.

"*The Corridor* is old-school. It's called *Midtown* now, a fancier name which helps bring in all the single urban hipster-wanna-bes that will eventually buy up these buildings, boot out the current tenants and triple the rent. Gentrification is coming, my friend. You and I, old people and struggling artists, we'll all be evicted for a better class of people or a new municipal stadium. We're all passé, at least as far as the movers and shakers are concerned. It is what it is. All hail the holy grail of progress. *The Corridor* is no more, we're *Midtown* now." Susan knows her history, knows it with an almost militant fervor. She must have been reading up on the Black Panthers.

"Thanks for the lesson, but I'll stick with old-school," Booker answers, undefeated by this breaking news. He's been here a long time and he's not going anywhere, not without a fight. Try as you might, it's very hard to extinguish the indigenous population of a place like The Corridor. They take refuge in the cracks and crevices of society, waiting out the temporary twists and turns of economic ups and downs without ever truly disappearing. They have patience. The Bookers of this world know something about survival.

"I thought you were heading over to Monica's?" I ask Booker, trying to lighten the tone.

"I was, but then I thought better of it. She's gonna need more time to cool down. Might be time to move on."

"What prompted this epiphany?" Susan interrogates him between bites of her burger, which she is enjoying with unrestrained vigor. She's off the Midtown lecture circuit for the time being.

"I must be getting wise in my old age," Booker smiles.

"So you changed your mind," I opine.

"So I changed my mind," he confirms.

"I don't know your girl Miss Monica, but I'm guessing you made the right choice," I kid him.

"You've probably known a whole bunch of Monicas in your time: so beautiful that you can't stand being away from them, so dangerous that you need to keep your distance. Right now she's in dangerous mode, and I need to keep my distance. No man in his right mind messes with Monica when she's in dangerous mode. Susan, you should change your name to Monica. No, I went into the office instead. That's the upside of my job: plenty of flex time, and I've got my own key. As long as the work gets done, the bosses don't seem to care too much when I go in."

"Must be nice," muses Susan.

"The job has its perks."

After a while Susan rises from her seat, yawns and stretches. "Well, I hate to be a party pooper, but it's nearly two o'clock. I'm going home. A girl's got to get her rest. Good-night, y'all. Happy housewarming. It was ... enlightening, to say the least."

"Goodnight, neighbor," Booker lazily waves a hand in her direction, then changes his mind and lays a clumsy hug across her shoulders.

"We'll talk later?" I ask her as she steps toward the door.

"Unless you decide to skip town in a hurry," she answers with a wink and a smile, and then she's gone. The wink and smile are much appreciated: at least I know that wherever we go from here, Susan and I, she's willing to talk to me. That's a start. We'll find a way to make this work. I momentarily bask in the glow of my success. The door is barely locked behind her when I'm hit with a different question, this one from the man inside my kitchen.

"What was that about?" Booker is more perceptive than I ever would have guessed.

"What was what about?" I respond, pleading innocence and stalling for time. He's not falling for it.

"That wink thing," he points out. "And '*enlightening.*' Whatever that was, it wasn't normal. What was so damn *enlightening* about your party? Nobody says 'enlightening' anymore. Are you two harboring some kind of a secret?" Despite the harsh tone he isn't intending to be mean or pushy, just curious: Booker is a guy who pays attention to detail.

"Nobody says 'harboring' anymore, so long as we're splitting hairs."

"I do."

"Well, you're one enlightening guy," I laugh, and he laughs with me.

"Anything you want to tell me?"

"Nothing that can't wait until later," I tell him, collapsing on the couch. I doubt it's anything I want to discuss in the morning, either. "I'm turning in. Are you going to be up much longer?"

"No. I'm turning in, too. You can kill the light. Hey, thanks again for letting me crash here." Booker's also a man who's smart enough to know when it's time to back off from a direct line of questioning. His shady love life and trouble with SpaghettiO's aside, Booker would appear to have his shit somewhat together.

"My pleasure. Thanks for the party."

"Don't tell me, tell Betty. It was her idea. I think she's adopting you."

"Betty's idea?" It never would have occurred to me. "Why would she do that? She hardly knows me."

"Maybe she's sweet on you, needs a man in her life," he jests. At least I hope he's kidding: Betty is pleasant enough, but what I don't need is an eighty-something-year-old girlfriend/stalker. I don't need *any* kind of a girlfriend right now. It would only complicate matters. "Now are you gonna tell me what was so enlightening?"

"Goodnight, Booker," I answer him, an indicator that the discussion is closed.

"Goodnight, roomie."

Thus for the second night in a row I find myself cocooned in this strange city, an unfamiliar world slowly sprouting and emerging from the ashes of the past. I wonder if every prodigal son feels this way; a sense of no longer belonging to any one place or time, combined with an inability to recognize what was once familiar. There's no clear path ahead, only a hazy and distant horizon. These are the thoughts that tumble through my mind as I lay alone in the dark, adrift and rudderless on an overwhelming sea of change.

"Count your blessings," I was told as a child, and so to comfort myself I begin to make a list of blessings. I have my health and a truck that works: blessings. A roof over my head: blessing. Davros: both a blessing and a curse. Susan: one-hundred-percent blessing. Janey: probably not a blessing. Janey will only provide turmoil to my world, if she's there at all. Pierogies and borscht: tasty blessings. That's all I've got so far. It's a short list, but still, a start. Maybe more will come to me later. Of course there is one enigma: I still can't decide how to categorize my new and unexpected roommate, a roommate who is now out cold and snoring spasmodically on my floor. His presence is an unwanted intrusion in my life. Yet, in a few brief days he's found a way to connect me to a community within the community: that's a good thing. Is Booker a blessing or a curse? Is he both? I'll go with blessing for now, though I reserve the right to change my mind. My thoughts drift elsewhere.

One of my first apartments in this city (back when I was young and foolish enough to think that I was impervious to the evil that lurks behind nearly every street corner) stood a few miles to the south and east of here. That 'apartment' was the left side of a freestanding, two-story duplex that had somehow survived the wrecking ball. Demolition was long overdue. Her brick facade was crumbling and there were visible holes in the exterior walls. There was dense ivy climbing the face of the brick, and while I was of the opinion that it gave the place a certain country charm, I also realized that the ivy was more than likely the only thing holding the joint together. I remember once sitting in the claw-foot, cast iron bathtub and sticking my hand through a hole in that second-story wall, grasping nothing but air. At the time it felt as if I could reach all the way to outer space, a feeling that leaves one disconnected from the world around him. Each of the other buildings on that solitary city block had long-before been torn down, and this building was merely awaiting the inevitable amidst a field of broken cement, knee-high weeds, and Norway rats.

Roaches, well, don't get me started on the cockroaches: they were everywhere. I have lived in a variety of conditions throughout my life, some good and some bad, but the one constant has been that I truly despise those filthy little beasts. My roommate at the time, he and I would play a game called "roach wars." We would turn out the lights in the kitchen and then, after five or ten minutes, flick the lights back on. He and I would be standing at the ready, each with a can of aerosol hair spray and a disposable lighter. The moment the lights came on, flaming tongues of death rained down upon the unsuspecting roaches, and we would chase around the room incinerating at will until there were no more roaches left to burn. The winner was determined by roach body count.

I'm thinking of that rental now, not because of any sense of nostalgia for a time long-forgotten. That place was a death trap, that's all it was: I'd be hard-pressed to conjure up one good memory of my brief stay in that dump. No, I'm remembering something that used to lull me to sleep amidst the sound of squealing tires and random gunfire. Behind this duplex stood a row of equally shabby, single-story commercial buildings fronting Grand River Avenue and the long-since eradicated tenements of the Jeffries Housing Projects on the other side. The backs of those shabby stores were visible just beyond the tall weeds of my backyard and the abandoned lots that lay between us. From my bedroom window in the upper back corner of that dilapidated duplex, I could barely make out the flickering neon cross from a storefront mission on the main drag. "Jesus Died for Your Sins," the sign flashed in a faltering red glow. Not "Our Sins," mind you, but "Your Sins." I took this particular choice of words as an accusation as much as any call to faith. "Your Sins" indeed. Why weren't the sins of the self-professed missionaries included on Jesus's scorecard, too? Were they claiming Jesus' death was entirely my fault, that their own personal sins played no part in it? It seemed presumptuous, to say the least, presumptuous bordering on arrogant.

Faith has never been my strong suit (as I mentioned earlier), but this message, well, it seemed a bit like a poke in the eye with a sharp stick. For a while this suggestion that I had somehow personally killed the messiah pissed me off, before I learned to let it go. You can't stay angry about everything all of the time: it's far too taxing. After a bit I learned to not worry about the message and instead appreciate the blinking neon nightlight as a comforting gift, a symbol that *somebody* was watching out for the rest of us, regardless of any misguided theology on their part. What did it really matter if a single pastor or slew of missionaries were right or they were wrong on the details? Irrespective of their personal judgments, God or no god, at least the storefront missionaries were *watching*, paying attention to the least among them (which is a big part of loving thy neighbor). It's hard to love someone if you're consistently averting your eyes. I gave them points for *trying* to save me: it was more than I was willing to give.

Lying here in the night I wonder if that duplex is still standing, and I make a mental note to drive by the place in the morning. I don't know if I want it to be standing or not; which would be better? Despite a lifelong desire to wipe the slate clean, it might be comforting to know that some evidence of my past still exists, somewhere, besides in the DNA of a girl in the apartment above me. I'm guessing that a big part of being a parent (even a belated parent) involves giving a child some sense of yourself and your family's history. What legacy do I have that I can leave to Susan? A suburban brother that I don't know all that well? An estranged, crazy sister, still waging war over the mythical family relics? An unrecognizable, abandoned house on the far west side of the city and either a dilapidated rental or a weed-choked vacant lot not far from a casino? What exactly do I bring to the table?

The one thing I'd really like to know (far more than whether or not that vermin-infested duplex still slumps wearily against the earth) is whether or not the storefront church on Grand River Avenue is still intact. More significantly, does the cross on the front of the mission still blink neon red into the night? Is anyone who cruises that lonely stretch of pavement late at night still reminded that Jesus died for *his* sins (but not necessarily the sins of the churchgoers), and that somebody, somewhere, is watching out for the welfare of the lonely driver? It occurs to me that possibly, just *possibly* this can be my gift to Susan, just as Booker's existence has become the Corridor's gift to me: my personal presence as a silent sentry. I'll be her guardian, not in the legal sense of the word (it's far too late for that), but in the sense of being an overseer, a watchdog, a protector and defender. With or without Susan's knowledge, with or without Janey's permission, it's the one gift I am still able to provide. I will become that neon cross from the mission, standing guard in the darkness.

CHAPTER THIRTEEN

Hindsight

Patrick was not in the least amused when I told him about my new apartment.

"You've got to be kidding me. You're going to live in the fricking *Corridor*?" he exclaims. For Patrick, that's as vulgar as language gets.

"Midtown," I correct him, using the hip new moniker to which I was so recently introduced.

"It's still the Corridor no matter what they want to call it. I love you brother, but that's just downright stupid. Do you have any idea what that neighborhood is like these days? The crime rate? Any idea how many murders there were in the city last year? Take a guess. This isn't the eighties, and you're not a kid anymore. There are predators down there. *Lots* of predators. You're making a mistake. You might want to rethink this one."

I'm quickly remembering what it was that I liked about living two-thousand miles from family. It is good to be loved: it's often better to be loved from afar. I find myself defending the place. "You'd be surprised at the improvements down there. It's a lot different, all kinds of redevelopment. Don't worry about me, I'll be fine," I reassure him. I'm not sure that I believe my own words.

"That's just it: we *do* worry about you. Judy and I, hell, even your sister Mary (I notice that she's *my* sister now, like we're playing a game of hot potato and I'm the loser). We don't have any choice in the matter. You *force us* to worry about you, and you're not doing much to make us believe we *shouldn't* worry. You've made some odd choices, but this might top them all. My kids barely know their uncle, and you getting shot or beaten to death won't strengthen that relationship. What am I going to tell them at the funeral? 'Sorry kids, your uncle was an idiot.' I'm not saying you need to buy a house, get married and have kids: but Christ, little brother, at some point you're going to have to settle down. Life doesn't get any easier in your old age, you know."

"Thanks for the lecture, Dad."

"Not funny." Apparently this strikes a nerve, but then, that remark always does. Comparisons to my father scare the hell out of the both of us. We're terrified that within the insult may lie some kernel of truth, that we are somehow predestined to follow in our father's angry, depressing footsteps.

"Sorry about the cheap shot. But honestly, you don't need to sweat it. I've gotten this far in life doing my own thing; I'm pretty sure the world will continue spinning no matter where I live. In the meantime, I've got some business to take care of in the city, and it's easier if I live close by."

"What do you possibly have to take care of in that city?"

"Business." I'm stonewalling.

"*Legit* business?"

"Is there any other kind?"

He knows that there are *many* other kinds, an entire business *spectrum* featuring varying shades of legitimacy. The look on his face suggests Patrick doesn't believe I've chosen the right side of the color wheel. He tries a different tactic. "You could stay here, in the spare bedroom. Judy wouldn't mind."

"You and I both know that's not likely to work." He has to admit that I'm right. He and Judy and three kids in no way need a strange uncle that keeps odd hours added to their household. As for me, I'm fairly certain I'd go bat shit crazy living in a town with no downtown, let alone in a house with kids. And Judy doesn't allow liquor in the house, a minor annoyance but one that could grow substantially.

"Just be sure to keep your head up," he finally tells me.

"I always do," I lie.

And so I hitched up the U-Haul and dragged the fragments of my old life to Midtown (I still prefer Cass Corridor, but I've been trying to put a positive spin on things) to meet the hollow shell of my latest incarnation.

The first thing that I realize, once I'm parked in front of my building, is that I'm going to need a hand getting the trailer unloaded and up to the apartment. When I get inside I discover that Booker isn't home. Andy isn't around, either, which surprises me even though it shouldn't. Wouldn't you think the superintendent of an apartment building should be somewhere on the premises during normal business hours? It's midmorning, so he can't be off to lunch. Sometimes the city moves to its own beat. In the meantime I'm more than a little worried that my truck and trailer will disappear from the street while I'm inside trying to locate help. I knock on a couple of doors, rousing nothing but the suspicions of Betty and Bruce, before finally giving up and moving on.

Davros is parked behind the counter of The Emporium, but he can't leave because he's running the store solo today. He doesn't know what Skinny Clerk Guy is up to, and seems unwilling to give out the kid's phone number for fear that I might somehow steal his prodigy away. He suggests I head back to my apartment and wait. If Booker or Andy don't show up, he'll send Skinny Clerk Guy my way for an hour or two later in the day. This isn't much of an offer, but I don't have any better ideas so I sheepishly agree.

"You owe me one," Davros points out, as if I didn't expect him to add the act of largess to his side of the ledger. I'm unclear on what he thinks I owe him *for,* exactly.

"Put it on my tab," I wave as I exit the building. Back to the apartment, still no Booker and still no Andy. Twenty minutes pass by, then an hour. It's nearly noon. I look out the second-floor window and two kids are trying to bust open the rear door of the U-Haul. Punks. Thirty-seconds later I'm down at the curb, swinging a broomstick wildly and screaming like a crazy man as the two kids hightail it down the street. This is what Susan sees as she rounds the corner and approaches the truck.

"Aren't you in fine form today," she quips.

"Just getting a little exercise," I tell her, panting for breath.

111

"You're lucky they didn't have a gun," she tells me, nodding in the direction of the two kids.

"They're lucky I didn't have a dustpan," I respond, and she laughs.

"Moving in, I assume?"

"Hoping to, anyhow. I was looking for Booker or somebody that could give me a hand with this stuff."

"Is there anything really big in there, like a sofa that you have to deal with?"

"Nothing bigger than a small bookshelf," I respond. "But at the very least I need someone to keep an eye on the trailer every time I carry a load up the stairs. Otherwise everything will walk away."

"I can do better than that. I've got an hour or so. We can alternate trips, and then you won't be so beat up by the time this thing is empty."

"Are you calling me old?"

"I'm offering you mercy."

"Thanks."

"Nada."

It doesn't take long before it's brought to my attention, bit by bit, that much of what I deemed worthy of hauling cross-country is utterly worthless junk.

"You're not really going to use this lamp in your apartment, are you?"

"Why, what's wrong with it?"

"It looks like something you discovered crammed underneath a manhole cover."

I look at her to see if she's kidding. She's not kidding. "It works," I plead, but she's not letting me off that easily. "There's nothing wrong with it," I plead some more.

"Are you sure you didn't just run electrical wires through a broken table leg?" Susan is one tough cookie.

"Fine, set it off to the side. I'll donate it to the Salvation Army," I give in.

"Are they gonna want it?" She asks, and I know she's not kidding. Will they want it? Probably not. We move on to the next item.

"What kind of raccoon was chewing on this end table?" Susan tests me. And so it goes. By the time the trailer is empty, there are more of my possessions in the discard pile than there are in my apartment.

"Susan, I'm not sure I can afford to replace all of this junk." I'm a pragmatist: if something still functions, however poorly, I'll use it until there's nothing left to use. I don't care what it looks like, and I hate buying new stuff. "It'll cost money."

"Twenty bucks should just about cover the lot of it."

"Heartless, that's what you are." The girl is right, but I don't want to admit it.

"You don't need to replace everything all at once, just buy what you need when you need it. You'll discover that you've been hauling around things you don't actually *require*. I'm sure you don't want people who visit you to think you hijacked a garbage truck, or that some homeless guy had his shopping cart explode inside of your apartment." Quite a sense of humor this one has.

I stare at her coldly for a moment, but she's not easily intimidated. She's right, and she knows she's right. "Just dandy. I'll give this stuff away," I give up on my end of the argument. "Thanks for all your help. Can I buy you dinner tonight as a token of appreciation?" This parental stuff is beginning to grow on me.

"Sure. Eight o'clock, City Fusion?"

"Not the best choice for me. How about Union Street Saloon?" I ask.

She doesn't question why City Fusion isn't my first selection. We both know. Janey. It would be uncomfortable for me, to say the least, to meet at the ex's place of business. "Union Street? That'll work for me. I'll meet you there." She's let me off the hook.

With that she helps me load the items from the discard pile back into the trailer, which I promptly haul down to the Fort Street Salvation Army for donation. At the Army donation center a shifty kid on the loading dock gives me a tax receipt for my bounty. A damn lot of good that will do: if I'm not working a regular job, how likely am I to itemize my tax return come April? Afterwards I return the trailer to a U-Haul neighborhood drop-off location. By the time I get back to Selden Avenue the day is mostly over. I'm hot, tired and cranky. All I wish for is to get upstairs, peel the dusty clothes from my back, and take a scalding shower. The universe has other ideas.

The shower is running, trying to suck a little bit of warm water from the antique boiler in the basement. Hot water takes upwards of ten minutes to arrive, an interesting feature that Andy failed to disclose when giving me the initial tour of this place. I'm stripped down to my shorts and draining a bottle of Pabst Blue Ribbon down my throat when there's a knock at the front door. I know it's not Booker (he has his own key).

"Coming," I yell as I scramble to find my jeans. The knock comes again, and I'm pulling my pants up as I hop through a maze of cardboard boxes toward the doorway. "Almost there," as the knock persists.

It turns out to be Skinny Clerk Guy, who Dav has finally sent over to help me. I tell him I've got everything under control. He stands in the hallway disappointed, palm outstretched, like he's some sort of bellhop waiting for a tip. I'm not going to give him a tip.

"Tell Davros I said thanks, though." I assure him. He doesn't flinch. I'm still not giving him a tip.

He peeks over my shoulder at the chaos of my living area and reluctantly accepts my explanation, but it's obvious the kid's not happy. I don't think he wanted to come here in the first place, and it turns out he's made the trip for nothing. "Can I get you a beer or something?" I offer as he turns to leave. It isn't much, but a consolation prize is better than no prize at all.

"No, thanks, I need to get back to the store. Davros would be mad if I get caught drinking on the job." And then he's gone.

Closing the door, I return to the shower, where the water temperature has finally climbed all the way up to "tepid." The water *pressure* is almost nonexistent: what trickles from the shower head can best be compared to a very old man with prostate problems, peeing softly in the night. I shed my jeans, waving one foot cautiously inside the fiberglass stall (shower only, no tub in this land of the dirt-cheap remodel). Tepid water is better than cold water. Some water is better than no water at all. That's two blessings, if I can keep a positive attitude and brace for the chill that I know is headed my way. I'm almost in the shower, ready to submit to the cold, when the knocking sounds again.

"Coming," I yell, and curse beneath my breath. I shut the water off (seeing any chance for a hot shower as a lost cause), dry my wet left leg, and once again hop into my filthy pants. Skinny Clerk must have changed his mind about that beer. "Almost there" I shout, making my shirtless way to the door. Skinny Clerk might be a nice guy, but he's had his chance. The kid should have just gone back to the store and left me alone. He's rapidly wearing out his welcome. The pounding on the door continues.

People have a tendency to search for moments in life: sharp, clearly identifiable points in time where the world changes, for better or for worse. Seven-forty-eight a.m. on December 7th, 1941 is one such example, the moment when the Imperial Japanese Navy bombed Pearl Harbor. Those who were there can tell you that in one precise second the world as they knew it ceased to exist: things for those folks would never again be the same. September 11, 2001 and the destruction of the World Trade Center was another such moment. Ask anyone and they can probably tell you exactly where they were and what they were doing when that attack occurred. Kennedy getting shot, the death of Dr. Martin Luther King, Jr., the first moon landing: those moments are game changers, embedded in our society's collective consciousness as waypoints to help us understand a world that's constantly morphing around us.

I've always believed that game-changing moments tend to be less common on the personal level. Sure, most people can recount the precise details of the birth of their first child, or how Uncle Al had a heart attack the day of their wedding, or that time they broke their leg while riding on a motorcycle, but for the most part the things that shape and define us tend to arrive in incremental fashion. That's why we don't notice them. It's rare that any single event indelibly inscribes your future, your hopes and dreams and personality.

"If only I had done this *one* thing differently," hindsight tells us. Hindsight is a bald-faced liar. It's a fluke for there to be one decision and one decision alone that permanently and irrevocably affects every decision thereafter. Sure, there will be exceptions to the rule, but in most instances we fool ourselves. Our screwed-up lives tend to be long-term, cumulative efforts, marathons of bad choices and general stupidity. We're afforded multiple opportunities to veer from any chosen path, and any one of those detours could have produced the same (or better) life results. Still we doubt that truth because we are too frightened, inattentive, or lazy to change course, and thus have no hard evidence to the contrary. It 's easier to blame our shortcomings on one solitary mistake. That's the nature of the game. Nearly everyone is afforded off-ramps; most of the time people refuse to admit it.

All of this brings me to this moment. I'm about to open the front door. I'm expecting that on the other side of the threshold stands a kid who's had a change of heart about whether or not he wants a beer. I hardly know this kid. In my mind as I currently know it, I allow that we will have one drink together and then he will be on his way. I'm wearing pants but I haven't bothered with a shirt, socks, or shoes. I'm sweaty and dusty and tired. I am neither searching for nor am I expecting any shining moment of lucidity, no waypoints or guideposts or thunderclaps that would serve to further rearrange my already precarious standing in life. This shows how little I know.

Even I have choices. I could refuse to open the door, get back in the shower and wait for my visitor to leave. I could yell "go away." I could do nothing. Instead I open the door, an unmarked portal to that place where past and future, reason and emotion all flow together, roiling in a turbulent mixture every bit as dirty as it is violent. In the hall stands Janey, waiting to greet me. She is visibly angry. Is this about to be one of those rare, life-altering encounters, or just another step down a well-beaten path?

CHAPTER FOURTEEN

Zombie Dogs in the City

"Stay away from my daughter."

"That's kind of hard to do." *For a variety of reasons*, I'm thinking, not the least of which is that Susan and I currently reside in the same tiny building. I don't necessarily appreciate the possessive "my" daughter, either. Shouldn't she be saying 'our' daughter? I don't speak those words, however: if there's one thing I've learned about Jane (and granted, my education in Janeology is more than a little out-of-date, so I might require a refresher course) it's that once she's angry, I need to stay the hell out of her way. Say no more than is absolutely required, and let her get everything out of her system.

"I mean it, stay away."

"We live in the same building, Jane. She's kind of hard to avoid."

"That was your choice, not mine."

Actually it was Susan's choice as much as it was mine, but again, I decide to avoid the incendiary. Jane doesn't need any help reaching her boiling point. "Well, it's still a fact," I tell her.

She gives me "The Look." I'd forgotten about The Look, but here it is, as vibrant today as it was twenty some years before. There might even be some new details that have been worked into the routine during my prolonged absence. I wonder if her husband gets to see The Look on a regular basis, or has it been tucked away in a special time capsule, awaiting my return? Does she practice The Look in front of the mirror in the privacy of her own room, exercising and perfecting the skill through repetition like an Olympic gymnast? I can't precisely define The Look, because it is a complex being that often takes on a life of its own. It is dynamic, rather than static. It expresses scorn, severe disappointment, unyielding dedication to a specific purpose, but there is more to it than just that. In its subtler tones you can detect all of your previous failures as a lover and as a person, etched one by one for time ever after. There exists both power and vulnerability in The Look, a reminder of what damage a person has caused, and the consequences that accompany such actions. Anger, resentment, recognition that this was all a foregone conclusion; it's all there. It lives in her eyes, in the twitching of her nose, and carves itself into the furrows of her brow. When Jane gets this way, her face becomes that of the All Knowing. "Don't even think about it," sayeth The Look, an instant slideshow of the past, present, and future.

"Then find a new place to live," she tells me angrily.

"I can't right now." This is true. I could afford to move, but I can't bring myself to relocate. Not now. I no longer feel as if I have a choice in the matter.

The Look slowly melts, washed away and replaced by the still-beautiful but timeworn face that I thought I once knew. It's the face that I fell in love with, only with creases and wrinkles and a whole lot more life lived. This is a complex face, the face of a girl that became a business woman. A very experienced, beautiful, tough business woman. Passion is quickly replaced by resolve and negotiation. "How much?"

"How much what?" I ask, thinking she means how much time before I'll finally go away and stay away or how much time do I intend to spend around our daughter.

"How much will it take for you to leave?"

She's offering me a bribe, and that catches me off guard. That's a new one for me, though I'm not sure why I'm so shocked. If anything I should be more shocked that no woman *before* has offered me compensation to get out of her life and stay out. A few might have found it cost-effective in the long haul. In Janey's case, it's absolutely the prudent thing to do.

"Please tell me you're joking." I know that she's not. "You're trying to buy me off?"

"I'm just saying. If it's because you can't afford to move again, I could help you. You know you don't belong here. Why would you want to move back to this place? There's nothing here for you. Is it about the money?"

118

"It's not about the money." Who's she kidding? She knows it's not about the money. Of all the things it could be about (for me in particular), well it sure as hell has never been about the money. *She* is the one that is all about the money, at least as far as I can tell. Money only matters to me when I don't have any, and I'm not yet broke.

"Look, you don't have a job. You don't have any friends here..."

"Not true," I cut her off. "I've got Davros. And Booker. And Betty." Who can forget my octogenarian paramour across the hall? It's a paltry list, but still... All are friends of mine, in a manner of speaking. In the case of Betty I'm stretching things a bit, but what does Janey know? Who is she to argue the finer points of friendship? "I've got friends, though I appreciate your pep talk. You really know how to shine a positive light on a guy's life."

"Who in the hell is Betty?" she's calling my bluff on that one. Janey always has been intuitive.

"A friend," I answer, figuring she doesn't need to know any more. "There's nothing between us. She and Bruce are a couple," like that explains anything.

She ponders this for a second. It sounds plausible enough to get her to let go and move on. She doesn't need to know that Betty is an octogenarian and that Bruce is a canine. "So you're staying put?"

"For now."

"You won't reconsider?" She's used to getting her way, and not happy that I've declined her opening bid.

"Not at the moment."

"Then leave Susan alone." That's Jane's Plan B. If you can't bribe, bully.

"I can't promise that. Besides, she's an adult." That other thing is left unsaid.

"She's still a kid. Stay away from her."

119

I know that Jane has a point, but I've already decided to stand my ground. Arguing with Jane is a force of habit. "She's old enough to think for herself."

"Susan's a young woman. A *vulnerable* young woman. You should know a lot about that sort of thing. Vulnerable woman, does it ring any bells? She doesn't need you around helping her to make bad decisions. I don't want to see you screw up her life, too."

Too. That word sticks out like a red flag. It's comforting to know that Jane's opinion of me hasn't become excessively elevated. Does she think I screwed up her life, my own, or both? "You sure know how to make a guy feel loved," I tell her. "Not all of my decisions have been bad." Not all of them.

"I'm serious," she blurts. She is definitely that: she's serious and then some. Serious as a heart attack. "Stay away from Susan," again.

"You know, there was a time when you didn't think I was all that bad." I recognize that I'm playing with fire here, but what have I got to lose? The woman is already angry. I don't want her as an enemy.

"That was a lifetime ago. I've learned since then. But as long as we're bringing up old times, do me one favor. I'm sure you'll agree that you owe me *at least* one favor. Stay away." Persistence.

"I'll see what I can do." That's pretty much all anyone can promise: essentially nothing. Even if I meant them, good intentions don't necessitate a desirable outcome, so why lie? I'll see what I can do.

"This is not a battle you want to pick," she sends one final warning, then turns and storms out without another word.

Jane is correct: this is not the battle that I wish to pick. I'm not a fighter. I've never been a fighter. I'm a *flighter*. My instinct is to get out of Dodge. Janey is a strong woman, a smart woman. She has resources and powerful friends and money. She's not a woman anyone would wish to cross. But sometimes life is not about the battles that you pick, but rather, the battles that pick *you*. I'm pondering this, the battles that have chosen me: there have been surprisingly few in my lifetime. Much of that comes from my own world view. I'm more of an observer or conscientious objector than a foot soldier in life's struggles. Things are safer this way.

Moments later I'm back in the shower, encouraged by the sudden deluge of warm water. A clot of rust and sediment must have kicked loose from a pipe somewhere in the bowels of the building. Like a heart recently cathed, a clear channel in the plumbing temporarily affords me a taste of what things were like when the place was newly built. I'm lathered up and enjoying this unexpected gift, blasting a day's worth of dirty and tired from my body and my soul with a steady stream of hot water. I spend fifteen minutes under the flood and relish every second. I hear the door slam in the living room and assume it's Booker, returned home. By the time I step out of the shower (warm water still in abundance) I feel like a new man.

"Booker, what's up, my friend?" I'm toweling off my hair, dressed in my now customary outfit of dirty jeans, no shirt.

"Hey, I didn't know you were still here. I want you to meet someone." I look up, and there's a young lady standing next to my roommate. I'm quickly having one of those "aw shit" moments with the expectation that the infamous Monica will be moving in with us next. She's a lot prettier than I'd anticipated: somewhere around thirty, tall and muscular but not overbearing, with smooth skin the shade of oil-rubbed bronze.

"You must be..." I start, but Booker cuts me off before I can do any further damage.

"Giselle," he informs me. "She's a professor over at the art college." Not the name I was expecting. Not the volatile, cut-your throat Monica of legend. Booker shifts gears faster than a Ferrari.

"Giselle. Pretty name," I recover nicely.

"Thank you," she smiles demurely. She doesn't look like any professor I've ever had. Maybe I should have stuck around school a little longer.

"Let me grab a shirt and I'll be right back out," I tell them, back stepping toward the bathroom.

"Don't bother. She's seen a man's chest before," Booker chides, and the woman winks at me, so I figure I might as well stay put. "Besides, we were just about to leave. I just wanted to show Giselle where I live." I don't bother to correct him: this is not "where he lives," not for long, anyway, but why rain on his parade? Let him spin his web.

"Well, take your time. I'm going out to dinner myself."

"Got a hot date?"

"I wouldn't exactly say that."

"A cold date's better than no date, that's what I say." Giselle doesn't appear to find this funny, and she scowls at Booker. Even her scowl is sexy, but I can tell she disapproves. It's not nice to make light of relationships when you're in the early stages of a newfound romance. Roomie is oblivious: Booker must have skipped this chapter while attending finishing school. "Are you seeing somebody new?" he asks.

"No, just meeting Susan for dinner."

"Interesting." I can tell he means a lot more when he says 'interesting,' but doesn't want to start a long Q & A session while his newfound friend is waiting. "You and Susan, what's that about?"

"It's not what you think."

"I'm not thinking anything. I'm a man without expectations, right honey?" He turns to Giselle.

"You better be," she lets him know.

"Strong woman," Booker nods his head toward the professor. I've got my own string of questions for Booker, including what happened to love-of-his-life Monica, but I figure I'll save them for later.

"Apparently so," I agree.

"And what exactly do you do?" the tall beauty asks me. She's got a good four inches of strength and beauty over Booker.

"I don't *exactly* do anything right now. I'm just sort of knocking around." I'm buttoning a shirt that I snagged from the back of the couch, one that I'm not entirely sure is clean. I give it a quick sniff test and decide that it will have to do. "Just a bit of this and a bit of that," I tell her, and immediately recognize how pathetic this sounds.

"I've been meaning to talk with you about that," Booker interjects. "I've got a position for you."

"Thanks, but I didn't know I was looking for one." I can only imagine what sort of *position* my association with Booker might place me in: locked in the trunk of a car, handcuffed to a police officer, the possibilities seem endless.

"Trust me, you're looking. You'll thank me later."

"I'm supposed to do a few things for Davros tomorrow afternoon. Maybe after I'm done with that."

"That's not a *job*, man. That's a *hobby*. I like Davros and everything, but come on... Seriously, this is totally above board and the pay is decent. I'm trying to keep a roof over our heads."

I laugh. He's trying to keep a roof over *our* heads? I thought that I was the one doling out charity, and now Booker believes that he's my benefactor. Did the tables turn when I wasn't watching? "Let's talk about it in the morning," I tell him.

"Trust me, this is good. You'll like it."

Trust needs to be earned. So far he seems to be doing fine, but I'm slow to come around in the trust department. I'm extremely wary of anything Booker has to offer. "We'll talk in the morning. It was great meeting you, Giselle."

"The same here," she answers with a warm smile. It's a smile that most men would kill for. They might not be willing to die for it, but certainly they would kill. She sways ever so slightly from side to side as she speaks, flashing just enough leg that I fully appreciate her powerful spell over my lodger. Not flirting, really, just letting me know that she holds the keys to this or any relationship. I am momentarily envious of my new friend, and at the same time profoundly grateful that I am not him: I'd never survive.

"Don't blow me off man. In the morning. You're going to like it," Booker guarantees me. Giselle is still grinning quietly alongside of him. The hypnotic sway of the ocean rolls across her hips, while he looks on like the cat that ate the canary. At first I surmise that Booker has no idea how good he has it, but then, maybe he does.

I casually wave my hand and slide out the door.

"Don't do anything I wouldn't do," I hear, as I'm traipsing down the stairs. I hop on one foot, pulling on one shoe and then the other like I need to make a hasty escape. I don't bother to turn around. *Anything Booker wouldn't do.* As I approach my vehicle, I'm still wondering what could *possibly* fall into that category.

Union Street Saloon isn't far, about a mile as the crow flies. By the time I get there and find a place to park the truck, I realize that it would have been simpler to walk. This is one of the downsides to a neighborhood riddled with one-way streets. On the other hand, having the truck nearby might come in handy. I might want to go somewhere after dinner, or flee midway through the meal. I pull the pickup alongside the curb on Woodward, lock the doors and head inside.

I'm early for our dinner date and Susan has yet to arrive. A smooth-talking hostess puts me at a tiny two-top not far from the bar and the kitchen. It's a little loud for my taste, but the place is packed and I'm not a regular here. Sometimes you take what you can get.

"Anything to drink?"

I hesitate, then figure that a small primer wouldn't hurt. I order a Rusty Nail on the rocks. A little lubrication may help with the tongue, or, if not, might at least reinforce my courage. I've barely touched my drink when Susan shows up.

"Been waiting long?" She asks as she slips into the seat across from me.

"Just a few minutes."

"Sorry I was late."

"Not to worry. I just ordered a drink. Do you want something to drink?"

"They know me here, so that's not going to fly. I'm underage, remember? I'll just have an iced tea."

"If you say so."

"Tea will be good." Like magic our waitress returns, takes the drink order, then disappears behind the swinging doors to the kitchen. A moment later she reappears with the tea in hand. We each order an appetizer, and the magic waitress disappears into the kitchen once again. There we sit in silence, me sipping whiskey and Susan sipping tea.

"So tell me about you and my mother," she implores, eyes wide open.

Where to start? How do you describe a part of your past that is indelibly etched into the mettle of what you've become? How many words would that take? And how do you tell a girl, no, how do you tell this *waif* that most of what she was taught regarding *her very existence* was founded upon a falsehood? I wouldn't even know where to begin. Maybe it's best to let sleeping dogs lie. "There's not much to tell," I mumble shyly.

"You're full of it," she answers. "I know there's more to the story."

"There's always more to a story."

"Then let me hear it." Our potato skins arrive at the table, and she begins to peel a thin layer of cheese delicately from the top of one before deciding to let it fall back into place. I should know by now that Susan is a girl who plays with her food.

"Is there really a point in rehashing this? Janey and I dated and then we broke up. By the time you came along we weren't even talking to one another. It's fairly mundane."

"Did you love her?"

"Did I love her...." I repeat, more to myself than to Susan.

"You must have loved her, right?"

"I loved her." I agree, a small concession to the past. I loved her the way only the young can love another, but I'm not admitting to that. Stupid Love. It's the kind of love that's both selfish and selfless at the same time. It was all-encompassing and totally self-absorbed, a love that is so intense it consumes ambition and foresight and reason and anything else of value until blind, Stupid Love is all that remains. Once you've experienced Stupid Love, it's nearly impossible to repeat. Not if you have a lick of sense.

125

"Do you still?"

"Love her?" I ask, answering a question with a question. That's a tough one: do I still love her in the "I want to be with you forever" sense of the word? Hell no. I'm guessing that some small part of me wants to hang onto the memory of what I once had, but only as a vague and fuzzy memory. I don't want the real thing, and I don't want to experience those emotions directly. I'm still afraid to be in the same room as Janey, even in a restaurant full of witnesses. I'm not afraid of what I'll say nor am I afraid of anything she'll do. I'm certainly not wary of old flames sparking to life. It's much bigger than that: I'm afraid of being haunted. There are ghosts I prefer not to visit, and those days of "in love" with Janey are so far in the rear view mirror that I can't even find them. I forget what they look like, and I'd like them to stay there. I've moved on, she's moved on, and that dog's not just sleeping, it was euthanized two decades ago. I don't want it to rise from the dead, don't want to see it make an encore appearance. What good might come from that? Who really wants to view Technicolor evidence of previous failures? In my head I'm picturing a zombie dog of love, a salivating, slathering collection of decayed pit bull parts chasing me as I run down an empty Woodward Avenue in the dead of night. Its jaws are open and there's a wild look in its eyes. I have no doubt that should the beast ever catch me, it would tear me to shreds.

"No, I don't love her" I tell Susan, and she looks down at the table in contemplation, quietly dissecting another cheese-filled potato skin. My answer isn't a lie, not exactly, but it certainly includes acts of omission. There's still a piece of me that the zombie dog could reach, if it tried hard enough.

"But you did once." A question spoken as a statement.

"But I did, once," I concede. "Can we talk about something else?"

"Why'd you come here, then, if you didn't want to talk to me? You're my dad, right? Isn't that why you're here? So we can discuss these kinds of things?"

"I thought maybe we'd talk a bit more about you," avoiding the first half of her sentence. I *could* be her dad. I am *probably* her dad. But I do not have

DNA evidence, and in the world of an avoider, this could be construed as cause for reasonable doubt. This could be cause for yet another relocation.

"This *is* about me. Isn't that how everything got started? Isn't the story of your relationship really the story of me?"

"Theoretically."

"You know what I'm saying..." She's wearing me down.

"Even if that's true, do we have to cover everything, all in one night?" I'm pleading for a little mercy: mercy or patience, whichever Susan will afford.

"I guess not," she replies, and sets her sights back on the potato skins. It's only a minute before Susan is back on the attack. "So where'd you two meet?" Her eyes barely fleeting from the plate. Mercy is not on tonight's agenda.

"She was a stripper at the Booby Trap Lounge, and I was a customer." Susan's jaw nearly hits the floor before she realizes I'm merely messing with her. "Your mom went to school with a friend of mine, and he sort of fixed us up," I clarify.

"No stripping, then?" to verify.

"She was not a stripper," I confirm. "At least that I'm aware of." I can't even draw that picture in my head. Mother Theresa as a stripper? Maybe, but not Janey.

"Was this friend a good friend?"

"Good enough."

"Are you still in touch with him?"

"No. I lost track of him somewhere along the line." A quiet pause, another piece of the picture surgically removed. I've abandoned a slew of pieces throughout the years.

"That happen a lot with you? Losing track of good friends?"

"More than you'd think." She takes a moment to digest this fact. "It's a gradual process."

"How long before you knew?"

"Before I knew?"

"That you loved her. How long?"

About five minutes, I'm thinking, but that sounds like a really bad thing to tell a girl who is now about the same age as Janey was when we were happily imploding, so I fudge the numbers. "It's hard to say. Jane and I went out a few times before we really clicked." That's not so much number-fudging as an outright lie. *I would have taken a bullet for her after the first date,* my inner demons remind me. Zombie dog is thinking about making a comeback.

"*A few times* before you knew?" She asks, in a way that implies she is not buying that which I am selling.

"Something like that," I respond, and plug my mouth with a stuffed mushroom cap in order to slow the tempo of her interrogation. "It's been a while since I've thought much about it."

"And it took you *a few times* before you knew, you say?"

This is one tough kid. Is it possible that *she* is the ghost that I fear? Or maybe she's just the ghost's envoy, bringing the message. "It wasn't instant karma or anything, if that's what you're asking. Look, life isn't always like you see in the movies. Relationships don't always blossom out of nowhere and then play themselves out in the course of two hours, as neat little packages with tidy endings." Except when they do. Jane and I took a lot longer than two hours for things to play out, but still, I'm sure that if you boiled out the fat from our relationship, a two hour docudrama would be adequate to sum things up (minus the tidy ending). We saw stars and fireworks right from the get-go. But instead of laying out the details of star-crossed love, I make the kind of speech a dad is supposed to give his daughter: "We went out a few times. I thought we could make it last, but it didn't. Sometimes things just don't work out."

"Wow! You're quite the philosopher."

"Wow, you're quite the smart aleck," I respond, and Susan smirks.

"Where do you think I get that from?"

"Nurture over nature," I respond, and just then the magic waitress returns to take our order.

Relief finally arrives via the fact that Susan allows the conversation to float to school, her future plans for employment, and more mundane topics. Now that we're no longer discussing dead romances, the evening flies by. Neither of us is interested in dessert, so when the tab comes I pay with cash and we both get up to leave.

"Thanks for dinner," she tells me.

"My pleasure. It was the least I could do."

"Let's do this again sometime."

"We should," I reply after a slightly awkward pause.

"Maybe my mom will come next time," Susan jokes. At least I hope she's joking.

"I wouldn't bet on it. She's not exactly enamored with the idea of you talking with me," I confess.

"And you know this how?"

"It was suggested to me by an unnamed source."

"You've been in town how many days, and you already have unnamed sources?"

"I'm an international man of mystery."

"Impressive."

"That's what I keep telling people," and her smirk reappears.

"Well, don't let my mother chase you off. I'm an adult and I can make my own decisions."

That attitude is instantly familiar. A moment later she's out the door and on her way. I step into the street after her and inhale deeply, feasting on the first cool hints of autumn. The city is surprisingly quiet, and I bask in the momentary calm. Somewhere in the faint distance sirens wail, and then, a few blocks over, the lonesome howl of a canine replies. Like Susan I'm on my way, too. I just haven't learned the destination.

CHAPTER FIFTEEN

Riding the Gift Horse

It is late. There's a package in the hallway, lying on the floor just outside my doorstep. The cardboard box is approximately eighteen inches long, twelve inches wide and twelve inches tall. It's sealed with gummed brown Kraft tape, the kind with little strips of fiberglass reinforcement running throughout. There's no address label affixed to the box, and thus I know it was not delivered by FedEx or UPS or whatever local delivery services they use in the Corridor. Besides, who delivers at this time of night? I circle it with suspicion. Is it a package bomb from Janey? I seriously doubt it, but then, one never knows.

"Are you going to pick that up or what?" Betty has appeared in the hallway with Bruce in her arms. She's wearing her ever-fashionable bath robe and big, fuzzy pink slippers that look brand new. "I thought I heard someone pacing around out here. Thought it might be a burglar."

"And you brought out the miniature poodle to scare him off?"

"Damn straight," she tells me. To the dog: "Right Brucey boy? You'll protect me."

I laugh. *Brucey boy* might lick a burglar to death, but I wouldn't expect much more out of him.

"So, this package. Are you going to pick it up, or will I have to do it for you?"

"Any idea where that came from?" I've ruled out the Janey/bomb theory, but I'm still not sure I want to know what's inside. Who else might be sending me mystery gifts in the middle of the night?

"Some skinny kid in black jeans and a T-shirt dropped it off. White kid. He knocked on the door, but Booker wasn't home." I'm not so sure that I like the way she, like Booker himself, has assumed that my apartment is now his "home."

"He doesn't really live with me, you know. Booker, I mean."

"Uh-huh."

"It's just supposed to be for a little while."

"That's how Bruce and I got started. Then those sad, brown eyes suck you in. Don't fool yourself. You've got yourself a roommate."

"It's temporary."

"Uh-huh. Isn't everything? I'm going inside. Let me know what you decide about that package. I can call a SWAT team if you think you'll need it." And with that she shuffles down the hall and back inside the safety of her own apartment. I hear the click of the lock and the metallic "thunk" of the deadbolt behind me.

Davros' guy, the skinny kid in black jeans and a T-shirt, must have brought the box. I pick up the package, fumble for my keys, and head inside. There's a note on the table from Booker:

Don't wait up. Won't be home 'till tomorrow. We'll talk about that position in the morning. B

I'd forgotten about that conversation. My imagination rolls through a few more positions that could possibly be achieved by way of my association with Booker. Again, none of these scenarios are enticing, entirely legal, or end happily. I will tell Booker "no" to whatever crazy shit he has brewing. I'm shocked to discover one beer in the fridge that he and the lovely Giselle must have missed in their previous visit. I pop the top and take a long pull from the icy bottle. My package sits on the table, waiting.

I cut carefully, using the one steak knife that I keep in the silverware drawer. Nothing explodes. The contents are packed carefully beneath layers of plastic bubble wrap. A note sits on top of the plastic. Two notes in one night: I haven't been this popular since Janey and I first swapped love letters, decades ago.

I picked this up at an estate sale: Merry Christmas and Happy Birthday. You owe me. Davros

I owe him. How many times has my friend told me this, and does he really believe it? You can never really tell. Dav recounts so many wild tales, both small and large, that it becomes hard to separate the truth from fiction. That's one of the dangers of living in a universe of your own creation. I wonder if there's any separation in his own mind, any line to be drawn between reality and desire. Does he believe his own twisted narrative, or is everything done in sport? Is he truly nuts, or is it just a facade? I'll be damned if I know.

At first glance the contents of the box look like any pile of miscellaneous junk. A steel ring with three old skeleton keys and one skateboard key. One brass doorknob. Ceramic salt and pepper shakers shaped like little yellow ducks. A ballpoint pen with a naked girl on it, the kind that when you hold the pen upside down, the girl's clothing disappears. The ink and water are so long gone from this particular pen that the girl is perpetually naked. I think I'd like her better with ink; it maintains the mystery. It is a collection of things that most people stuff into a kitchen drawer and promptly forget about until one day when they need a rubber band or a paper clip or a key to that forgotten lock in the basement, or until the owner dies and someone has to come and empty out the house.

I'm wondering why Davros bothered to send me a box of trash and trinkets when I stumble across the padlock, a Master lock with the dial on the front, just like about one-hundred million other padlocks with the dial on the front. I almost overlook it. There's nothing exceptional about the lock, other than the fact that this particular lock has the combination written in ink on a scrap of index card and taped to the back of it: zero-six-zero, my old combination from grade school. I sit in stunned silence. This isn't just any box of crap from the junk drawer, it's *my* box of crap from the junk drawer. God only knows how Davros stumbled across it, but this came from my parents' house.

I move over to the couch and sift cautiously now, finding things that I recognize from long ago amidst the debris. There's a magnifying glass that pivots from its vinyl sheath (my favorite ant-burning tool), compliments of Downriver Federal Savings. A stack of baseball cards rubber-banded together, not one piece retaining any value because they spent most of their formative years lodged between the spokes of a Schwinn three-speed.

133

Assorted nuts, bolts, springs, and clips from I-don't-know-what, and four broken wristwatches (one of which was mine, a green Timex Camper with plastic casing). Four pieces of chalk, a pencil sharpener, eight golf pencils and a small paper envelope with three baby teeth inside (previous owner not identified). While the junk drawer runs deep in memories, it is woefully lacking in anything worth more than a dollar. Two fountain pens, a stamp pad devoid of ink. A glass baby food jar full of steel ball bearings. Two rulers and a rusted tape measure.

The trip down memory lane is an intriguing but largely unfulfilling ride, and I'm about to quit for the night when I stumble across a smaller package in the bottom of the larger box. This tiny package is sealed up tighter than a bank vault. I tear through an outer skin of duct tape, a second layer consisting of a gallon-sized, zippered plastic bag, another layer of duct tape, and then half of a box of cotton batting. Beneath the cotton batting is a manila mailing envelope, and inside the envelope lies one fold of tissue paper and finally the prize: a minute collection of what appears to be bones, and a lone piece of yellowed parchment with writing in what I immediately recognize as Insular Script. Most would call this writing 'Gaelic' if they recognized it at all, but it's actually 'Insular,' not 'Gaelic.' 'Gaelic' is a language, a font, something you type but not something you write. I only know this because I've heard the stories. I didn't think this day was possible, but after seven long years, it has arrived. I'm not sure whether I should feel elated or cursed. Either way, Davros has given me something special, something I never would have expected: possession of the relics.

It's the next morning before I decide to contact him. Patrick, my brother, has never been fond of late night phone calls. There were a few times, back in those early days when I was young and reckless, that I needed a quick rescue. Not bail money or anything serious like that, but a car pulled out of a ditch or a ride home from some godforsaken dump on the outskirts of town. The call usually went to Patrick, because I knew he wouldn't rat me out for my misdeeds and because his overriding sense of responsibility would require him to help his little brother out. He wouldn't tell: he'd be too embarrassed, for one thing. No one wants to admit that his brother is a total idiot.

"Patrick, how are you?"

"Good." I can hear the wariness in his voice, like there exists the possibility of a snake biting him through the wires. "To what do I owe the pleasure? Did you get a job yet?"

"Some." There is truth to this statement. "I've been doing some side work for Davros." Just then Booker waltzes through the door, waving as he walks past. He makes a beeline for the kitchen, where he grabs a saucepan and a can of SpaghettiO's. "I have a promising lead on something bigger, even as we speak."

"Doing what?"

"Network solutions," I answer, remembering Booker's brief description of what he does for a living.

"What do *you* know about network solutions?" Patrick asks with wonder.

"Very little, but it's more of an entry-level thing. We're still working out the details." Booker gives me a thumbs up from across the room as he shovels a spoonful of salty red noodles into his mouth. "That's not why I'm calling, though."

"No?" Hesitation, like he already knows this can't be a good thing.

"You sound tired. Is everything okay?"

"Everything's fine," he replies, but I don't believe that and neither does he. "Is there something you needed?"

"No. Hey, you ever get a chance to talk with Mary?"

"Not really. About three times in the last seven years. You know all about the argument, right?"

"I know all about it."

"We're not speaking to one another. I'm not complaining about it."

"Lucky you."

"Sometimes. I don't really want to go into it."

"Well, here's the thing: I have a present for you."

"No thanks." Emphatically. My brother's guard is up.

"You don't even know what the present is."

"Doesn't matter."

"Don't you want to know what it is?"

"Not particularly. Whatever it is, in the context of this conversation, it can't be good."

"It's good." I tell him about coming home from dinner (I conveniently leave out the parts about Susan, because that's a much more complicated discussion than I'm ready to initiate) and finding the box on my doorstep. I describe the contents of box, the junk and the padlock, and finally the discovery of the relics. Then I make Patrick an offer.

"Hell no," my brother tells me.

"I give them to you, you can give them to Mary, and then things will be right."

"That's flawed logic!" he shouts into the phone.

"Flawed how?"

"You *know* how. If I have the relics, Mary will swear I've had them all along. It doesn't matter if I give them to her now. The mere fact that they're in my possession suggests that I've been hiding them from her since this whole thing started. I stole them, I hid them, and I tortured her for my own entertainment. Now I'm not only a thief, but I'm a petty and vindictive thief who took them just to spite her. Hell no. You give them to her if you want to. I'm not having a damn thing to do with it." There is finality in his voice. He's right. That's *precisely* how things would go down.

I ruminate on this for a minute before I finally break the silence. "Well, *I* can't give them to her."

"Why not?"

"Same reason."

"There you have it. Throw them away. Give them to the Church. Feed them to the hogs."

"What hogs?" It's not as if we'd ever lived on a farm.

"You know what I mean. Just don't bring them to my house."

"Why would I bring hogs to your house?"

"The relics, idiot. Don't bring them here."

"You don't want to make amends with your sister?" I know the answer.

"*Our* sister, and I'm not stepping into that minefield. This wouldn't fix anything; it would only make things worse. In Mary's eyes, this would be *evidence*. Think of something else." And that's the end of our conversation.

I close the phone and slide it into my pocket, turning just in time to catch Booker wiping the last of the sticky tomato sauce from his lips onto my one and only clean dish towel.

"Please don't do that." My request isn't even acknowledged. Dishcloth, washcloth, what's the difference?

"Are you going to come work with me, or what?" he asks.

"You haven't actually described what it is you're offering here, Booker."

"I was getting to that. You didn't give me a chance to talk last night, with you being in such a hurry to rush off to your hot date with Susan."

"It wasn't a date."

"Whatever you say, man."

"It wasn't."

"I believe you," duly corrected.

"So what's this job you've got for me?"

137

"Network solutions."

That's a fairly broad and vague concept. It could mean a lot of things, most of which I don't understand and am completely unqualified to perform. "You do realize I've got practically no experience in that field, right? Look around: I don't even own a computer. I don't know anything about networks. I'm not what you would call a tech guy."

"Doesn't matter. Even a monkey could do this job, and you're no monkey."

"Thanks."

"You know what I mean. I'll train you. This is entry level, the work isn't that hard, and the pay's decent. It's full time, comes with benefits, and you could practically walk to work from here. All you need to do is come in and talk to my boss. I'll hook you up."

"You told me your job doesn't even have benefits."

"My choice. I like it that way. Contract employees have certain liberties, and it's a trade I was willing to make. The job I'm telling you about has got'em."

"Is this an office job or in the field? I don't travel well." A lie. Traveling is what I do best.

"Office, at least for now. Mostly just taking phone calls, listening to people gripe and sounding sympathetic. We've got tech guys that do the real work. Eventually you'd have to do some service calls, but they're all local."

"How soon?"

"We need someone that can start next Monday."

"Let me think about it."

"Ain't nothing to think about. What are you gonna do, odd jobs for Davros the rest of your life? This is a *real position,* man. This city's got, what, twenty-five, forty percent unemployment, and you're turning down a good paying job with maybe benefits down the road? Think about what you're saying."

"Didn't say I was turning it down; I just asked you to let me think about it."

"Five o'clock today, let me know. Otherwise I know a dozen folks'll line up begging for this one. I'm doing you a *favor* here."

That and the package from Davros makes two. I'm not sure I can handle many more favors. "I appreciate the gesture, I do. Just let me stew on it for a few hours. I really do appreciate it. Thanks, Booker."

He eyes me warily. "Don't think too long. You'd better say yes."

"I need a couple of hours," I tell him, and he reluctantly agrees.

"So what's this shit about some *relics*?" he asks me, moving on to the next topic. "You talking about old folks, or what?"

So once again I describe the previous evening (Booker gets the full version, which includes my dinner with Susan) and the box in the hallway with its contents from the old house.

"No shit? Exactly how old are these bones?"

"I don't really know. I can't read the writing."

"But it was your mom's, this box of bones, when you were a kid?"

"Pretty sure."

"Where'd Davros get them, again?"

"He claims that he bought them at an estate sale."

"I call bullshit on that one. You know that guy is full of something. He's your friend and all, but...come on...you know he's soaking in it."

"Probably," I agree, and then we are speechless. You could 'call bullshit' on most of what Davros says, but right now I can't think of any better explanation. Where else could he have gotten the relics, the chicken bones, whatever they are? He'd never even met my parents, didn't know where they lived. I'm pondering this as if within the riddle is a key to all that lays before me. Booker is lost in his own thoughts, then he quietly breaks the spell.

"Giselle," he murmurs, more to himself than to me.

"Huh?" I must have skipped a beat in the conversation. I can't figure out what his girl from last night has to do with my box of childhood memories.

"Giselle can help you out with that."

"How's she going to help? I thought you said she was a professor at the *art* school."

"She is, but she knows people. People at the DIA, Wayne State. I guarantee she knows someone who can help us out with this. Giselle is what you'd call *connected.* She'll help us out."

There it is again: "us," that sneaky plural pronoun that suggests Booker and I are partners in something bigger, but I decide to let it slide for now. Booker is only trying to help, and I *am* intrigued by his friend Giselle. Who wouldn't be intrigued, a beautiful woman with smarts like that? "She knows people at the Detroit Institute of Arts?"

"Some. They're all connected, these academic-types, historians. Brainiacs. Smart people like to hang out with other smart people. It's like a cabal or whatever you'd call it. Trust me. She'll know somebody that reads Irish."

"Insular."

"Whatever."

A few phone calls and forty minutes later I have an appointment with a dean of languages at the University. Two hours later, both the parchment and the bones are in the hands of this dean, who assures me he'll get to the bottom of my story, eventually. It's not as if I have anything to lose.

CHAPTER SIXTEEN

Old Habits

Color. It's the thing that nobody in this town does anything about, at least not in any significant way. Sure, the subject is splattered across the news, satiates local politics, and is perpetually embedded in the anonymous comments that permeate both the street and the World Wide Web. Race is the straw man for every societal ill, every move to the suburbs, every prosecution, non-prosecution, carjacking, every failed or thriving school system. It's both the cause and the symptom of corruption, negligence, abject poverty and lost hope. Race is omnipresent, the ringing bell that elicits response from Pavlov's dog. The charge of racism becomes the proverbial man yelling "fire!" in a crowded movie theater, guaranteed to send them running in all directions. It is alluded to, mentioned in code. Yet for all the shouting and the posturing, the finger-pointing and the denial, the whispering in the dark corridors where sane men fear to tread, race is rarely *acknowledged* in any meaningful way.

It has soaked deeply into the fiber of nearly everything that does or doesn't occur in this embittered place. We talk about it, we talk *around* it, we dance with it. It's our unwilling partner. We accommodate it and still we attempt to avoid it. In the end, nobody knows what to *do* about anything. There are too many facets, too many extenuating circumstances and related issues, too many long-standing convictions and too much anecdotal evidence for anyone to fully grasp the complexity of our dysfunction. Too much mistrust, too much history. Too many dead ends and detours. We are blinded by the sheer extent of the problem, light dwellers forced beneath the surface into a subterranean cave of oppression, and yet we can feel its presence everywhere. Hatred and misunderstanding brew beneath the surface, and still the region comprehends so little of how it's all intertwined. Forest for the trees, all of that. It is bigger than Detroit, sure, but it's also of a magnitude endemic to this town. There's no word big enough to sum up the problem. We are ground zero for a centuries-old plague. Prophecies become self-fulfilling, legend and lore, and then, finally and conclusively, reality. In the end we are left exhausted and beaten. Race is a god in this city.

I say this because, upon leaving the offices of one dean of languages at the University, I stroll leisurely across campus toward the North, where, in an uncharacteristic burst of naiveté, I had parked my truck alongside the curb on a largely abandoned block between here and the New Center. Honestly, I still don't know what the hell I was thinking. The Wayne State campus is a world unto itself. Sure, it is teeming with petty theft and constant invasion by the neighborhood dregs and scammers for miles around. But the school also comes with its own police force and nearly 850 high-definition security cameras that constantly monitor the ebb and flow of human traffic. Bad things happen here, but not nearly on the scale of bad things happening just a few blocks in any direction. And when bad things do happen, the Wayne State police actually show up with some degree of regularity. There's also a fairly comprehensive and fluid mix of people of all ages, ethnicities, and incomes walking about freely, NOT constantly looking over their shoulders. In short, the campus itself can (at times) be mistaken for any other college campus or thriving area in any number of large, successful cities. Only it isn't.

Approximately one-quarter mile to the North and three deserted city blocks later, I arrive at my truck only to find that all four tires are missing. The rims are missing, too (that goes without saying). I shouldn't have parked on the street, not even in broad daylight. I pause, staring at the vehicle like it cannot possibly belong to me. *It must be someone else's*, I surmise. This truck is the same color as my truck, but it cannot possibly be mine. Maybe I'm on the wrong block. I check the street sign suspended from a lamp post: I'm (unfortunately) not on the wrong block. I look closely for dents or signs of rust, and the truck in front of me matches my memory, the minor signs of abuse and neglect that I've accumulated on my own vehicle squaring solidly with the dings and scratches seen here. Denial. Disbelief. Disappointment. This is very disheartening. *Damn.* Four cinderblocks support the axles of my now-stationary ride, a sight not uncommon in this crime-riddled swamp. *I wasn't gone that long*, I think.

My truck's tires are gone, and my mind immediately leaps to that one subject that (until now) I thought I was above and beyond: the thieving bastards who did this and their assumed ethnic background. I swear, mutter some profoundly racial epitaphs beneath my breath (words that I never expected to come out of my mouth), before finally grabbing a small slice of composure. Then I curse myself for having ever returned to this place, curse myself for parking on the street when I should have known better, curse myself for thinking that I could exist in this "renaissance" world where nothing ever truly rises. Things might *appear* to rise, but it's only the vortex of the whirlpool creating an illusion, a lifting tide that is prelude to the whole damn thing getting flushed down the crapper. *I was not cut out for this*, the runner within me chimes. I don't belong here. *They should drop a bomb on this whole stinking city.*

"Shit man, you got a problem."

The voice is behind me and I just about jump out of my skin. Usually I'm more aware of my surroundings. You have to be. But the bedraggled man sidling up to me appeared out of nowhere. He'd snuck up without a sound (though that's probably an overstatement: the man probably didn't have to do any "sneaking," as lost as I'd been in my pool of self-pity). I'm lucky he's just some street urchin and not a group of the younger thugs that make their living preying on this world's vulnerable.

"Shit, man, you need to announce yourself when you come up on someone," I chastise.

"You was daydreaming," he explains. "Excuse me sir," he starts with a voice dripping in bold sarcasm and false modesty, "it would appear you got a problem." The man smiles broadly. He's missing most of his front teeth. There's something both sad and comical in his grin.

"Very funny," I mumble.

"Here to amuse," he answers. "Spare a dollar?" Five feet away and the putrid smell is already turning my stomach. He not only *looks* rough, he *is* rough. I take a step backwards.

"Not at the moment," I tell him, but still find myself fishing around in my front pocket to see if there's any cash tucked away. Long ago I'd learned to keep my wallet fairly empty, maintain just enough cash in there to look like there might be something. Mostly ones. The real money stays hidden somewhere else: in a pocket, in your shoe, in your hat. Then if you get a gun in your face, you can hand over the wallet and come out alive, with minimal loss. "Any chance you see who did this?"

"Spare five dollars?" He replies.

"Is that a yes?"

"Got ten dollars?"

Christ on a crutch. I'm not sure if the clown actually knows anything, or if this is some new form of reverse negotiation. I make a quick decision to give him whatever bill first comes out of my front pocket before the price goes any higher. "Here's a five, it's all I've got," I lie as I hand the wrinkled cash over to my new best friend. "Did you see who took my tires?" He takes the money, but I can tell that he doesn't remotely believe that it's all the dough I have.

"You didn't hear it from me," he whispers slyly, swiveling his head left and right like there might be some high-tech eavesdropping equipment around the corner.

"Okay, I didn't hear it from you."

"I didn't exactly *see* anything, and if anybody asks, I don't even know what you're talking about. I never met you, man."

"That works for me," I assure him, taking a slight step back to let my nose get a breath of moderately less rancid air. Never having met him is smelling better by the moment.

"You gonna need some new tires soon, ain't you?"

It's about what I figured: he doesn't know anything, and this was part of his not-so-elaborate plan to get whatever cash is in my pocket. He's going to give me a song and dance about hard times and how he got mugged and needs bus fare for him and his wife and three starving kids to another city and a cousin who can give me a discount at a store somewhere far, far from here. A five-dollar lesson in street economics, but at this point I might as well hear him out. I've paid more.

"And?" My impatience is building.

"You know that place on Michigan Avenue near Trumbull, purple and yellow building sells used tires on the cheap? Big sign, tires twenty dollars and up, that shit?"

"Yeah, I know the place," I lie. It wouldn't be hard to find, if the place exists at all. Purple and yellow: gaudy is in vogue this year, but then isn't it always? My guess is this is one big line of B.S. and that there's no such business on Michigan Avenue near Trumbull, but I may as well play along. It's not as if I can just get in my truck and leave.

"You go in there tomorrow early morning, I bet they got a set of four tires fits your truck perfectly. I bet they even come with a set of rims fits your truck perfectly, too. In fact, I *guarantee* they will."

"You guarantee? Is that a *bonafide* guarantee?" I ask mockingly, although I'm beginning to believe that he's giving me some variant of the truth. I've heard tell of more than a few seemingly legitimate enterprises around here stealing your goods, only to sell them back at a "discounted" price. And "legitimate" has become a subjective concept. "You've seen this? You saw them take my tires?"

"Not exactly today, but I know who done it. Ain't the first time, won't be the last." The grin again.

"No shit?"

"No shit, honest to God. You didn't hear it from me, though. Got another five bucks?" He prods hopefully. I guess if you're living on the street, dressed like a dumpster and smelling like a sewer, hope must spring eternal. It's a requirement. What else does he have? For me, personally, I don't know how you get it, this hope. Hope must be a kissing cousin to faith.

"Why the hell not?" I tell him, and pull another fin from my pocket. At least somebody will be having a good day. "Make sure you don't blow it all on food and shelter, though. Get yourself some booze, too."

"Thanks, friend," he winks, and then Mr. Homeless slinks off before I get a chance to reconsider my cash donation.

I'm not here to catalog all the woes that plague my hometown. It's a long list, goes back generations, and I'm the last guy to come up with viable solutions. Corruption, greed, poverty, ignorance, neglect; take your pick. All I know is that race is the god in the center of this maelstrom. I'm just one man in this world, one man with a dependable truck that's missing four rims and four tires. I look to the heavens, where a single jet cuts a swath high across the cloudless dome, a contrail of white trailing behind. Oh, to be so free. At least the pilot of that plane doesn't have to worry about someone stealing his tires. This little fiasco is going to run about a thousand bucks unless I can somehow get my stuff back. That's a thousand bucks I don't have. *Shit.*

When I finally snap back to the situation at hand, I see four surly youths coming down the next block, moving at a rapid clip in my direction. *Shit again.* I turn tail casually, like I haven't noticed them. I take a few leisurely steps, enough to make them think I'm not frightened, before breaking into a full-out sprint toward campus. I turn South at Second Avenue, crossing Burroughs, York, and Antoinette. I look back and they're charging hard. I'm winded, but I know that stopping to rest will not be good for my long-term health. My legs keep pumping. I look over my shoulder again and the pack is still coming, but losing ground. Two of the youths are lagging way, way behind, hacking and wheezing. For once I am grateful to the American tobacco industry. I cut hard around the side of a campus parking structure, cross Palmer, and quickly merge amongst the crowded sidewalks near the law library. Five minutes later I look casually back over my shoulder, a final check. Much like the condensation from the jet plane above, my four fearless pursuers have evaporated.

CHAPTER SEVENTEEN

Family Reunions

"You're going to have to get that vehicle off the street before dark, or there'll be nothing left. You know anybody with a tow truck?"

This from Davros, or as I'd like to call him now, Captain Obvious. I was out of ideas, stranded on foot in a world where city busses might not come for hours, and precariously low on solutions. My apartment was a quarter mile to the South, but The Emporium was only a couple of blocks away and seemed like a good base station for the rescue operation.

"No, I don't know anybody with a tow truck," I answer. It seemed like a stupid question, but Dav often likes to talk in riddles. Cryptic messages are his usual forte. You have to humor him if you want his help.

"Yes, you do."

"You own a tow truck?" I didn't think he owned one, but maybe the old horse trader has a new trick (or an old truck) up his sleeve.

"Not me, but I've got a friend with one." *There's a surprise.*

"Do I know your friend?"

"No, but you will. Do you want me to call him?"

"I don't know, do you want me to beg you to call him?" Sometimes this game gets a little frustrating. It's like playing twenty questions, only there's no upper limit on how many questions you have to ask before Davros reveals the answer. Sometimes the answer is totally unrelated to the original discussion. The game is only over when he decides it's over. So far I'm up to three.

"I'll call him if you'd like me to."

"Damn, Davros, can you just give the guy a call? I need a tow truck."

"No need to get chippy with me. I'm just trying to be helpful." That's one way of putting it.

An hour later my truck has been hoisted onto a flatbed, hauled and stored securely inside a warehouse on the lower east side that I didn't even know my friend owned. The truck still won't roll, though: that would require wheels. We're standing by the register inside Dav's store. Three or four tourists are wandering through the aisles. "Tourists" is short for suburbanites, wealthy gawkers passing time so that they'll have stories about the Crazy Things In the City that they can tell to their friends back in Birmingham and Bloomfield Hills over spritzers. It's clear from what they're wearing that these ladies are not here to buy.

"How are you going to pay me back for this?" Davros asks (ignoring the non-customers). I should have seen this coming.

"I thought the tow truck guy was a friend of yours."

"He's a friend, not a missionary. You owe him a hundred and twenty-five bucks for the tow, and you owe me twenty-five a day for storage."

"A hundred bucks for a tow?" It seems a little high. "It would have been nice to know that in advance."

"A hundred and twenty-five," he corrects me. "That's cheap."

"Twenty-five a day to park inside an empty building you're not even using?"

"That's the family rate. Hey, the other guys are all charging fifty a day." *Family rate. The other guys.* Big, kindhearted Davros. "We'll see about your tires in the morning."

"Sure. Have you ever heard of this tire place on Michigan Avenue, or was my odiferous buddy making it up?"

"Don't worry about it. We'll see in the morning. You want some chips?" He's working on a big, greasy bag of potato chips that's his afternoon substitute for nutrition. It doesn't look appetizing.

"No thanks, I'm trying to watch my cholesterol."

148

"They're cholesterol free," he tells me with a deadpan face.

"Really?" I ask with feigned interest. I'm distracted by one of the cuter tourists in the back of his store, a thirty-something woman who looks like she just stepped out of a Neiman Marcus catalog. She's not my type, but at the moment that doesn't matter. I don't know where she's from, though I'm sure it's a place where the valet doesn't steal your tires while you're sampling hors d'oeuvres. She and her boisterous friends crack wise about who would be caught dead wearing this item or that before finally waving us goodbye and heading out the door. They're off to safer regions, far from here. I find myself wishing she'd take me with her.

"Yeah, cholesterol free. It says right here on the bag, *no extra charge for cholesterol.*" Davros, Comedian of the Corridor.

"Huh?"

"The cholesterol. It's free." He chuckles to himself.

"Funny stuff," I tell him.

"*I* like to think so."

I look out the front windows, peer beyond the thick iron security bars into the filthy street beyond. Not even five o'clock and we're losing daylight. That's one of the many downsides of living in Michigan during the fall and winter; daylight dies quickly. It never bothered me while I was living in other northern latitudes, but I think part of it is the fact that in those other places, you can safely leave your house after sunset.

"Hey Dav, I need to get moving." For a man on foot, walking around at night isn't a great idea.

"You need a lift somewhere?"

"Nah, just hoofing it back to my place." It's only a quarter mile. As long as I get going soon, I'll be alright.

"I'll pick you up at eight tomorrow morning, your place. Be ready."

149

"Where are we headed?" I didn't get any of his odd jobs done this afternoon, and I don't rightly know what he has in mind. Another scenic tour of the warehouse district, perhaps? Eastern Market for another load of treasure?

"We're going to get your tires back."

I don't ask how, although I'm certain I know where.

Back at the apartment, Booker's nowhere in sight. It's kind of bizarre, I realize: I almost miss the man. I didn't want to let him into my place, not even for one night, and now he's grown on me. I guess you can get used to anything. There's a note on the table.

Sorry I missed you. Creole in the fridge, help yourself. See you in the a.m.
B

I check the refrigerator, and indeed there's a half-full carryout container of shrimp gumbo and another partial of jambalaya with three corn biscuits. I could get used to this treatment. I pop the two cardboard boxes in the microwave and push the buttons for three minutes cook time. I wander out into the hallway and knock on Betty's door, but there's no sound inside other than the mild yapping of Bruce. "Shut up, Bruce," I tell the little dog, and surprisingly he shuts up as I retreat to the solitude of my own quarters.

The food is excellent, and I make a mental note to find out where Booker got it. There used to be a little tinderbox on Gratiot that cooked like this, but that place is undoubtedly long gone: moved, burned, relocated or otherwise departed. Everything I once cared about in this city seems to have incinerated or evaporated. I utilize the last of the biscuits to wipe the last of the juice from my cardboard dinnerware, smacking my lips with contentment. It's the best meal I've had in a long time. But now I've got a more pressing issue: it's barely past six in the evening, and I've got nothing to read. I've got no television, no transistor radio, and, worst of all, no Booker or even Betty to speak with. It's way too early for me to fall asleep. Maybe I can borrow a book somewhere. I head out into the hall, up the stairs, and rap on Susan's door. She's not home either. Back to my place, my quiet, lonely place. I could go out, but not very far, not without a car.

I contemplate my choices. There's that hole in the wall bar on Third Street, that of the damp basement smell and the surly waiter. I could *probably* get there and back in one piece, but that's a big probably. Not that the odds of running into trouble are actually *that* high, but there were fourteen people shot in this city (that I'm aware of) within the last four days, six of whom are dead. That's just the official count. A solitary white guy walking the streets at night sticks out. And while the risk of violence isn't astronomical (it's only six blocks, after all, and this is a big city), the cost of being wrong certainly could be. I decide to pass on Third Street.

City Fusion is only three blocks, and while that wouldn't be my first choice for a night on the town, I can do the math: three blocks rather than six should cut the risk of getting jumped by half. Hell, if I have to I can run for three blocks. I proved that earlier today. If I'm lucky Janey will have gone home for the evening, and will have left some anonymous floor manager in charge. If I'm lucky I can get a quiet table in the back, down a drink or two and kill part of the evening before retreating to my silent homestead. I figure I'm overdue for some luck.

I cover the three blocks without incident. It turns out that Janey is indeed gone for the night, another mark in the win column. They have a table for two available in the back. Chalk one more up for the good guys. I'm beginning to believe that things are finally going my way, and maybe my ten bucks to the chatty homeless guy earlier today bought some positive karma. Maybe there will even be a set of truck tires in my future. I order a beer and some nachos, not that I need the nachos, but it will give me something to pick at while I people watch. This isn't the kind of place where you can just sit and drink. I'm half a beer into my evening when karma decides to elicit her backlash.

"You son of a bitch." It's a woman's voice, and while it's coming from somewhere behind my back, I'm pretty certain the title is directed towards me. It's not Jane's, but the voice is familiar nonetheless. I duck instinctively, as if there may be a blow coming at my head, but the blow never arrives. Instead I whirl my neck around and immediately become the recipient of a heated verbal harangue, the words streaming as if channeled directly from the voice of my long-departed father. Dad's voice, Mom's face. "You worthless little S.O.B., snuck back into town and you're sitting around drinking on money which you probably got from selling what is rightfully mine from the tailgate of your beaten down, gypsy-wagon, sheeny man truck. Didn't even have the decency to tell anyone you were here. If I weren't a lady I'd kick your ass from here to Seven Mile and back again." Strong words from a "lady," and the lady is my sister Mary. "Patrick said you had the relics," she finishes, "this whole time." Like that justifies her spiel.

People are staring. Not all of them, but certainly enough to make things uncomfortable. The waiter is staring, too, from his station across the room. I need to defuse the ticking time bomb.

"Mary, why don't you grab a seat?" I ask, rising to give her a hug. She deflects the hug, giving me more of a football-style shoulder bump than anything else, but at least she's piped down. "I'm sorry, have we met?" My hand extends to her friend. I'm hoping if I first get them to sit down, getting them to shut up will be easier.

"Gwen," the friend answers, like she knows all about me and whatever evil I've done might be contagious. Gwen does not take my hand.

"Nice to meet you, Gwen." I lie. I reach against the wall and grab an extra chair, cramming the three seats around the perimeter of my tiny table. "Please, sit down." Mary gives me the snide eye but takes a chair anyway. "What brings you two down this way?" I'm thinking maybe Satan has started his own limousine service.

"Theater tickets," Mary mumbles. She never struck me as the theatergoing kind, but who knows? People can change. Maybe her boss or someone else gave her a set of freebies. Maybe it was Gwen's idea.

"Sounds great. Which theater?"

"The Bonstelle."

"Good choice," although (from what I recall) my sister wouldn't recognize good theater if it bit her on the ass. The Bonstelle is run by the University's Performing Arts department. The place seats twelve-hundred and they usually put on a comparatively good show, or so I've heard. It's been a while. "What's playing?"

"Guys and Dolls," Gwen chimes in enthusiastically. Gwen appears to like musicals. It's hard to go wrong with the classics.

"Where's my inheritance?" My sister plows straight ahead. Subtlety has never been her strong suit.

"Out for appraisal," I tell her, which is almost accurate. "I don't know what Patrick told you, but I just received them the other day. I thought one of the cousins took them." I know it's the truth, and even *I* think it sounds like I'm stalling. There's no way she's going to believe me. I explain the whole story, the ride to Eastern Market with Davros and the bumpy roads and having to find an apartment and then the story of an estate sale and finally the box with the bones. I can tell by the expression on her face that she's not buying any of it. Who would? It's like a plot some third grader would concoct.

"And you claim they're out for *appraisal*?" That last word hangs like a fresh turd in the air.

"Trying to determine what they are, and then maybe what they're worth. Mostly what they are," I assure her.

"There was a note in that box describing the relics," she states with authority. "I know exactly what they are."

"You could read that script?"

"No, but Mom once told me what it said."

"Do you really think Mom could read that stuff?" I can tell Mary hasn't thought this through.

"That's what she told me." There are no shadows in my sister's world, only truth and fiction.

"Do you believe everything our parents ever said?" I ask, and she gives me a look of disdain. Of course she does.

"When do I get them back?"

That's a tricky one, because at no point in this discussion had I committed to the idea that the relics *belong* to Mary. Don't get me wrong, I don't necessarily intend to keep the relics: in this family, they're more trouble than they're worth. If she were asking nicely that would be a different story. I don't want them, never did, but that's not really the point. Nobody likes to be *told* what they're going to do, especially by someone who presents themselves as entitled to whatever they want. Especially by a sibling.

153

There's still a little childhood spite hiding inside of every individual, and I'm no exception. The child in me wants to call dibs. On the other hand, why poke the bear?

"I'm not really sure how long it'll take," I tell her. "We can talk once I hear something."

"It had better be soon."

Or what? I'm thinking, but I don't bother to ask. *If you get them today or ten years from today or not at all, how could it possibly matter?*

Just then I see a familiar face cutting across the room, a face I've never been so happy to see. At least, that's what I think for a fleeting moment. I rise up to greet the man. I grab him by the arm and drag him to my sister.

"Booker, my friend, how are you?"

"Who's this gentleman?" Mary asks. The tone of her voice says she already disapproves of him, but then, that's her everyday tone.

"My new boss." I blurt out quickly. I'm not sure if this means that I'm accepting his job offer or merely that lies come easily.

"We're roommates," Booker states, while slapping me across the back. He's passing through on his way to meet his girl Giselle. She's sequestered at a table in the back nook. "Glad you're on board, roomie."

Mary gives me a contorted glare, a look that could intimate any number of things. Who can guess what narrative she's weaving in her head? "Your new boss or your roommate?" The idea that he might be both is beyond her grasp. Suspicion is growing. "Which one is it?"

"Oh don't worry, it's nothing serious, just a sexual thing," Booker jokes before shooting off toward the beautiful woman in the next room.

"A *sexual thing*? What was that?" She recoils and stares directly at me. "Are you gay???" I can see the wheels are still spinning inside her head. Booker's attempt at humor just fed the flames of conspiracy.

"His idea of a joke," I reassure her. I'm convinced she doesn't believe me.

154

"If that's his idea of humor, you have some deranged friends," she states warily.

"Always have," I agree, my eyes scanning the room for an escape route. Conversations with my sister have a tendency to tire me out.

"Is there anything else you'd like to tell us?" You've got to credit the Irish, we like confessionals.

Us. I'd practically forgotten about her friend Gwen, seated across the table. How lucky I am. *Yes,* I'm thinking, *There is something I'd like to tell you. I'd like to tell you both to get the hell out of here and let me finish my drink in peace.* "Nope," I answer, just as I spy Jane walking through the dining room and into the kitchen. Could things get any better? Like I said: karma. Jane's dressed to the nines, definitely not work attire. She must have been en route to a more formal affair (the Bonstelle, perhaps? The opera? Some charity shindig?) and got called in for some minor calamity or another. Jane doesn't notice me, and I'm good with that. I've had enough excitement for one evening. Mary and karma, on the other hand, have other plans. The wheel of fortune keeps landing squarely on black.

"Didn't you used to date that woman?" My sister is more observant than I'd have guessed. At least we have that in common.

"What? Oh, yeah, decades ago."

"Weren't you two rather serious?"

"Yeah." I answer distractedly. "Rather." Janey's talking with the chef, happier tones this time around. I'm mesmerized: it's always been hard for me to keep my eyes off of her. Susan is lingering in the back.

"She's held up well," my sister opines.

"Yep."

"Looks way better than you do." Possibly the understatement of the year.

"Indeed," I reply dryly, but my sister has never been quick to take a hint.

"You're getting gray hair. Hers still looks good."

"Yup. She probably dyes it," I lie. Anybody can see that it's natural. All this time I'm watching Janey floating around the kitchen, a hummingbird flitting from one spot to the next.

"You'd have done well to hang onto that one."

I don't even bother to acknowledge my sister's latest barb. Why feed the troll?

"She dumped you, right?" Now she's deep mining for treasure.

"Something like that."

"Who's that girl tagging behind?" Mary is the dog that never lets go of a bone. "She's a knockout." Janey and Susan are slipping through a different doorway, away from the dining room and back into the night. I am both saddened and relieved to see them go.

"That's her daughter." I leave it at that. Why throw another slab of fat into the fire?

"Well, she's got her mother's looks, but there's something about that girl that seems familiar." I'm not delving into the "why" of that.

"Can't imagine what that would be," I fire back. I'm already exhausted. Twenty minutes with family and I'm already thinking about moving to a different town, a different state, a different country. This is a new world's record.

A little while later, after a few more reminders about her "Goddamned inheritance" (I'm glad to see her Catholic schooling finally paying dividends, and respect for the divinity of these alleged religious artifacts is still intact) Mary and Gwen scamper off to catch their play. I down my drink in one gulp and begin the brisk walk home.

CHAPTER EIGHTEEN

Walking the Dog

Fire trucks, and lots of them. There are emergency vehicles up and down my block. I spot two engine rigs, a ladder truck, two paramedic units and two cop cruisers. You don't get a cooperative response like that in Detroit, not unless someone accidentally shoots the mayor of Highland Park outside of a nightclub. At first I'm thinking that Booker burned my apartment down so that he could have a matched set, but then I recall that he was still in the rear dining room of City Fusion when I left the joint. Did he leave SpaghettiO's on the stove again? Unlikely. Why go out to eat if you've got SpaghettiO's?

"What's up?" I ask one of the two firemen leaning casually against the back corner of a truck from Ladder Company Twenty. We are fortunate in that the fire station is only a few blocks away, and doubly fortunate that no one has (as of yet) stolen or otherwise disabled their equipment.

"Old lady had a heart attack," he grunts.

"All this for an old lady having a heart attack?" It seems unlikely. It looks more like a bomb threat or a presidential visit, and I doubt the president is dropping by tonight.

"Someone called it in as a major fire with multiple injuries." He grunts again.

It figures. An old woman having a heart attack is commonplace in this town In most instances such an event would barely warrant a nod. Emergency response time is notoriously slow; getting better, but notoriously slow. If you stumble across someone that's dying, in most cases you'd be better off placing her in your car and driving her to the hospital yourself. That assumes, of course, that your car still has rims and tires. Call in a major fire with casualties, however, and the world *might* conceivably take notice. At least for a moment.

"That's not good," I mutter to no one in particular.

"This come as breaking news to you? That someone would do something like that? You find it humorous?" The second, older fireman chimes in this time. There's anger in his voice. He thinks I'm toying with him. Maybe he thinks that *I* phoned in the semi-false alarm. I've offended him, or maybe life itself has offended him. He looks both angry *and* beaten, like he's watched this opera one-hundred too many times. Dark bags hang beneath his eyes, suggesting he hasn't had a good night's sleep in years. He probably hasn't. A man signs up for a noble cause, chooses a career that puts his life in danger every single day in order to help others, and instead watches as his soul slowly gets ground into dust. He's probably counting the days until retirement when his pension may or may not still be there. The city is, after all, in bankruptcy court.

"Not anymore," I answer, fully reprimanded. "It doesn't come as news, I mean. I know it's not a joke."

"Cause we get this shit every night," to reinforce his point. Just in case I didn't know. Maybe I didn't hear him the first time. Maybe he thinks I'm slow. This man wants somebody to understand what his life has become, wants someone to share his pain, and I'm the nearest candidate. He's offering to share. My job is to stand there and take it.

"Thanks for coming," I tell him with downcast eyes, and shuffle away towards my building. "We appreciate it," added as an afterthought.

"Huh," he answers, staring up at the blackened sky. "Asshole."

The paramedics slam the back doors of their battered box van and prepare to pull away. Old neighborhood, old equipment, old woman, same familiar story. Old woman with a heart attack, whoever she is, will be getting a brief ride over to Detroit Receiving Hospital. It's probably less than two miles in total. If the good folks over there can't fix her, she'll get a more leisurely escort to the Wayne County Morgue. The rest of the responders, police and fire alike, are taking their time about leaving as they mill about in the street. Why race back to the station only to get called out for the next run? Who wants to charge head-first into Armageddon? They might as well finish their coffee, catch a breath of cool night air, and prepare for whatever's coming next. It's advice we could all stand to follow: there's always something coming next. Three minutes later I hear someone yell "Heidelberg," and the trucks peel out of there.

A small covey of residents huddle on the front steps to the building, but there's no one in particular that I recognize. I step inside and scamper up the stairs.

My feet clear the first landing, slowly making their way up to the second floor. They're rounding the bend, my hand is on the bannister, and I'm stepping into the hallway when I'm struck by the first sounds of the coming apocalypse. The apocalypse sounds an awful lot like a dog barking, a dog barking inside of my apartment. Superintendent Andy is standing just outside my door.

"Do I even want to know?"

"Hey, good, you're home," he answers cheerfully.

I pause. I'm not sure that I want to know what's inside, but I have a fairly accurate guess. "God, I hope not. Please tell me there's not a dog in my apartment."

"It's Bruce. Betty said you'd take care of him."

"She did." A question as much as a statement. I'm rapidly putting two and two together. Old woman, heart attack, uninvited dog in my apartment. Betty.

"Said you'd know what to do."

"Not really."

"You'll figure it out." Another moment of silence.

"Where'd they take her?" I ask.

"Henry Ford." The other hospital, not quite as close as Detroit Receiving, but not much farther away.

"She gonna make it?"

"She's old." Like that explains anything.

"But she could still talk when they loaded her into the wagon?"

"So far. She said you'd know what to do. Said you should keep Bruce for as long as necessary."

"How long do you think?"

"Your guess is as good as mine." Another pause.

"Has Betty got any kids or family that you know of?" I'm thinking that 'as long as necessary' had better not be for long. I'm not big on commitment.

"Not that I know of. Look, I've got to get going. I'll waive the monthly pet fee as long as he's here. I put a bag of his dog food in there, too, and his bowl's on the floor. I'm gone for the night, back in the morning. Good luck with your dog."

"He's not my dog," I remind him. "And the dog won't be here that long," I add.

"She said she could trust you," he confides, waving his hand in the air and disappearing down the staircase.

She can trust me. There's the second sign of the apocalypse.

I unlock the door and the first thing I see is Bruce, comfortably snuggled against my pillow at one end of the couch. My pillow. My couch, also functioning as my bed. His tail wags tentatively, a sign he's no more confident with this arrangement than I am. Bruce is comfortable, but not confident. He's met me but he still doesn't trust me. Who can blame him? I'm not sure that *I* can even trust myself. Evidence dictates that we should proceed with caution.

"You're not going to sleep there," I tell him. "That's my bed you're lying on." He tilts his head to one side, not understanding or possibly just wondering if he's heard me correctly. In any event, he's not getting down anytime soon. My pillow is already half covered in dog hair. "Don't even think about it," I warn him. He lays his head back down and burps into the pillow. It's a loud, smelly dog burp. "You're not."

I wander over to the kitchen looking for something to drink. The fridge is largely empty save a few packets of ketchup, some mustard and a jar of pickles. There's no food, but my friend Booker has generously stashed a fifth of Absolut vodka in the freezer. I open the booze and take a long pull straight from the bottle. It's already been a long night. I stare menacingly back at my newfound friend. Perhaps I need to try talking to him as a peer. We can have a meeting of the minds, a man-to-dog summit.

"So Bruce, how long has it been since you've gone outside?" The dog doesn't answer, and I've got no way of knowing. I take another pull from the vodka. Harsh but not too harsh. Do I take my chances, wait until morning to walk him? Somehow I don't think this would be such a hot idea. How big is a dog's bladder? What is a dog's bladder capacity? More vodka. Of course, walking around the Corridor alone at night might not be such a hot idea, either. How often *does* a dog really need to pee? I've no clue. If I had a computer, I could look it up. Again, this falls outside my area of expertise. I decide to err on the side of caution since I hate cleaning up after roommates. I've had too many of them pee on the floor before.

"Where's your leash, boy?" Bruce looks up momentarily, burps loudly, and then lays his head back down. I'm going to have to buy another pillow. On the counter is a bag of dry dog food, an empty bowl, but no leash. I scan my tiny apartment for any hidden dog leash: the back of a door knob, draped over the couch, the kitchen sink. Still no leash. It probably never occurred to Andy that a dog would need to be walked. Why would he give me a dog with no leash? I've no way of getting into Betty's apartment, not without a key, so I can't look there. Another splash of vodka. Time to get creative.

There's a thick leather belt around my waist, which I slide from its loops while still magically managing to keep my pants up. So far so good. I slip the belt through Bruce's collar and coil the strap around my hand. The dog doesn't growl when I touch his neck, which is comforting, but my belt is far too short for the task at hand: I'd have to crawl alongside him for this to work, and I have no intention of crawling. I look around some more, my eyes eventually focusing on Booker's bath robe: his robe has a terrycloth belt of its own, which I appropriate for the common good. One improved clinch knot later I have a butt-ugly leash that is of appropriate length and may or may not be strong enough for what I'm about to ask of it. Half leather, half terry, I'll take my chances.

"Come on, Brucey boy!" I exclaim with false joy and enthusiasm. The dog momentarily moves his head from the pillow, decides he's not interested, and lays his head back down. "Come on, Brucey!" I try a little louder this time and with even greater vigor. "Let's go for a walk!" I'm trying to sell used cars, here but clearly Bruce isn't falling for it. He raises his head again, wags his tail ever-so-slightly, then lays back down and belches. Smelly belch. An "I ate something that died" belch. I make a mental note to find him some different dog food. "Let's go for a little walk," I cajole. Nothing, not even a burp this time. *Bastard.* "Get up, you lazy son of a bitch!" I finally yell in frustration: it would appear that tough love inspires him. Bruce slowly rises to his feet, stretches, and launches himself toward the floor. I'm in awe. Who'd have guessed? He stands in front of the door, ready to walk. "Good boy," I tell him. He wags his tail slowly in my direction; I'm guessing that's only because the dog doesn't possess a middle finger. "Let's go take a leak!" Real joy and enthusiasm shine through this time. Now the dog's tail beats faster, and barely a few seconds elapse before he's dragging me down the steps.

We descend from the porch and I realize that the night air has dropped ten degrees during the brief time I was in the apartment. The temperature hovers just above freezing, that not-quite-fog density in the atmosphere that intimates the immediate onset of winter. It might even snow before the night is through.

Bruce leads me to the corner and we walk north on Second Avenue, past Alexandrine and Willis Street and beyond West Canfield and Prentis towards the University. The city has become suddenly quiet, save the occasional squeal of a car's tires or a siren in the distance. The Forest Arms Apartments loom to my left, a four story turn-of-the-century beauty once inhabited by artists and students and just Plain Old Folk that worked in this city. There were something like one hundred units inside, and I'd been in there many times during my earlier days. Friends, acquaintances, parties. While the grand dame had suffered years of abuse and neglect, you could still (at that time) find ornate bannisters and fancy wainscoting hiding behind her shabby demeanor. It needed a little love, sure, but you could tell the place had good bones.

All of that has since been ravaged by fire and a collapsed roof. Like so many buildings it's an empty shell, a parking lot in waiting. Somebody or other has recently devised a grand plan to fix her up, but then, somebody or other always has a grand plan to fix something in the City of Detroit. We are the land of grand plans. What we are *not* is the land of adequate financing, follow through, or a collective will to accomplish much of anything. We are not the land of political expediency, though that too might be changing with the city in bankruptcy court. In certain individuals there exists the drive for rebirth and initiative, and this drive appears to have become mildly contagious: there are pockets of infectious good, but they're isolated. What we really need is an epidemic. I wish the grand planner well. I really do, because I think it would be a great thing if he can bring the Forest Arms back again. It would be a victory. I can offer him hope, but I cannot offer him faith.

We reach Warren Avenue, the main street that borders the Southern edge of campus. Warren Avenue is busy, not busy like you might find in Manhattan or Chicago, but busy in a "holy shit, there's people actually driving the city's roads at night" sort of way. Busy enough that I have to wait for the light to change before I can cross. It's a small thing, but it's something no less. Traffic. A sign of better things to come. Ghosts and ghouls aren't the only creatures stirring this evening.

I should turn back and go home, but Bruce forges on and I'm tethered to him by belt and by cotton. We keep walking, east to the next corner, then northbound on Cass Avenue. New buildings and major renovations dot the Wayne State campus, things I hadn't noticed before. I have yet to be accosted, solicited, or otherwise harassed on this walk, and I wonder if it's the ferocious poodle on the end of a line that protects me. The dog's stopped to pee about every thirty yards since we first started walking, and I've begun to suspect (at this point) that he's lifting his leg largely for show (unless Andy gave him a sixty-four ounce Big Gulp just before I arrived). Maybe bad guys are frightened by tiny dogs with prostate problems. Two miles and fifty-five minutes later we are standing at the front entrance to Henry Ford Hospital, Bruce and I.

"Sir, you can't bring that animal in here." The security guard is armed, a pistol on his belt. He rests his hand on his hip, just to let me know that he can reach it if he needs to. We've come a long ways since the days of doormen in velvet long coats and braided hats, but then, who the hell am I kidding? That was the stuff that punks used to play dress-up with, back in the eighties. Now nobody dresses up and everybody's got a gun.

"I know, I was just thinking."

"Well, could you step to the side and think somewhere else? You're blocking the entrance."

I look over my shoulder. There's no rush to get in, maybe a dozen cars in the parking lot and not a soul in sight. Maybe over at the emergency entrance, sure, but out here, with visiting hours long past? I could stand here for five more hours and not impede anybody. "No problem," I tell him. Why cause trouble?

"Are you looking for someone?"

It hadn't occurred to me that I was, but yes, I'm looking for someone. I suddenly have no doubt as to why I'm here. "A friend of mine was admitted tonight with heart problems."

"E.R.," he tells me as a matter of fact. He nods his head toward the side. The guard still hasn't taken his eyes off me; threats can come in all colors, shapes and sizes. Maybe I'm one of the crazies.

"Thanks," I answer, and slink around to the far side of the building.

The E.R. is much busier than the main entrance: ambulances come and go, smokers huddle around cars and trees and the handful of bushes that separate the parking lot into tidy rectangular segments. The waiting area is packed with the sick, the injured, the obligated. *Just another night in paradise*, I murmur, barely in time to catch the attention of Security Guard Number Two.

"Sir, you can't bring that animal in here."

I wasn't intending to. "I think I just met your brother at the other entrance."

"Are you saying we all look alike?" His definition of *we* is immediately understood. "You some kind of wise-ass, or are you high on something?" he asks suspiciously. Hand on his hip (just like the other guy) but this man's finger is twitching. Not quite as cool and collected as Guard Number One.

"Wise-ass," I confirm. "Sober wise-ass," I add, just to be clear.

"Well, knock that shit off," he tells me. "We've got a full house in here tonight. No animals allowed, keep the dog outside," he warns me, in case I didn't hear him the first time. His eyes scream "don't make me shoot you."

"Yes sir."

I step to the side before he can tell me to take my wise-ass thinking somewhere else, that I'm blocking traffic. Two ladies come out of the E.R., one bawling her eyes out and the other one wanting to bawl her eyes out but too strong and too busy consoling her shattered friend to be messing with that kind of nonsense. Four young guys, maybe early twenties, are passing a cigarette between them on the sidewalk just behind me only it's not just a cigarette. They inhale and hold it, then pass the joint to the left. A shaky old man, probably in his late seventies (but then it's hard to tell) sits in a wheelchair just outside the doors, an oxygen tank strapped to the back and a hand-rolled smoke between his lips. Hardcore. You've got to love the nicotine to be lighting up while a bomb is strapped to your back. Hanging out at the hospital is a never-ending side show of broken humanity.

"Mister, watch my dog for a couple minutes?" Shaky looks at me like I just offered to give him a complimentary case of the clap.

"Why the hell would I wanna do that? I'm a old man. I'm in a wheelchair. What'sa matter with you, anyways?"

Plenty. "I just need to dash inside for a second, check on a friend. Give me a break here. She just came in an hour ago. Hang on to my dog for five minutes while I run inside and find out how she's doing."

"You got a girlfriend, huh?"

"Friend, not a girlfriend." I clarify. "All you've got to do is not let him run away. Five minutes."

"Ain't nothing gets done around here in five minutes or less. It'll take you fifteen, at least. Maybe twenty. Pack of cigarettes." That's his asking price.

"I don't smoke. I'll give you five bucks."

"Don't help me none. How the hell am I gonna get to a store sitting in a wheelchair with a oxygen tank glued to my ass? And you can't buy smokes

165

for no five bucks. You want me to watch that mutt, it'll cost you a pack of cigarettes."

"I don't smoke, and I don't have time to run to any store. Look, do me this solid. I'll give you ten bucks, five now and five when I get back. You can pay somebody else a few bucks to go and get your smokes for you."

He considers my offer. "Sounds fair."

"Five minutes is all I need."

"I'll give you fifteen, after that, the dog's on his own."

"Tie him to that tree if you have to," I nod toward the dying ornamental in a hard-packed triangle between the sidewalk and the building.

I hand him the terry cloth end of the leash and slip quickly inside. Hopefully Bruce won't have emphysema by the time I get back. Security Guard Number Two gives me the once over like maybe I'm smuggling a poodle beneath my shirt, but finally decides to let me pass inside. There are two people ahead of me waiting to get at the counter: a middle-aged man with what looks like a gunshot wound to his leg (I've seen worse) and a large woman (indeterminate age) with a cough that sounds like end stage tuberculosis. I'm trying hard not to inhale the air, but fifteen minutes is way too long to hold your breath. At least I know that the gunshot wound isn't contagious. Shaky was right, this is going to take a while.

Thankfully the gunshot man gets placed in a wheelchair of his own and ushered to a special section of the waiting room. Guard Number Two gets to babysit until the police arrive, protocol with anything that involves a bullet. Next in line (Ms. Tubercular) gets an immediate escort to a private room where her germs might be contained. Three minutes and counting, probably a world's record for service at this desk.

"Next." That would mean me.

"Hi. A friend of mine was brought here a couple of hours ago by ambulance. I was wondering how she's doing."

"Name?"

"Betty."

"Betty...?" Clerk Lady is waiting.

"Or Eliza." Suddenly I feel like an idiot. I can't remember Betty's last name. I've seen it on the mailbox and on the buzzer outside our front entrance, but for the life of me I can't remember. Polish, I think, or something from Eastern Europe.

"Your friend have a last name?" Still waiting.

"Starts with an S, I think."

"Sweetie, you're going to have to do a lot better than that. This is a big hospital." There's a line growing behind me, a line of impatient, miserable patients six people deep and growing. She's right, I'm going to have to do better or a few of these angry and injured waiting to be "next" are going to want to kill me.

"She owns a dog, and I believe she had a heart attack."

"Um-hum..." She's now certain that I'm a dolt. "Seriously. You might want to do a little research and come back once you've got a better answer. Maybe you can call a friend."

It suddenly comes to me: "Sobczak," I blurt out.

"God bless you."

"No, Sobczak. Betty Sobczak. Eliza Sobczak. That's her name."

"You want to spell that?"

"S-O-B-C...." I go through the letters. I actually get it right on the first try. She asks for *my* name, and I spell that out, too. Clerk Lady looks down, pecks the letters into a keyboard, then asks me to take a seat. Someone will be with me in a minute. I check the time, and I've already burned eight minutes total of my allotted fifteen. I'm worried about Bruce. I don't want him to end up tied to a tree.

"Look, can't you just give me her room number and tell me how she's doing? I'm kind of on a tight schedule."

"Sir, if you'll just wait over there, someone will be with you in two minutes. Next!"

I wait off to one, side trying hard not to make eye contact with any of the would-be patients that surround me. Tempers flare easily in a place like this, and why wouldn't they? Sick, injured, in pain, and waiting around hoping that someone will get around to helping you. It's not the hospital's fault, and it's not the clients' fault. It's the sheer volume of need that clogs the process.

Four minutes later (I've now got three to spare) a man in scrubs appears next to Clerk Lady. She whispers something in his ear and points to me. The man slips out through a locking door and comes around to my side of the counter. We introduce ourselves and shake hands, that perfunctory meeting of two men who will never remember the other man's name. He's got a serious look on his face that probably comes from working extreme hours and bathing daily in other people's misery.

"Long night, huh?" This is all I can think to say. I realize how stupid I sound. He looks like he's had a long night. He doesn't answer. "I'm sort of on a tight timetable here. How's she doing?"

"Mrs. Sobczak had an acute myocardial infarction..."

"Plain English, please," I cut him off. "I get it, but keep it basic. I'm kind of tired and I don't think as clearly when I'm tired."

"Massive heart attack."

"How massive?"

"Massive." He leaves it at that, and I mull the word over for a second or ten.

"Is she going to make it?" I'm watching his face, and his serious look has grown even more serious, something I hadn't thought possible. Not a good sign.

"I'm really sorry. We did everything we could, but Mrs. Sobczak didn't make it."

"Shit." It's all I can think to say. I feel as if I've been punched in the gut. I don't know why, but I didn't expect this. I thought she was a tough old bird. I figured she'd live.

"These things aren't easy. I'm sorry for your loss," says Doctor What's-His-Name. I believe that's something he's legally required to say.

"Thanks." There was a brief wave of nausea, but now it's gone. I don't know what would be better, but "I'm sorry for your loss" sounds like such generic crap. I know that it's meant to be comforting, but really, what does it imply? Generic bullshit. Perhaps he should try "How's that dog of hers doing?" or something a little more relevant. He's watching me. I'm feeling a little better, and he's standing there patiently.

"We hadn't known each other all that long," I finally confide.

"Really?" The doctor's face shows genuine surprise. "That seems a bit unusual, since she put you down as next of kin and Durable Power of Attorney."

With that I am shown to a room around the back, where a different Clerk Lady anxiously awaits. There are forms to sign, a few administrative details to remedy. I'm convinced that I'm not the guy who should be doing this, but still I agree to sign on every X on every form. First I dodge outside to renegotiate my deal with Shaky (another ten bucks buys me another half hour. I must be getting the wholesale discount). I go back into the hospital and sign what seems like an entire ream of legal documents. I don't have the answers to ninety percent of their questions, but I fill out what I can and scribble my name when asked. I'll have to make arrangements for Betty's body in the morning. She must have some kind of relative I can find before then. They give me her meager possessions: a purse containing one State of Michigan I.D. card, a Medicare card, two tubes of lipstick, and one eyeliner pencil. A receipt for $23.49 in groceries from the local market, twelve dollars in cash round out the lot. That's it. Back outside I reclaim Bruce, who is now curled up on Shaky's lap.

"Sorry 'bout your friend," Shaky tells me, and offers a cigarette which I gratefully accept. I don't smoke, but this seems like a good time to start. "You got a good dog here."

"Thanks," I tell him, and together we puff away in the darkness.

"It ain't easy losing a friend."

"No, it sure isn't." I'm still in a bit of shock. Betty and I barely knew one another, yet somehow I'm still feeling a hurt inside. And there's also the fact that Bruce is going to be living with me until I figure this out. What am I going to do with a dog? That's an awful lot to explain to a complete stranger. "This is all completely unexpected." It's the best I can offer to the man on oxygen.

"We all got our problems."

"It's the truth."

"But losing a good friend, now that blows some serious donkey pecker."

I look at the man and for the first time tonight, I smile. *Now there's a line they should teach those doctors.*

Walking home we take Second Avenue southbound and then cut down Gullen Mall, which is the fancy name for a broad sidewalk that runs north-south across the campus. It's deserted at this time of night, and I should probably know better than to walk such an isolated stretch in the wee hours but I'm far too exhausted to care. If someone wants to jump me, well, have at it. Take me for all I'm worth. It will probably amount to a net loss.

We eventually come to a fountain (there are a few on campus, none on the massive scale of Grant Park in Chicago or that big stainless donut in Hart Plaza, but hey, you get what you pay for) where Bruce and I pause to rest on a bench. The water is purling peacefully, and if I didn't know any better I could be sitting streamside at my favorite campsite. Bruce jumps up on my lap. He's tired and cold. I'm feeling tired and lost.

"You're alright, buddy. We'll figure it out." The dog shivers and burrows tighter against my jacket. I look to the sky, but the combination of city lights and cloud cover obliterate any chance of seeing a star. They're out there somewhere, I'm still sure of that. I wonder what time it is, but then, what does it really matter? I don't start work until Monday. Tomorrow is Thursday. A few more minutes of sitting and a few memories percolate to the surface. I recall a favorite camping trip alongside a babbling river up in Oscoda County. I've always loved water; water and solitude. There were many times that I would head to the forest with not much more than a

170

sleeping bag, some fishing gear, a fillet knife, and a roll of aluminum foil. A potato, one square of butter, and a packet of loose tea, one cowboy coffee pot and I could live for a week. Life was simpler then.

Time flits by and I drift back to another time, a time when I was sitting by a different fountain in the middle of the night. Only it wasn't Bruce snuggled with his head in my lap, it was Janey, and this must have been early in the fall because it was a lot warmer then. The Scott Fountain, Belle Isle: we were wearing T-shirts and, while it was chilly in the dark, we weren't cold. At least I wasn't cold. Maybe Janey was, and maybe that's why she was stretched out on the bench with her head in my lap. Did she ask for a blanket? I don't remember. We weren't *doing* anything that night, at least we weren't doing anything special like running naked through a fountain or going to prom or driving to Ann Arbor. It was a night, a *regular old night.* We were just, how can I explain this, *being.* We were young and living in a moment, and we were wholly occupied with being young and living in a moment. Wholly occupied.

I don't know why this comes to me now, because those times are the times that I rarely reflect upon. They're over and done with. Nothing good can come from worrying about the past. As someone once told me, "If you don't want shit to stink, don't move it." Words to live by, those are. Memory is a tricky thing. You have to be careful not to let yourself airbrush over the things you did or didn't like in the past for the convenience of a more palatable present.

But tonight I'm reminded of the *warmth* of that particular moment, that moment long ago on a bench by a fountain that was not this fountain. I'm reminded of that sense of *belonging*, not just to another person but to a world of boundless opportunity, something bigger than myself. In that moment on a bench, by a fountain much larger than this fountain, all of what life had to offer still seemed to lie before us. The *both* of us, *together.* They were waiting, all of those big, indescribable things, diamonds in the sky just waiting for us to reach out and grasp them. And then they were gone.

Voices echo in the distance, and the sound drags me back to the present. It's time to get moving. Anybody out at this time of the morning is probably up to no good, and I'm proof positive of that. The fog still suspends in the air and dims the early morning sky, but a mile or so to the south and east a luminous glow projects from ground level. A faint whiff of smoke dances across the lower atmosphere, remnants of another dream turning to ash. Bruce is snoring, a miniature canine chainsaw. I give him a nudge and he awakens, gives me a short growl, then jumps to the ground. He's ready to go home and so am I. Together. We get to the crosswalk at Warren Avenue, only a few more blocks to go. It's only then that I realize I've been sobbing like a baby.

CHAPTER NINETEEN

Heidelberg is Burning

"We're taking the tires, motherhumper!" Davros isn't exactly *yelling,* but neither is he using his inside voice. I'm standing alongside of him (really more like a half-step behind and slightly to his left, in case things really hit the fan). It turns out there *is* (in fact) a purple and yellow building on Michigan near Trumbull, and it turns out that the guy behind the counter at Tires Cheap is not particularly intimidated by Davros' use of a loud voice and salty language. The guy has, on the other hand, noticed the small cannon tucked inside my friend's belt (for which he does indeed have the proper license and permits). I can tell that the man's weighing whether or not to fight for possession of the rubber or take his lumps and let us wheel them out the front door.

"Who says *motherhumper*? I'm not sure that's even a word." This from someone with a very thick accent of his own.

"*I* say it, motherhumper. The tires!"

"I still do not believe it is a word. You swear incorrectly."

Dav came to my apartment at eight this morning and I'd honest-to-God forgotten he was even coming. I was functioning (if you can call it that) on about three hours of sleep. Bruce was pressed between my knees and the back cushions of the couch, which is an exceptionally cozy position for the dog and not a bad way for me to stay warm. Still, I wasn't prepared for that eight o'clock wakeup call and I'd forgotten that I now own a pet. Thursday. It's hard to keep track of the days when you have no schedule.

"I need to walk the dog," I'd told him.

"You don't have time."

"I don't have time to *not* walk him. Any idea what a pain it is to clean up dog whizz from the cracks in a hardwood floor?"

"Make it quick."

I did, racing downstairs with Bruce on his makeshift leash and letting him take a leak against the cast iron porch railing. Funny that Davros didn't even question why I had a dog in my apartment. Bruce paced back and forth on the tiny strip of grass that separates the sidewalk from the street, but eventually decided that porch pissing was all that he was up for this morning. We shuttled back upstairs and Davros and I left Bruce inside.

Two minutes later we stepped into Dav's Cadillac.

"Can we at least stop and get some coffee?" I'd asked, and The Big Man didn't even bother to answer. *Hell no we didn't have time for coffee.* I forgot my cell phone at the apartment, but knew he wasn't turning back to get it. What would I need a phone for? Davros started driving and it didn't take long for me to figure out where we were headed. "This place really exists then?" Still no answer. We wouldn't be in his car if the place didn't exist. Now we're standing inside of Tires Cheap and Dav looks like he's about to shoot up the joint if we don't get the answers we want from our friendly neighborhood car stripper.

"I am not sure what you're talking about. Are you saying you would like to buy a set of tires? You don't need to come in here with all your 'motherhumper' talk and shit. Ask nicely; I do have tires for sale." The owner is a young man of Middle Eastern descent, maybe thirty if that and built like he spends all of his spare time at the gym: that, or boosting heavy tires off the street. I've got to hand it to him, he's calm under pressure. If I didn't know any better I could almost fall for his line.

"We're not *buying* anything, dipshit. You're giving my friend here his tires and rims back, *these tires* sitting right in front of your shitty-assed counter. You're even going to give him two bills for the tow you cost him. Two hundred bucks, asshole. Scumbags like you are ruining my city." *His* city. I'm hanging back a full two steps now, debating whether Davros is merely posturing or if he's truly ready to start shooting up the place. My money is on shooting. I also find it curious that the tow truck which cost me a hundred and twenty-five smackaroos only yesterday has now gone up to two hundred, but that's the least of my concerns. Stray bullets head the list.

"Surely you're mistaken. I just purchased those wheels from a salvage yard last night. I didn't even have time to put them on the rack." His voice is getting loud now, matching fire with fire. "They're kickass tires, still have a ton of life left in them. If you're interested, I could make you an incredible deal." It's telling that at no point has this guy mentioned *police*, *strong arm* or *robbery*, all words that that I'd be shouting to the heavens. A legit businessman would be screaming bloody murder by now, that or crapping his pants. It's also telling that the wheel on top of this four-stack has some red, green and blue paint on its center hub, as if the previous owner had been involved in a minor collision with a Molson Brewery truck. Coincidentally, I once hit just such a truck myself, and the accident managed to leave an identical stripe. Funny, that.

"They're mine. I recognize the paint on that rim. You stole them."

"Surely there is some misunderstanding. I bought them from a reputable dealer just yesterday. I haven't *stolen* anything."

"A reputable dealer? Look, genius, they were stolen from my truck just yesterday, a few blocks north of here. A witness told me where I might be able to find them, and here they are. That paint? (I point to the tri-colored smear in the middle) I've got an accident report from three years ago that mentions where I acquired that paint (a total lie). A *police* report. I want my tires back."

The guy behind the counter chews on this for a second, because a witness could complicate his flimsy cover story. A witness would make our story more credible in the eyes of the law, and the law isn't really something he wants here, not under any circumstances. This is one set of tires amongst many, and he's weighing whether it's worth fighting over. *Was there a witness?* He's not sure. There *could* be a witness. There is always that possibility. My accident report is total bullshit, a complete fabrication. He probably suspects as much, but he has no way of knowing for sure. I can tell the gears are spinning in his head. Davros is suddenly quiet, letting the man stew in his own fears. I do notice that Dav's hand is casually resting on the butt of his gun, just as a reminder. A little "bonus fear," to put the man over the edge.

"You know, it has just occurred to me," the esteemed representative of Tires Cheap now tells us, "perhaps my reputable associate purchased these tires from someone, how should I say this, *slightly less reputable*? You can never be certain about these transactions, especially when they involve a third party. People make mistakes. It is possible that my supplier was misled by the original supplier. Perhaps there is some truth to what you say. I have no way of knowing, as I run a legitimate business here. Maybe we could strike a bargain. Half price." He smiles the smile of a hungry crocodile.

"You want a bargain? We just offered you one," Davros pipes back up. "You load these into the back of my car, give my friend two hundred bucks for his trouble, and we don't call the police. That's the bargain. Don't scuff the upholstery. A one-time-only offer. If it happens again, I'll decide whether to call the police or blow a .45 caliber hole right through your nut sack." I'm fairly certain Dav means it, and Tires Cheap looks convinced as well. The blood rushes from his face. If it were me on the other side of that counter, the blood would also have rushed from my nut sack.

"We have a deal," the man responds. "*Motherhumpers.*"

Now we're bumping along, two tires in the trunk and two in the back seat of Dav's big Cadillac. I feel like I'm going to throw up, but just haven't gotten around to it yet. The criminal life can be stressful.

"That went well," my friend tells me. "Better than expected, when you get down to it."

I don't want to know what constitutes "expected" in his equation. *Did he expect shooting? Fatalities? Cops? Prison?* "I'm feeling a little sick, Davros. You might need to pull over."

"Suck it up, Nancy. You're getting soft in your old age. We did good. We'll slap these babies back on your truck and you'll be on the road again in no time. By the way, you owe me another seventy-five bucks."

I know now why the cost of towing expanded from one-and-a-quarter to two hundred dollars. "Let me guess..."

"Collection fee," he cuts me off. "My time is worth *something*, right?"

Who am I to argue? I've probably just participated in a felony, possibly multiple felonies. Do I really want to bang heads over chump change? "Yep," I let it go at that.

"You're lucky he didn't sell them before we got there. When did you find time to adopt a dog, by the way?" What we just did, robbery or repo depending on how one looks at it, is now ancient history. He has moved on.

So I tell him about Bruce and about Betty, about my night-time stroll to Henry Ford Hospital and my late walk home. I do *not* tell him about sitting by the fountain, about ghosts and memories of my youth coming back to haunt me. I'm not ready for that conversation, and even if I were, Davros is not the man with who I'd have it.

"It sounds as if you're settling right in. Next thing you know you'll be getting married."

To whom? I almost ask. The only person I'm seeing much of these days is Booker, and while he's a pleasant enough guy, he's definitely not my type. I make a face instead.

"Just kidding with that whole marriage thing. But you do seem to be settling in."

I don't answer, but Lord, I truly hope not.

We pull up at his warehouse, and my truck is still safely inside. Chalk one up for the good guys. An hour later the wheels are on the axles and my truck is back on the road. Davros secures the building behind us. There are a couple of locks and some kind of security cage involved.

"Are you coming by the store?" He asks as he climbs behind the wheel of the Caddy.

"Can't. I've got to try to track down Betty's family. Right now I'm next of kin, and I'd like to ditch that designation."

"Then swing by the store later today or sometime tomorrow. I've got a few things we need to talk about."

"I will. Thanks again."

"Don't worry about it. You owe me. And you still need to toughen up," he warns before driving off. The morning sun is to his back. I get into my truck and embrace the freedom of having a vehicle with wheels back. I set off more or less in the same direction.

My first stop is at an auto parts store, where I procure a set of locking lug nuts for the truck. It might not prevent another round of tire theft, but at least it will slow the bad guys down. In the old days I'd have purchased a locking gas cap, too, but nobody bothers to siphon gas in this modern era, the filler neck on a newer vehicle is designed to stop that sort of thing (the tube to the tank is kinked). This redesign deterred gas theft for a while, until thieves discovered that they could just drill a hole in your gas tank and drain it from the bottom. Now instead of simply being out one tank of gas, you'll need a five or six-hundred dollar repair if someone gets to you. So much for progress.

Stop number two is the gas station. Nobody siphoned or drilled my tank, but I've learned never to let myself get low on fuel. You don't want to be filling up in the dead of night around here. Ever. I'm below a quarter of a tank, so it's time to top things off. The best part of this stop is that, while I'm paying in advance (you can no longer pump fuel first in this world of drive-offs), I notice that this particular station happens to sell dog leashes from a pegboard display behind the register. It makes no sense: but then, many things about my hometown don't make sense. Dog leashes at a gas station. Why? I'm not going to question it. I buy a leash and secretly think that maybe there *is* a god after all.

The third stop on my post-shakedown at Tires Cheap tour is the apartment. Bruce needs to be walked, and this time when I open the door the dog is genuinely happy to see me. I take him for a long stroll, all the way around the block and over to the freeway, then up and down another street. The leash works as advertised and is far more attractive than the bathrobe belt was in my hand. Bruce craps on a vacant parcel behind my building, and I turn back home. It's not quite ten in the morning and I feel like I've already had a full day.

Back to the felony: is it really a crime when you steal your own stuff? Undoubtedly. Rules is rules. But in a lawless society people carve out their own forms of justice. The system as it currently exists is fatally broken. This may seem wrong, but the only way I was getting my property back was to take it back. Davros is right. I do need to toughen up. Still, twelve years of Catholic schooling has imbedded a mean guilt streak in me. I'm contemplating this guilt when I stumble across a familiar face.

"You're out and about early," Susan tells me. She doesn't know the half of it. We're both walking up the front steps to the building, having arrived from opposite directions. She seems unusually chipper, which means she hasn't heard the news.

"Hey there, kiddo."

"Hey yourself, old man." We're becoming familiar, finding our way in this fresh relationship.

"You're coming in kind-of early this morning. No classes today?"

"Just a break between classes."

"You weren't home last night?" I ask.

"Why, you worried about Heidelberg?"

"Heidelberg?" I wasn't thinking about that, but then that was why the trucks left last night.

"Another fire. The Penny House burned to the ground last night. Some kids were talking about it this morning. It seems as if the whole city is going up in flames lately."

I thought I was the only one to notice. "I'm sorry to hear that. No, I wasn't thinking about Heidelberg. I was just wondering if you knew about all the commotion around here."

"I must have missed it. As a matter of fact, I did get in really late last night. Why, what came up? More SpaghettiO's flambé?" Still chipper. She definitely hasn't heard.

"No. Betty had a heart attack."

"I was about to ask why you're walking Bruce! How's she doing?"

"She didn't make it."

179

"She died?" Astonishment.

"Last night."

"Oh no!" Susan steps inside the foyer. "I'm so sorry! How'd you find out about it?"

On the walk up to my floor, I give her a brief synopsis. "The long and the short of it is that Bruce landed in my lap, and I've got to track down her family. Any ideas where I should start?"

"I didn't think you two were all that close."

"Neither did I."

"I'm sorry. I really didn't know her that well, not any better than you do. I liked her. I have no idea."

"Well, if you think of anything let me know. *Please.* Maybe she mentioned a relative in conversation?"

"Nothing. I never really talked with her that much, at least not about her family. Sorry."

Not very helpful, but maybe she can solve one of my other problems. "Hey, have you given any thought to acquiring a pet? Maybe a cuddly canine?" I ask hopefully.

"Fat chance, but I'm sorry for your loss. That's what I'm supposed to say, right? *I'm sorry for your loss?*" She looks at the dog, then at me. "You two *do* make a cute couple." Susan continues up the next flight of steps, and Bruce and I reluctantly enter our unit. Booker is waiting for us inside, or more precisely, Booker is on his way out the door but pauses long enough to bark some information in my general direction as he races by.

"You need to hire a secretary, dude. Messages are on the refrigerator door."

"Whoa, whoa," I stop him at the threshold, "what messages?"

"All kinds of people calling. You really ought to take your phone when you go out. You, my friend, are extraordinarily popular this morning. Your sister called (*I don't care to know why*). That professor from the University (*could be good news*). Henry Ford Hospital. The landlord (*I have no idea what that's about*). That chick that runs City Fusion. Being your roommate is starting to turn into a full-time job, and I've already got a full-time job, only it pays part-time. I'm getting out of here before that damn thing rings again. Any word on Betty?"

"Died."

"Shit."

"You said it."

"Got yourself a dog, it would appear."

"It's temporary."

"Isn't everything?"

"Point taken. I swear I've heard that somewhere before."

"You're starting work with me on Monday, right?"

"Monday morning, bright eyed and bushy tailed [now that I've got another mouth to feed]. You tell me when and where."

"Alright, then."

"Alright, then," I agree, and then Booker, too, is gone in a flash.

Where do I begin? I call the hospital first. They need some additional forms signed, but nothing that can't wait. Betty's body has been sent to the basement morgue, and someone will have to claim it eventually. Routine stuff. I tell them I'm still searching for relatives, I'll have to get back later, and we leave it at that.

Then the real work begins: knocking on doors. I figure that *somebody* in this building must have a scrap of knowledge about Betty's past. So far all I know is that she was once married and her husband is now dead. What I haven't counted on is that most people who live in this building are either working or in school during the day. I start on the top floor and begin working my way down.

Susan is the only person on the third floor this mid-morning. That makes me zero for one. My floor turns out to be equally unproductive. That doesn't surprise me: cross off yours truly, Booker's burned out place and Betty's now-vacant apartment, and there aren't many residents left. In fact, my search of the building as a whole turns out to be very unproductive. Watchdog Mike, the half-clothed neighbor who was banging on doors the night of Booker's fire, he's around but is otherwise useless. For a man that keeps such a close eye on the world, Mike sure doesn't remember much.

The best lead arrives in the form of Andy, our property manager/superintendent. He doesn't know anything at all about Betty's past, but he has no ethical concerns whatsoever about giving me the keys to her place. In Andy's eyes, possession of the dog is nine-tenths of the law.

"Have at it. Somebody's going to have to clean it out before the end of the month anyway. Let me know what you decide."

What I decide; I decide I don't want this responsibility. On the other hand, maybe I can learn something by casing Betty's apartment. Nobody else is going to do it. Bruce and I head down the hall and let ourselves in. The dog is happy: no, the dog is ECSTATIC to be back on familiar turf. He runs from one end of the place to the other, back and forth like he's been snorting cocaine. His tail wags. He stops to howl, then runs some more. Then a little panic sets in, and he's eagerly searching for something. Someone.

"Settle down, my friend, she's not here." The dog cocks his head to one side, trying to comprehend what I just told him, then decides to go back to doing what he was doing. Crazy dog. I look around and decide that the only thing I can do is dig in and keep shoveling through her life.

I find a leash. I find another bag of burp-inducing dog food. I find an exceptionally clean one-bedroom place decorated with the things you might expect to find in the home of an ancient Polish lady: slightly tired but well-kept furniture, an assortment of afghans and woven throw rugs, coasters and doilies and tchotchkes and one gold framed picture of the pope (John Paul II, not the current one). I discover kitchen cabinets laden with green Anchor Hocking glasses and Corelle dinnerware circa 1970, an electric coffee pot and a griddle and one good cast iron skillet that Betty probably referred to as her "spider." I find a hodgepodge of framed snapshots, most featuring a man I can only assume was the former Mr. Jozef Sobczak, a handsome fellow back in his time (which appears to have ended somewhere around 1979, when wide sport coat lapels were still marginally in style). I find a small stack of envelopes under a wicker basket in the kitchen: gas bill, electric bill, bank statement. Nothing personal.

I enter the bedroom, which I must say makes me slightly uncomfortable. I've been in the bedrooms of strange women before (some stranger than others), but not under these circumstances. Not as a snoop, a ghoul prying through the decedent's past. This is entirely new. The bed is unmade, sheets thrown askew.   I avoid that. To the right sits a nightstand with an alarm clock/radio and yet another picture of Jozef alongside a recent copy of Reader's Digest. I go through the drawers and find a pair of fuzzy slippers, a few nightgowns, and a handful of costume jewelry. Then a rosary, a ball composed of various rubber bands, a box of envelopes, two ballpoint pens, and four first-class postage stamps. It reminds me of the box that Davros sent.

Two dress suits, (one black and one pink) hang in the closet and not much else. Some sweaters lay on the shelf. A coat, a lightweight jacket (pockets are empty) and one jaunty hat. The dresser holds more clothing, underwear and brassieres and short-sleeved shirts. Tucked inside the top drawer is a jeweler's box with a simple wedding band inside. There's a short stack of love letters from Jozef, the most recent of which was written in 1965. A bank book: a passbook savings account containing one-hundred forty-seven dollars and fifty-six cents. That's it.

What I don't find is a picture of any kids. I don't find any cards or correspondence from friends or relatives and I don't find any messages on her vintage telephone answering machine from a long-lost sister-in-law or niece or nephew wondering how she's been. No computer, no address book. *How is it possible that a woman that age doesn't have a personal phone book? A Rolodex? Did she keep addresses and phone numbers in her head?* In short, there's no indication that Betty had any life whatsoever outside of the dog Bruce and occasional contact with her immediate neighbors. This mission is a failure. It's sad, really. This could easily be me in thirty years.

I grab the leash, a pillow for the pooch, and the bag of dog chow. I carefully lock the door behind me, then Bruce and I shuttle down the hall to our own joint. He's bummed out to be leaving Betty's (I can tell), but once we're inside my apartment, the dog quickly makes himself at home on the couch. Dogs are easy. I give him the pillow, scratch behind his ears, and he's out cold within minutes.

The list on the fridge beckons me. *What do I have to deal with? What is critical?* I look at the first item. I have absolutely no intention of calling my sister Mary back, at least not today. Cross that off. The professor at Wayne State? Important but not urgent. That, too, can wait. Henry Ford Hospital I've put in a temporary holding pattern. *What can I tell them? That I have no idea where to start? Keep her on ice?* I should probably pick a funeral home but it still doesn't seem right. Not yet. Betty's family should be at the funeral (if she has any family). I'll keep looking. The landlord. *What does he want?* I run downstairs and ask Andy, who assures me that the building's owner merely wishes to know when I'll be emptying out Betty's place, no need to call him back immediately. The owner is anxious, but Andy's already spoken with him. The clock is ticking and he's hoping he can lease the apartment before the first of the month. I'm not knocking myself out here. If the landlord doesn't like my work ethic, let him be the next of kin. Let him clean it out. Last on Booker's list is "that chick that runs City Fusion." *Absolutely not.*

CHAPTER TWENTY

Unclaimed Persons

Three o'clock and I'm at my wits' end. I've tried the local police, social services and the Secretary of State (Betty hadn't driven a car in over sixteen years and that's as much as they could tell me). All of this has led me nowhere. I ask the hospital for suggestions. They put me in touch with a warm and fuzzy woman in case management who tells me to try the things I'd already tried. She says that if that doesn't work, then use my own best judgment. My own best judgment: it has served me so well in life. Finally she reminds me that I was listed as next of kin, and thus Betty must have trusted me to do the right thing. If I can't make a decision, she'll provide a list of local funeral parlors that might help me with my decision. Every word she spoke sounded like "tag, you're it!"

"What if I just don't show up? I mean, what if nobody claims her body?" It's a bluff, but I'm curious what her response will be.

"Sir, you can't do that."

"Technically I wouldn't be *doing* anything. I'm not legally obligated to claim my neighbor's corpse, am I? What we're talking about is *not* doing something that I'm in no way required to do in the first place." I've got some logic in there, somewhere.

"Sir, I realize that in times like this we all deal with grief in our own way. Trust me, this isn't a road you want to follow..."

How does she know which road I'd like to follow? I almost call her a bad name, but then I settle down. I've spent a lifetime following dirt roads and blue highways. Maybe I'm Jack Kerouac. Maybe I'd like another detour, a little jaunt through the countryside. It's just possible that, while I've enjoyed visiting Armageddon, I've decided not to stay. "Why not?" I finally ask. "Please explain to me again why I don't want to take this road?"

"I feel your sorrow, I truly do." (She must be reading from a counselor's handbook at this point, either that or gazing at tea leaves in the bottom of a cup. There's *no way* she is feeling my particular feelings at this moment, because "sorrow" is *way* down on the list of what I've got inside. I'd start with frustration, lead to hopelessness, and work my way down from there). "I'd be glad to put you in touch with someone who can assist you with that. But in the meantime, we can't just have unclaimed persons stacking up at the hospital. It isn't moral. It isn't *right*."

"Unclaimed persons." What the hell kind of a term is that? It sounds so impersonal. A picture scrolls through my head of an Unclaimed Persons Department, except that these unclaimed persons are very much alive. They are lives somehow forgotten or abandoned, an Unclaimed Persons Room stashed inside every airport, every library basement, every Chuck E. Cheese pizzeria. Every UPS hub, every post office, every train station and every child care center could have a little space in the back where they keep their stash of unclaimed persons. I'm envisioning entire warehouses full of unclaimed persons, shrink wrapped, neatly tagged and labelled, organized on industrial shelves and waiting for someone to come and get them, waiting for someone to give meaning to their lives. There might be thousands of them, maybe *tens of thousands* throughout the country, millions worldwide; suspended lives, waiting for one kind soul to take them home, to claim them.

"Sir? Are you still there?"

I don't know how long I've been lost in thought. "Yeah, I'm still here."

"I'm sorry, did you hear what I just said?"

"It wouldn't be *right*?" I respond. I think that's what she said. Who the hell is she to define what's *right*?

"Exactly. So when might we expect this issue to be resolved?" She's looking for a timetable, or a hard date, or better yet, an exact time. Preferably today. Persons can't remain unclaimed forever.

"Unclaimed persons?"

"That's how we've been asked to describe them. Sir? About resolving this issue?"

There's no sense in arguing. "I'm hoping it won't take more than another day or two. I'm working on it."

"That would be wonderful. We really appreciate your cooperation in this matter. These things are never easy. Is there anything else with which I might assist you?"

"No, I'm good," I tell her, and hang up. I'm at my nadir, the lowest possible point in a trajectory.

It's then that luck intercedes. Luck, fate, karma, God; call it what you will, although I'm certain that if it is God that's involved, his messenger wouldn't be cloaked in the drab uniform of the United States Postal Service. There are faster ways to get your point across. In my frustration with the world at large, I decide to take a break from calling and walk the dog. MY dog, it would seem. I keep forgetting that he's officially mine, and officially needs to be walked. Bruce is excited and ready to go. I clip the leash on his collar and we bounce out the door. Just as I get to the landing at the bottom of the stairs, I spy the postman coming my way with his heavy leather satchel. Expectations are low, but I ask him anyhow.

"Anything in there for Betty Sobczak?"

"You're not Betty Sobczak." He's a swift one.

"No, I live across the hall from her. *Did* live across the hall from her," I correct myself. "Betty died last night, and I'm trying to track down any relatives."

"I'm sorry to hear that. Never met the lady."

"She was a good person."

"So you say." Then an awkward pause. "You're not her," in case I need to be reminded.

"So no mail for Betty?"

"I didn't say that, but even if there were, I can't give it to you. Federal regulations. You'll have to go through the appropriate channels."

"I'm working as her intermediary, and I don't have a lot of time. There are some issues that need to be resolved, and I can't locate any of her relatives."

"Got a warrant?"

"No."

"Not good enough."

"Someone needs to make funeral arrangements."

"Good for you."

I'm not getting anywhere. We stare menacingly at one another. I try another approach. "The dog lives in that apartment. Can he collect her mail?"

"You're kidding, right?"

"About the dog?"

"Yeah. You don't really think I'm going to fork over the mail to a dog."

"He's a retriever." I know, I'm grasping at straws.

The letter carrier grimaces and looks closely at Bruce. "He's a poodle."

"A hybrid. One of those designer dogs: a Golden Poo-Triever. Half-and-half." I immediately realize that I should have attempted *Re-Troodle*, instead. No way is he going to fall for *Poo-Triever*.

"A poodle-retriever? No chance in hell. He's a runt. A dog that size would need a step ladder to get laid by a Golden."

"Alright," I admit, "He's all miniature poodle. But the dog *is* a tenant. Betty Sobczak's dog."

"I hear a butt load of lies on this job, pal; scammers looking for social security checks, credit card numbers, bank statements. I don't even know you. Can't do it, even if I wanted to."

"Come on, give me a break, would you? This is her dog. He *lives* with her. I'm trying to do the right thing here."

"Dogs ain't people. Sorry, no can do." He opens the little metal wall box with his key and slides something inside. "I could get canned over something like that, and then who's gonna support my two exes? You'll have to go through the proper channels."

"Can you at least tell me if there's anything inside Betty's mailbox, other than bills?"

"Against regulations. Again, sorry." He looks me dead in the eye, gives me a shrug, then looks back at the mailboxes: Betty Sobczak's mailbox door is slightly ajar, not locked tight like the rest of them. "Huh, would you look at that?" He asks, and then turns and leaves. Pity is a powerful tool.

One envelope. One small envelope rests inside the little postal cave. I take it out with care and examine it closely: it's addressed in flowing, girlish cursive to Mrs. Jozef Sobczak. Betty. The return address reads *L. Wojtkowiak, New Britain, Connecticut.* I slip the envelope inside my pocket, hoping against hope that L. Wojtkowiak can bring me some answers. It's a long shot at best, but better than nothing. I should tear it open here and now, find out if it holds a clue, but I don't. Bruce needs his walk.

We take the usual route, down to Second Avenue, around the block, and pee in the empty lot (Bruce, not me). Broken whiskey bottles are everywhere, empty condom wrappers and used hypodermic needles litter the abandoned properties. People have quit caring. How can they do this? Why would you soil your own city? It occurs to me that if I indeed decide to keep Bruce, I'd better make sure that his shots are up to date. I don't want him coming down with hepatitis.

Watchdog Mike is sitting on the stoop when we return, surveying the terrain while he puffs away on a cigarette.

"What's up, cat?"

"How are you, Mike?"

"I heard about Betty. Looks like you inherited her dog."

"Looks that way."

"That is one good dog there. I've never heard him growl or nothing. He'll make you a good friend."

"Thanks," I accept the compliment (like I contributed in any way to Bruce's upbringing). My ownership of Bruce is somewhat like my relationship with Susan in one respect: In both cases, I'm reaping the fruits of somebody else's labor.

"When's the funeral gonna be?"

"Still working on that."

He takes another drag. "She was alright for an old lady," he muses.

"That she was. You ever hear her mention any family?" I've asked him once already, when I was knocking on every door in the building. Still, I'm hoping he might have a flashback to a previous conversation with Betty. Maybe his perpetual flightiness has worn off.

"Just a dead husband."

"What I thought," I tell him, and reflexively pat the envelope in my breast pocket to make sure it's still there. "Catch you later, Mike."

"You know where to find me."

Once upstairs and in the sanctity of my own place I slice the envelope open with a butter knife, taking caution not to destroy the return address (such that it is). The greeting card has a simple message and not much else:

Aunt Eliza-

I'm not sure that you remember me, but I'm Lisa Wojtkowiak, your "niece" (my grandmother Irenka was your husband's first cousin by marriage). I haven't seen you since I was a little girl, but I remember the time that you came to visit at our house for Christmas. I was just a toddler, and you brought me the most beautiful handmade doll! I'm in college now, and while I was cleaning out my room, I found that doll and thought of you. Thank you again! I loved that doll when I was little, and I still do today. Someday I intend to pass it on to a little girl of my own. I hope this letter finds you well:

I don't hear much about your side of the family since my parents passed.
Take care, and I'll try to write again soon. - Love, Lisa

This might be as close as I'll ever come to hitting the lottery. Is the mystery solved? I'm not sure that the young granddaughter of a first cousin by marriage is going to be the answer to my problems, but it's better than nothing. I'm going to require internet access in order to track Lisa down. I've got a (pretty damn distinctive) name and city in Connecticut to help narrow things down. I head upstairs to Susan's apartment and knock on her door.

Luck is still running strong. Susan is home and she has a laptop with web access. In less than five minutes I have Lisa's full mailing address, as well as her cell phone number, Twitter account (whatever that is) and email address.

"Does that help?"

"I certainly hope so. Thanks, Susan. I appreciate it."

"No problem. That's all you needed?"

"For now."

"Want me to run a quick search, see if there are any other relatives around?"

"Can't hurt. That would be great."

She punches in a bunch of information, waits, and tries again and again. Fifteen minutes and still nothing good turns up. I may need her to give me a quick tutorial before I start the job on Monday. I'm not *incompetent,* but my last few jobs required limited tech skills. I'm worried that what little I do know could use a major-league refresher course.

"It turns out Sobczak is a highly common name, at least in certain communities. Milwaukee is one of them, Detroit is not. Not too many around here, and I'm not seeing any connections, at least nothing to suggest a direct relative. Nothing to suggest any relative at all. It looks like Betty was more or less a loner, other than this New Britain girl. Sorry."

"Thanks for trying, anyhow. I appreciate your looking. I'll give this Lisa a call and see where things go from there. Let me know if you come up with any brilliant ideas."

"I will. You know, I was talking with my mother this morning. She's been trying to get ahold of you. She says you've been...what was the word she used? *Unresponsive.*"

"Yeah. I've been a little busy."

"And unresponsive."

"That too."

"She's not used to people making her wait."

"I bet."

"I'm just letting you know. I have no idea what it is she wants to talk about, but you might want to call her back."

"As soon as I can." This conversation is beginning to make me a little uneasy.

"Don't shoot me. I'm just the messenger," with her hands raised high in the air.

"Thanks," I soften. "I'll get to it as soon as I can."

I head back to my place. I'm about to call Lisa in New Britain when my phone rings Caller ID says it's my sister, so I ignore the call. Before I can dial out she calls again, so again I open my flip phone and immediately press "end." This is a little game that we used to play (back when she was still speaking to me). On the third call I decide she's not going to quit, so I answer.

"Hello, Mary."

"Why'd you hang up on me?" Just like old times.

"Me? Hang up on you? When?" As if I don't know.

"Just now. Don't claim it wasn't intentional." She's testier than usual.

"You tried to call me just now?" Feigning disbelief. "Are you sure you dialed the right number?"

"Of course I had the right number! You're on speed dial for Christ's sake!" Again, there she goes, that parochial schooling really paying dividends.

"There must be something wrong with my phone. Maybe I had the ringer turned off."

"Well, turn it back on. You are the most technologically incompetent man I've ever known. How's anybody supposed to reach you if your phone never rings?"

"I'd never thought about it like that." Maybe I *should* turn the ringer off and leave the ringer off. "Thanks for that tip about the ringer, but I've got to go. Much appreciated."

"Wait a minute!" She practically screams. "That's not why I called."

I'd been hoping if I confused her enough she'd forget why she rang. "Why'd you call then?"

"The relics. Where are they?"

"I told you last night: out for study. I'll let you know the minute I learn anything."

"You're trying to sell them out from under my nose, aren't you? That is my legacy you're messing with!" Hotter still: volcano angry. "I'm not kidding! You are not going to hock them." She still thinks that increased volume makes up for absence of reason in any argument.

"I'm not planning to sell anything. I'm trying to get a determination on what they are, maybe what they're worth. You want to know what you've got, right? If you had a Monet you'd get it authenticated, right? [I'm reaching]. People won't just *believe* it's a Monet. You need some sort of proof. Certification. Maybe these things are of historical importance. Maybe these things belong in Rome." This is the *most* unlikely of outcomes; I don't know how those words came to mind. But now I've planted a seed in her head: the chicken bones from our house should be hanging in the Vatican. She can already imagine herself dining at the right hand of the pope, Mary the Finder of Lost Treasure, resurrector of the faith in the eyes of all the Church. Grandeur awaits, and I'm the only thing holding it back.

"I guess," she reluctantly agrees. She doesn't trust me. She doesn't trust anyone, which is at the root of most of her life's problems. Still, Mary has taken the bait. "Rome, you say?"

"Maybe. Or Dublin," I add. It never hurts to mention the old homeland.

"How would you know?"

"Experts. I've got a couple of them working on it. They probably need to do some carbon dating and such. I think one is an anthropologist. He'll maybe call in a linguistics specialist. Not many people read ancient script." That last part (about not many people reading ancient script) is true.

"How long will that take?"

"Beats me. These things take time. Maybe a week or two? A month? I really can't say." Total B.S., I'm making it up as I go along.

"Call me," she barks and hangs up. There's one nuisance delayed.

I immediately dial Lisa of New Britain, Connecticut. Miracle of miracles, the long-lost niece herself answers the phone.

"Hello?"

"Lisa Wojtkowiak?"

"Who's calling please?"

I tell her. "I'm a friend of your aunt Betty...Eliza," I correct myself, remembering her letter. "From Detroit?" I sense confusion on the other end of the line.

"And you got my number how?" Savvy for a girl her age.

I consider being tactful, but if I do that she'll probably hang up before I can get to the point. "I'd like to say I got it from your aunt, but unfortunately that is not true. Betty...er...Eliza passed away yesterday. I found your name on an envelope. I'm trying to locate her closest living relative." It wasn't the most delicate way to break the bad news. There's another long delay from her end.

"I'm sorry, and what is your relation, exactly?" Finally she speaks.

"I'm her neighbor. A friend, I guess. I was at the hospital last night, shortly after she passed. I'm trying to find her nearest relative. *Any* relative, really." The girl is now sniffling on the far edge of the continent. This was probably not the best way to break the news of Betty's death, but what else could I do? "She'd just received a letter from you [I don't mention that I've read it], and I assumed you two were close."

"Not really." Still crying. "Close, I mean [sniffle...]. How'd she die?"

"Heart attack."

More tears. "Did she suffer much?"

"No, not much. It was all over in an instant."

"That's good at least."

"There are worse ways to go."

"I guess." Silence. "Did she get a chance to read my letter?"

"She did," I lie. "Yesterday afternoon, in fact."

"I barely knew her, you know. She was my grandmother's cousin by marriage. I only met her once when I was tiny."

"She told me all about that trip. She was quite excited by your note. Said it was wonderful, brought back all kinds of good memories."

"Not *too* excited I hope? I mean, you don't think..."

"Trust me; it had nothing to do with her heart attack. Nothing like that. Her doctors tell me this had been building up for years." I'm getting good at this. The sniffles are drying up on the other end of the line.

"So, again, just why is it you're calling me?"

Here I tell her about the hospital, and how somebody needs to sign for Betty/Eliza's body and arrange for a funeral or cremation or whatever, and that she is the best and closest thing to a relative I've been able to locate, even if she is the granddaughter of a first cousin's wife by marriage or something.

"I'm sorry, there's just no way I can do any of that. I'm in mid-semester here, and I can't afford to miss any more classes. Plus, I hate to say this, but I'm broke. Majorly broke. I really don't have any money. There's no way I could afford to fly out there and do those things. We weren't that close."

"I understand. Is there anybody else in your family, somebody she *was* close to or someone with a little more, how should I say it, means to travel?"

"You mean money? Sorry. Both my parents died years ago, and I'm an only child. As far as I know, both my aunt and her husband were only children themselves, and they never had any kids of their own. I'm sort-of the last of the line."

"No distant cousins that you can think of? Aunts, uncles, in-laws?"

"None that I know of. You can always try a web search, but I suspect you'd be wasting your time. That's why I sent Aunt Eliza that note: I figured she doesn't get a lot of mail. She was the only one left on that side of the family. She might have appreciated hearing that the bloodlines go on, in an indirect sort-of way. How old was she? Do you know?"

"Her state I.D. says eighty-four. I would have guessed she was younger, maybe seventy or seventy-two by looking at her. She held up well."

She processes that thought. "Funerals are kind-of expensive. You should be able pay for that with her savings, right?"

"Not really."

"Didn't she have any savings?"

"About a hundred bucks, as far as I can tell."

"Didn't she have any insurance? I mean, isn't that what insurance is for?"

"No insurance, at least not that I can find. She was living what they call *a very modest lifestyle*." *Modest* is code for "broke." Another pause, maybe five or six seconds of silence.

"What happens if nobody shows up, at the hospital I mean?"

"You mean to claim her body?"

"Yeah," she says sheepishly. She doesn't want to say the thing outright. "What if nobody does that? Do they just throw her away or something? Bury her in a pauper's grave?"

"Don't worry about it. I won't let that happen." I can tell that she's relieved. We swap a little more small talk, Lisa thanks me, and we say our farewells and hang up. *Tag, you're it.*

CHAPTER TWENTY-ONE

Roomies

The five o'clock hour is fast approaching, thus I assume that the productive part of my day is spent. I'm wrong. No sooner am I off the phone with Lisa from New Britain than my brother calls. He has just gotten off the phone with our sister Mary, so you can guess where their conversation went. I fill him in on a few details, we laugh, we hang up.

Two seconds later my phone rings again. *Grand Central Station*, I'm thinking. This time it's that professor from Wayne State.

"I've been trying to reach you," he tells me. "I left a message earlier with your associate." *Associate.* I'm guessing Booker has been called worse.

"Sorry about that. I've been tied up with a little family matter."

"I hope it's nothing serious."

Serious as a heart attack, I think, but that would probably be disrespectful, although I suspect that Betty would have found it humorous, too. I didn't know her for long, but she didn't seem like one to stand on ceremony. "Just a small medical issue, nothing *too* serious."

"Well, I'm glad to hear that. I was calling about those items you brought me." The relics.

"Yes..." I expect that he's got more questions, though I've told him all that I know. My knowledge on the subject is skimpy at best. You could knock me over with a feather when I hear what he has to say.

"I have some information for you, but I'd like to deliver it in person. When might be convenient for you?"

"Seriously? Already?"

"My research was fairly forthright."

"Good news or bad news?"

"That's for you to decide. I hope you won't be disappointed."

"That makes two of us."

"What works best for you? My classes are on Mondays, Wednesdays and Thursdays. I have office hours blocked out at different times, depending on the day of the week."

I almost tell him Monday, but then I remember that I've promised to start a new job on Monday. I have no idea what my schedule will be like after that. Is it five days a week? Nine to five? Booker wasn't entirely clear on the matter. Booker isn't entirely clear about most things. "I've got a rather busy week coming up. Any chance we could meet tomorrow or sometime over the weekend?

"I don't normally keep Friday hours. Let's see...no, tomorrow's no good, not good at all...the day after is... Saturday. I'm not usually in on weekends, either, but I've got some papers that I need to grade. I could make a little time in the morning. How about nine Saturday morning, my office?"

"Works for me. I look forward to meeting with you."

"I think you'll find this information...extremely interesting. I found it so. Nine o'clock, see you then."

Does the Vatican await?

I don't know about that. Either way, this is one positive development in an otherwise frustrating time. Five-thirty now and I'm thinking about dinner. Have I eaten today? I can't remember. I should eat something, but there's no "something" in my house. Was there food in Betty's fridge? I failed to check, but I expect there is. I could walk down the hall, open her door, and help myself to whatever is inside. Yet it seems somehow *morbid* to be stealing food from the dead. I'll wait.

I'm debating another trip down the hall when I notice my ward: Bruce has something on his tiny dog brain. He's standing by the door wagging his tail frantically. "We're not going outside," I warn him. The tail keeps moving.

199

"You just went." I tell him. He cocks his head to one side. "No." Maybe if I reduce the amount of words, it will sink in. "No."

Before I can determine what's wrong with the little twerp, there's a knock on my door. The dog knew. Turns out it's Andy. Again.

"Hey, I forgot to tell you something. Bruno...."

I stop him there. "Wait. Who's Bruno?"

"Your landlord. You know, the man who owns this building."

"Sure, I get it now." I had not as yet heard that name.

"Bruno says you've got until the end of the month to either move that stuff out of Betty's place or pony up another thirty days' rent."

"I figured as much. That hasn't exactly been my highest priority, if you get what I mean. I'm still trying to locate a relative." He couldn't have come here to tell me this.

"Well, it just occurred to me. Since you've still got a chunk of the month left, and Booker's place isn't going to be fixed up for a while, maybe you'd like to move your roommate down the hall. Get him out of your hair. Just tell him not to set it on fire. Hell, maybe you'd rather take that place for yourself. Betty's place is in nicer condition than yours. Bigger, too." He has a point. "On the other hand, now that you've got yourself a dog, you'll need to start paying the monthly pet fee."

Part "A" was good news, Part "B" not so much. "You're kidding, right?" It's not as if I went out and adopted the pooch. My expenses are going up based on an unwelcome inheritance? "You're kidding about the pet fee?"

"Thirty bucks a month." He's not kidding.

"I thought you said you'd waive the fee."

"Short term. Bruce was still Betty's dog back then."

"*Back then* was just this morning."

200

"The times they are a changing. Just ask Dylan."

Shit. "How about twenty bucks a month?"

"Bruno says thirty, non-negotiable. Dogs can do a world of damage to a place."

"He's been living here for... (I realize I don't have the foggiest idea how old the dog truly is)...a long time. Betty's place looks mostly impeccable. He's not going to tear anything up. Can't you just grandfather him in? I'm not even sure that I can keep him."

"That dog is no grandfather: he's only four years old. Charges won't start 'til the first of next month, though."

"That's the best you can do?"

"That's the best."

"Thanks, tell your boss he's a sweetheart."

"Bruno's rules, not mine. I'm just trying to help. For what it's worth, I'd keep the dog if I were you. He's well-behaved, and everybody likes him. The dog needs somebody, and Betty trusted that you'd take care of him. He seems to like you Put him in the shelter and he'll be dead within the month. Too many dogs, not enough suckers. Say what you will, the woman was a good judge of character."

This day keeps getting better. "Give Bruno my love, and tell him he's a cheap S.O.B."

"Trust me, Bruno is not a man you wish to love. He's ugly and old and mean and bald and *incredibly* tightfisted. Takes ugly to a whole new level. Even his wife doesn't love him. He *is* cheap but he knows it, and he hates to be reminded of the fact. Let me know what you want to do about that other apartment."

"Aye aye, captain."

Once Andy is out of my hair I'm quickly overcome by exhaustion. My butt drops down on the couch and I stretch out, just for a bit. Five minutes, that's all it should require. *Five minutes*, I tell myself. Bruce quickly joins me, wedging into his now-familiar spot between my knees and the cushions. It's been an extraordinary day, particularly if you include the moonlight walk in the wee hours, which was really but an extension of the *previous* extraordinary day: Davros, the chaos at Tires Cheap, my ransacking of Betty's apartment, my sister's insanity, and an impending chat with a professor at the U. My mind swirls thinking about all that has transpired in the last twenty-four hours. Moments later the dog and I are both sound asleep.

It's hours later that a door slams, and I wake with a start. Booker is home, late but energetic.

"Rise and shine, and give God your glory, glory!" He's singing. Sober, although you'd be hard pressed to tell.

"What the hell is all that caterwauling?" I ask, getting up slowly and forcing Bruce from atop my legs.

"My mother used to sing it to me in the mornings," like that makes any sense whatsoever. "Catchy, ain't it?"

"Good lord. What time is it Booker?" I'm finally sitting upright. Bruce has crawled down to the far end of the sofa and is falling back asleep, proving that "guard dog" does not come under his official list of duties.

"Three o'clock, roomie."

"In the morning?"

"Indeed."

"Then why am I awake?"

"Thought you might like some company. I was here at dinnertime and you were asleep then. It's not good for anybody to sleep that much. Did somebody slip you a roofie or something?"

I have to think for a minute, trying to remember what a "roofie" would be. A modern Mickey Finn, I suddenly remember: knockout drops slipped inside a beverage. "No roofies, just a long day."

"Anything I need to worry about?"

"I doubt it. What have you been up to?"

"I had a date with Giselle, but it ended early and she didn't want me sticking around all night. She thinks it would be better if we *take things slow*. Her words, not mine."

"It didn't seem like things were moving too *slow* the other night when she was here."

"Not if I have anything to say about it. I've got one speed, and that's throttle wide open. Slow is a relative thing. I think she just didn't want to see my ugly face when she woke up in the morning."

"So instead you decided I needed to have an early look, eh?"

"Indeed, you lucky devil. Want to do a shot of vodka?"

"You're a little late for that..."

"Aw, roomie!" He pulls the empty bottle from the freezer. "That's just not right! Taking the last of a man's drink."

"It was a medical emergency," I explain. He nods at me like he's been there, too.

"It's alright. I've been thinking about cutting back, anyway." I can tell he's not too happy, but we all make sacrifices.

"Cutting back? What would inspire that kind of irrational behavior?" From what little I know of Booker, 'cutting back' would indicate a behavioral shift of seismic proportions.

"Giselle says she wants a *serious* man. I think that means if I want to be with her, I need to be within wandering distance of the straight and narrow."

"Good luck with that." Giselle is lot of woman, the kind most men would kill just to be with, should they discover themselves lucky enough to seize the opportunity.   If any woman could inspire change, she'd be on the short list. That said, what Booker is proposing reminds me of a story about an old dog and new tricks. This would be a case of *wholesale reformation.* I just can't envision it.

"That girl is something else. She might just be worth it." I'm not sure whether he's trying to convince me or trying to convince himself.

"Worth forsaking all others? Worth giving up drinking? Worth settling down?"

"I said *wandering distance* of the straight and narrow, *my* friend, not straddling the line," and he chuckles.

CHAPTER TWENTY-TWO

On Short Notice

The blood flow to my legs has been cut off and they're rife with that pins-and-needles pain that comes from poor circulation.

"Bruce, you need to get up."

The dog lifts his head slowly from the crook of my knees, decides it's not worth it, and lies back down.

"Bruce, get up, buddy. I can't move." He's on top of me.

This time he rises slowly, stretching out behind my back like maybe his legs, too, have fallen asleep. Eventually the dog jumps to the floor and, nails clicking against the hardwood floor, makes his way over to the water bowl.

I pull myself to a sitting position on the edge of the couch, having momentarily forgotten where I am. After my conversation with Booker last night (this morning, technically), I'd drifted off to sleep. It must have been around four when Bruce decided that he needed to go outside once again. I have to wonder why the dog is becoming so fond of these late-night strolls. These walks are putting my life in jeopardy on a semi-consistent basis. I have to ask, *why?* Because I'm one-hundred percent sure that Betty wasn't getting up and walking around Selden Street in the middle of the night, every night. I would have noticed the early morning patter of footsteps in the hall. *What has changed?* Is dog insomnia a symptom of Bruce's mourning?

So I'd walked Bruce, mostly just us pacing back and forth on the skinny strip of grass in front of our building until he did his business. He must have led me back to Betty's door since here I sit, on the edge of her couch. The sun is streaming through the blinds and I guess that it's now somewhere around eight or eight-thirty in the morning. Friday. I get up, walk to the fridge, and discover it to be surprisingly well stocked. I unearth a glass in the cupboard and pour myself some orange juice, wander back to the couch, and turn on the television.

Television. I can't guess how long it's been since I've last owned one. Not that I've *never* watched TV. For a man who has worked a variety of jobs, many of which were in bars and restaurants and other segments of what is commonly known as "the service industry," my life has been littered with the constant blare of sporting events, "reality programming," and breaking news. Pasted to the walls, cluttering up the lobbies and waiting rooms of life: they are ubiquitous, or (as my pal Watchdog Mike might say) *freakin' everywhere, man*. I've just chosen not to *own* one, at least not in a long while. Having a television set in my life, front and center in the living room, only encourages this particular drifter to stagnate in his lair. I've never required the incentive.

In this case the television is here, I am here, and Bruce is here. I turn it on. The set is old, a nineteen-inch RCA unit with an actual DIAL to change the channels. No remote. The local news is on, and much of it is the same as you'd hear in any other large town: weather, traffic, an accident on the Lodge and two on the Fisher Freeway. The first real snowstorm of the season arrives tomorrow night. Then they get to the meat of the matter: an emergency financial manager is overseeing the city's functions, if you can claim that this city is functioning. Detroit Public Schools have lost two-thirds of their enrollment over the past decade, just one part of the latest Great Exodus. A new mayor-elect and the city council are posturing for position and occasionally grandstanding for the camera. The county jail project is stalled with over one-hundred million dollars wasted, a partially built failure ready for the next round of scrappers. Eight fires in seven months on Heidelberg, over half of the original structures razed to the ground. They're trying to raise money for security. Twelve shot dead in the last seven days, a carjacking at a gas station, and an armed robbery at a popular jazz club. Puppies in dumpsters and an unidentified toddler found wandering the streets. The bankruptcy appears to be more than just financial, it's moral, too. There's enough to make me pack up and leave. I might forego the packing, just get up and leave, but for a knock on the door.

"Hey, are you in there?" It's Susan, tapping lightly.

"Just a second," I answer, switching off the TV and hurrying to open the door. "Hi. How'd you find me?"

"I heard the television, figured it had to be you in here." She steps inside.

"I think Bruce was getting homesick."

"I can see where he might. That's a big change for a dog." Bruce is lying in the other room, sprawled across the unmade bed.

"So, what brings you around this time of the morning? Can I get you a glass of juice or some instant coffee?" I'm dead certain that I saw a jar of Taster's Choice around here somewhere.

"No thanks. I just wanted to see how you're holding up. I've got a 9:30 class and I'm on my way out. Any luck reaching that girl in Connecticut?"

"I spoke with her, but it was a dead end. I think I'm on my own with this one."

"Got a plan?" she points the toe of her shoe into the floor board, twisting from side to side with nervous energy. Fidgety, the wasted energy of youth.

"Not really," I answer truthfully.

"Do your best. That's all anybody can do."

Sage advice; I'm wondering which one of us is the parent. "Thanks," I tell her gratefully.

"Keep your chin up. Things will get better."

To this I only smile silently. Optimism is one more thing wasted on the young. Optimism and faith.

Susan reads my mind. "It *will*," she assures me, before skipping out the door.

Bruce and I get the leash and head off on our merry way. Booker is not home, not in *our* apartment, at least. I don't know how one man can operate on such a minimal amount of sleep. I wave to Mike, who is back at his familiar station on the stoop. The dog and I keep walking. I'm thinking breakfast; I'm thinking Coney King, a tiny diner that squats on Second Avenue closer to the University. *Did* squat, it turns out. What I've failed to account for is that Coney King is no more; burned, leveled, and otherwise made nonexistent at some point between my memories and the present world. A coin laundromat has taken its place. At least I *think* the laundromat has taken its place. Is this even the right block? I can't tell. There's no residue to suggest that Coney King, site of hundreds of thousands of cheap and greasy meals, ever was. Another piece of the past slides by without memorial, another part of my history gone without leaving so much as a stain on the pavement.

What else have I missed? I'm standing on the sidewalk, staring blankly at a coin laundry and wondering what else is gone, when Davros pulls to the curb in his big car.

"Yo, Dummy! Quit staring in the windows and get in the car!"

We obey, the dog and I.

"Don't let that thing shed all over my upholstery. What were you staring at, anyway?"

"Just thinking about progress, I guess."

"Did you find any?" His idea of a joke. "Less thinking and more doing, that's what you need. Where are you headed? I'll give you a lift. I'm on my way to the Fisher Building." That's in the New Center area, north of campus.

"Wrong direction. Just drop me at Second and Brainard and I'll take my truck."

"That means I'll have to turn around."

"Then turn around." He circles the block.

"So what's on tap for you today?" He asks.

"Burying the dead."

"That is a significant task."

I tell him my plan. It is a good plan. At least I'd like to think so. Davros doesn't necessarily agree, but neither does he object. If I want to tilt at windmills, well, they're my windmills. Tilt away. "Have at it, Don Quixote" is all he can say.

Second Avenue is a one-way street, and like so many other things in this world, leads in the opposite direction from where I wish to go. I loop around the block, pick up Third Avenue southbound to Temple Boulevard, Temple two blocks westbound to Fifth Street, and Fifth two blocks south to ground zero. Ground zero is my old duplex, a duplex which has gone the way of Coney King.

I pull over in front of the vacant lot where the duplex used to be. I *know* that this is the place, because the squat little factory next door still stands. Boarded up, tagged with gang signs and neglected, but still standing. Where the duplex once stood is a field of knee-high grass delineated by a series of evenly spaced eight-foot high galvanized poles. It's an improvement over the past. There was a chain-link fence here, once, somewhere between my time and now, only the fence didn't last, either. Across the street is another abandoned factory, this building two stories of once-white brick covered with graffiti. I've found the place.

A stroll to the corner unveils another surprise. I knew about it, of course, but things sometimes don't hit you until they're witnessed firsthand: the casino. The casino itself is imposing, a mammoth, multi-story complex of gaming and hotel and parking that takes up an entire city block. It's of a style that has been referred to (architecturally speaking) as "retro-futuristic." One might also describe it as "imposing fortress of brick and glass." It's not ugly, not by any means, but it *is* massive. It most certainly is *not* a bakery. It, too, is an improvement, although I still miss the HOS_E_S sign and the sweet smell of yeast in the air.

This neighborhood (not that it was ever truly a *neighborhood,* at least, not that I can recall during *my* lifetime) has not fared as well. It has seen enormous change, and most of that change hasn't been for the better. A gas station has gone vacant on the corner of Grand River and the Lodge Freeway. Most of the storefronts that backed up to my duplex are long gone, too, though one shuttered pioneer is still hanging in there. A two-story motor lodge, one of those anachronisms left over from the 1950s, hunches low on the far side of the road. I'm sure that they get an interesting tourist trade. Carl's Chop House, fine dining known throughout the city and only a few blocks up the road, gone.

Don't get me wrong, there are good changes, too. The Jeffries Projects, those high-rise tombs of poverty that covered the north side of Grand River Avenue for as far as the eye could see, they're being slowly replaced by quaint new townhouses. I don't know if these new townhouses are low income or not, but either way, they're a vast improvement over Detroit's version of Cabrini Green. The problem is that I'm trying to establish a picture from memory while most of the pieces have gone missing. If a person had been here, had seen the demise and growth of a city as it occurred in real time, a person could fill in the blanks. He'd have lived it. As things sit, I'm playing a game of connect-the-dots where I can only see half of the dots. God only knows what picture I'm likely to draw.

'Jesus Died for Your Sins.' I can't find the damn sign. I remember where it *used* to be, more or less. In my mind's eye I can picture it clear as day from the back window of that second floor apartment. It should be right here, down the street from the casino. In reality, in the present *here and now* in which I stand, there's no sign. It doesn't exist. For the second time today I find myself dumbfounded: *Did someone steal it? Did the storefront church move to a new location, taking their beacon of hope with them? Is it possible that all of this time, all of these years, that sign was really somewhere else, somewhere farther up or down the road or in a completely different part of the city? Was the Jesus sign but a false memory, a counterfeit souvenir from my younger self to the present?*

I can knock on doors, ask around, but in a world of "shoot first and ask questions later" that's a risky tactic. What businesses have been here long enough that anyone will even remember that sign? I look up and down the street for answers and come up empty. The Twinkie Men are all retired. No Carl of Chop House fame, no gas jockeys, no tenants on the right side of my missing duplex. That little motor inn is the one constant, but when I ask at the front desk, the kid has no idea what I'm talking about. It, too, has since changed hands.

"What's with the dog, man?" The kid behind the counter is not interested in my quest for the missing church, but he's very interested in my partner. We provide a distraction from his usual pay-by-the-week clientele. I'd forgotten Bruce is still with me, a silent extension of my arm connected by way of nylon webbing and one brass clasp.

"Oh, just a dog."

"Cool dog. He's a happy little dude."

"Thanks," and I leave it at that. Even Don Quixote needed a sidekick: perhaps this dog is my Sancho.

I give up. I've tried and failed. I walk back across Grand River and Bruce and I get into the truck. The engine is started and the transmission dropped into drive, tires swinging onto Grand River Avenue. Back toward Cass Avenue, towards defeat, towards home. The windmills have won. I quit. My best has proven inadequate. I am only a block along when something catches my eye and I pull quickly to the curb.

"Wait here a minute, buddy." The dog doesn't answer.

Bruce stays in the vehicle this time. I lock the truck door and head over to a swaybacked, single-story commercial building with seven different entryways (six of which are permanently shuttered). The one that is not nailed shut, a door second from the end, behind which lies a space of no more than two-thousand square feet, is a church. "Church" is a term used loosely in these parts. This place professes no neon salvation, no high-tech damnation, just a hand-painted, plywood sheet that extolls the "New Radiance Church of Life Eternal." Scrawled across the bottom in small letters, almost as an afterthought, is a note that reads 'all are welcome.' *We'll see.*

"Can I help you?" I'm greeted by a woman, a very sweet, soft spoken fifty-something-ish African-American woman who can't be much more than five-two and one-hundred and fifty pounds: not what I was expecting. I expected big and gruff, a sizable man with a voice and disposition to match the harsh environment. I expected someone who looked like a fighter, not this.

Behind me the windows are covered with brown butcher paper, protecting the sanctuary (such that it is) from those distractions of the big street outside. Four rows of movie-theater seats, probably salvaged from one of the city's abandoned cinemas, are laid out with their backs to the glass. There are five seats to a side, a narrow aisle down the middle. *Maximum capacity forty,* I'm thinking. Against the far wall stands a makeshift altar, a raised plywood platform eight-inches high covered with silver garage floor paint. On the platform sits a simple wooden pulpit, two chairs, and a pounded nickel cross upon the wall. It seems like the whole place was slapped together on short notice.

"I'm sorry, is there something I can help you with?" she asks again.

"I was looking for a sign," I start, and realize that my words could be taken many ways. "A church, I mean, it used to be around here somewhere. It had a very distinctive sign out front. I was hoping that someone might remember it."

"Me? That would be unlikely, if your church is indeed gone. We've only been here for two years, though I'd certainly be willing to ask around. My husband might recall if he were here, but he's at work right now. He grew up in the neighborhood. Maybe one of the parishioners, but they're not around, either. I'm Pastor June, by the way."

So I introduce myself. I describe the neon sign from my past, and what I'm seeking. Pastor June has a soothing manner about her. We chat some more. The cold front they'd been predicting finally arrived. Eventually she tells me to bring Bruce inside, let him warm up, so I do, a beast in the chapel. It *is* warm in here, the "Radiance" of the place physical as well as spiritual. She asks me about myself, a topic I respectfully skimp on: there isn't enough time for my story. *No conversion happening here, lady.* She tells me about her growing outreach to the community, some of the many good things she's doing, though Sundays generally draw but a dozen or so of the hardcore locals, people down on their luck and many with addictions. "A dozen more getting help than otherwise would," she points out. The money is tight but her husband (Pastor Al) has a full-time job driving trucks and between them they find a way to keep the doors open. A likeable preacher, one with modest aspirations and what seem like sound convictions. Eventually I tell her about Betty and what I have in mind. We make a deal.

CHAPTER TWENTY-THREE

The Hound of Ulster

"So let me get this straight, we're talking Celtic mythology, somewhere around the first century?"

"Correct."

"You're a language specialist?"

"A dual role actually: I am an Associate Dean of Linguistics, but I'm also a Professor of History. My true specialty is referred to as 'Linguistic Anthropology.' There's an awful lot of crossover between the two areas, as you might well imagine."

I'm sitting in the professor's office, which is not as impressive as one might imagine. There are no overstuffed leather chairs, no mahogany paneled walls. This is not a movie. This eight-by-eight, windowless room contains one locking metal file cabinet, an industrial grey Steelcase desk, one padded desk chair with casters (office supply store quality), and one wooden straight-backed chair. There is a computer (desktop model) which still has the old, fat style monitor attached. Even I know that it's a dinosaur as far as technology goes. I see stacks and stacks of paper, despite common claims that we are becoming a paperless society. There are piles everywhere. Wherever the money is being spent in education, it most certainly is not being spent here. I can't imagine a more depressing place to spend a Saturday morning.

"The Hound of Ulster?"

"The Hound of Culainn, or Cuchulainn (he pronounces it Koo-Hoo-Lin), if you prefer."

"I'll stick with *Ulster,* if it's all the same to you. A tad easier on the tongue."

"Ulster it is, then. There are also Scottish variations..."

"Please, let's go with *Ulster.*"

"Very well, then."

He seems a bit disappointed that I won't let him flaunt his knowledge, but I've got a funeral to attend. It's nine-fifty now and I've promised Pastor June I'll be at the church no later than eleven. I'm still not sure I follow this story.

"Can you run it by me one more time, but dumb it down a bit? Give me the children's version, if you will."

"I'll try," he answers, and so he does. "It takes place in Ireland, in the time of clans and chieftains and no central governance. There was once a boy named Setanta being raised by his uncle, King Conor of Ulster. Conor was not *the* king; he was *a* king, if you get my drift. There were many local sovereigns in various parts of the island. It was a fragmented society at that time. This boy, Setanta, a child especially fond of hurling..."

"Puking???" What boy would be fond of vomiting?"

"Hurling: it's an Irish sport. Try to keep up. Imagine lacrosse, only with something resembling axe handles instead of those netted hoops that lacrosse players use. Hurling uses a big field, nets the size of soccer goals. Twenty plus guys to a side running around smashing a sphere about the diameter of a baseball into the net. You get hit with the stick a lot; it's an exceptionally violent pastime. That's not really my point, however." He takes a sip of water.

"In any event, Setanta's uncle, King Conor of Ulster, and his uncle's friends are invited to a party put on by the blacksmith Culain. They all go, all except Setanta who stays behind to practice his hurling. He's got a big match going on; *hurling*. The blacksmith Culain is known far and wide for his particularly ferocious guard dog. The party guests show up. Once his guests are seated, he asks if everybody has arrived. The guests say yes, so he puts his legendary dog out to guard the house and the grounds. Only they've forgotten about Setanta, who comes along after his hurling match has ended."

"I'm with you so far."

"Seven-year-old Setanta decides to join the feast, but when he shows up, the vicious dog attacks him. Culain's dog. A dog feared throughout the region, legendary in his own right. Crazy vicious. Those folks at the party hear the ruckus, and suddenly they remember that the boy was due to arrive late. They think he must be getting ripped to shreds. But instead, the child defends himself by flinging his hurling ball down the dog's throat, then smashing the dog's head against a post. The dog dies. A gory tale indeed. While the party participants are amazed and gratified to discover that the boy has survived, the blacksmith, Culain, is anguished over the loss of his prized guardian. It's not the boy's fault, but the boy feels responsible no less. Setanta promises the man that henceforth *he* will guard the pass to Ulster in the dead animal's stead. The child becomes known as the Hound of Culain, Cuchulain, or, more commonly, the Hound of Ulster, a fierce protector in his own right. There are other spellings, other variants. The kid went on to do other stuff. In later tales and legends Cuchulain is referenced as possessing almost superhuman strength, a mythical beast, but this is the primary episode that involves *your* find."

"So you're telling me that these *relics,* as my family has come to call them, are somehow related to this legend of a boy and a dead dog?"

"It would appear so. The paper which you've provided would purport to have been written in the year sixteen-hundred and forty-three. I'm inclined to believe that's an accurate account. There was a rebellion of Gaelic Catholics in 1641, and eleven years of fighting in the land thereafter. It was a time of nationalism and religious fervor, not to mention widespread death and destruction. People were trying to stay alive, and at the same time trying to preserve and salvage religious and cultural artifacts. This would fit the bill." He takes another sip of water, and I nod my head to indicate that I'm still with him.

"The script this document was written in," he continues, "*Insular script*, was developed in Ireland sometime in the seventh century. It became popular in Ireland, and Catholic missionaries helped it spread to continental Europe thereafter. Its peak usage was from the late seventh until about the mid-ninth century. It became increasingly obscure thereafter, though there are a handful of documents as late as the early twentieth century which provide examples. They're rare. I would venture that if this *were* a forgery, a good forger would have invented a much earlier date: there's no *advantage* to forging a date that late in the game, especially when referring to something that allegedly took place in the first century A.D. Everything about this document passes preliminary inspection. Thus I think the note, such that it exists, is authentic. Of course, we can always send it out for carbon dating, test the paper and the ink, but that stuff gets expensive. It would be helpful if we still had the original display box."

I look at my watch. It's eight minutes after ten and I'm still not sure what this man is trying to tell me. "How can this be *authentic* if we're talking about a fictional character?" I ask. "This Setanta, the Hound of Ulster, whatever you want to call him; he's just a figure in a Celtic fable, right? Grimm's Fairy Tales For the Irish? Where does *authentic* come in?"

The professor leans back in his chair, slides his reading glasses to the top of his balding pate and rubs his eyes wearily. Finally he addresses my question. "Don't confuse *mythological* with *fictional*. Sometimes legend and lore are rooted in substance. This is *authentic* in the sense that I believe this note, truthful or not, was indeed written in the year of our Lord, sixteen-hundred and forty-three. Very few in Ireland were literate at that time, and thus the chances are extremely good that this document was created by a member of the upper class, i.e. a wealthy aristocrat or a member of the clergy. Neither would have an obvious motive to lie, although we can't rule out that possibility. It they were *intending* to lie, they would certainly have concocted a more lucrative one. The value of this documentation fifteen centuries after the fact is hardly worth the trouble of lying. At the very least, I suspect the author *believed* that the content of his missive was truthful."

"And the bones?" There's not much bone to work with.

"The fragments *look* old, but those would be easier to fake. Without proper lab testing, I'd just be guessing. The document holds the key here."

"So you're telling me these *could be* bone fragments from the legendary Hound of Ulster, KookyLin, whatever you call him?" I'm blown away. Maybe the family stories contained some grain of truth after all. Not religious relics, per se, but historical artifacts. The Vatican won't be calling, but someone will. My bubble of excitement lasts for but a second.

"Oh, hell no!" the professor bursts out laughing. "Not the Hound of Ulster himself. That would be a find! There's nothing to imply that, and I'm sorry if you misunderstood me. The note, roughly translated, claims that these bone fragments came from Culain's beast."

Again I'm stunned, and then I realize what he's telling me. "The dog?" Bewildered.

"The dog."

"And their value?" How much are a few bones from a dead dog, *mythical at that*, truly worth?

"Strictly academic. Of interest to scholars, for certain. You might even find a pub in Dublin willing to give you fifty euro for them, as a conversation piece. That would be about it. You should consider donating this to a folklore museum."

Now it's my turn to break into hysterics. I cannot wait to tell my sister.

CHAPTER TWENTY-FOUR

Burying the Dead

I was worried about having enough pallbearers. Pastor June sent a few men to the hospital, where they picked up Betty's body and brought it back to New Radiance. I'd supplied the casket, which it turns out you can buy, dirt cheap, at Costco. I kid you not, walk right in, buy a casket, load it into the back of your truck and you're done. Six hundred bucks, tax included, out the door. I took care of that last night, Friday night, dropping the casket off at the church around eight. One of the parishioners is taking classes at the Amazon School of Beauty and Cosmetology, and she volunteered to do Betty's hair and makeup at no charge. The woman said she needed the practice anyway. The whole thing, the way it has come together, seems rather haphazard. Part of me feels guilty, but I believe Betty would have preferred it this way. From what little I know of her, spontaneity was her forte. The pallbearer thing, though, has me worried. I'm not certain who's going to show.

A good chunk of the previous evening was spent spreading the word about the funeral. I wasn't sure who to contact, but I did my best. People get strange when confronted with death: they're afraid maybe they'll catch something. Nobody wants to be reminded of their own mortality, and nothing says 'mortality' like watching a former acquaintance getting fed to the worms. When people were told about the arrangements, I heard an awful lot of "check my schedules" and "see if I can make its." The service was less than a day away and nobody wanted to commit. That's fine, that's their choice. We're chickens, most of us, but then why shouldn't we be? Even the faithful have their doubts. It might be better to play it safe. I'm just hoping we get six that show.

It turns out I needn't have worried. I'd promised Pastor June my arrival by eleven, and I make it with five minutes to spare. I was still laughing about the relics the entire ride over here. Mary is going to have a hemorrhage when I tell her. The funeral service is set for noon, and June and I have a couple of things to discuss beforehand, music, for one, scripture, for another. Pastor Al is there, too, a quiet, reserved man who prefers to let his wife do the talking. He's big, tall, and wide, but one of the least threatening men I've ever met. Just a steady presence, I guess you'd say. June hits me with a handful of concerns Did Betty have a favorite passage? Was she particularly fond of a given hymn? There are no answers. I'd only known the woman for a week. June can choose. I put my trust in her.

People start to trickle in around a quarter-to-twelve and I'm silently counting able bodies. *Please let there be six.* Myself, Davros, Watchdog Mike and Booker are here. That makes four. It's a good start, though I'm not sure we'll get two more. The service is only fifteen minutes out. Andy arrives, but he dropped something on his foot while working in the boiler room, and is hobbled with a limp; not pallbearer material. Susan shows up at ten before the hour, and heaven-knows-why but Janey is with her. Maybe she's just providing moral support for her daughter. I could draft Susan in a pinch, but I can't see asking Janey to carry someone she'd never met. It's a sparse crowd, and I'm starting to get nervous.

By five-minutes-to there's a quick flood of people rushing in, folks I don't really know but recognize from our building. The seats begin to fill. At the last moment Pete and Mark, the couple from upstairs, arrive. I've found my missing pallbearers. There might be eight faces in total that I don't know. These are June's parishioners, come to share our grief. All told we've got thirty-seven, which packs New Radiance Church like Carnegie Hall on opening night. June props the front door open in order to let some air in.

The service is short, thirty-five minutes in total. Most of it is standard fare, ashes to ashes and Amazing Grace, the usual thing. I'm glad she skips the platitudes about "eternal rest" and "greener pastures." June gives out a brief but poignant eulogy. She avoids any pretense that she knew the deceased personally, for which I'm also grateful (I truly despise when a preacher salts his sermon with juicy tidbits about the person he has never met). Pastor June instead focuses on the value of community and friendship, the love and support shown here today by those that have lost one of their own. Her summation gets me where it hurts.

"You are not alone," she preaches. "You have *all* been claimed by the heart of God, whether you recognize it or not." I know, it sounds a little corny, but you can tell that she's feeling it, and thus we're feeling it, too. June is no wide-eyed doe in this world. She has seen some of the worst this city can dish out, and still she has chosen to stand and serve alongside her husband

Al, here in this storefront dive. Pastor June and Pastor Al understand humanity. "And yet it is not enough to look to Jesus, to Mohammed, to Buddha or to whatever your individual beliefs. I know that there are those among us who do not believe, and that, too, is alright. That is your prerogative, that is your right, that is your burden. You are still part of the Almighty's project, in one way or another. No, it is not enough to pine for the glories of a life ever after. For it is what we do here, *now*, in our brief time on this dirty little planet, that truly matters. In the end, the only question you need to ask yourself, the only question that *truly* matters, is *did I love?*" That is all.

The New Radiance choir (four of the eight faces that I didn't recognize) breaks out in song. They bite into A Mighty Fortress, incredibly smooth and powerful voices flowing from our midst. They hit the highs and lows with ease, the walls reverberating in that tiny sanctuary. By the end I'm tearing up, taking great pains to make sure that Davros and the others don't take notice. I don't need to be called a sissy. We walk Betty down the aisle and out the door, carefully sliding her casket into the bed of my truck. The crowd gathers round to watch the spectacle as I raise the tailgate and make sure that it closes tightly. Pastor June gives a quick, final blessing, and we are on our way. I'm driving and Davros rides shotgun in the front. The crematorium is only a few miles up the road, a straight run up the Edsel Ford Freeway to Harper Avenue. We'll deliver the casket, and then meet up with the rest of my neighbors at the luncheon.

"Are you going to be okay?" Dav asks me as I merge into the first lane of traffic.

"Yeah. Why wouldn't I be?"

He gives me that look, with one eyebrow raised and a twist to his lips as if to say 'who do you think you're kidding?'

"I'm fine. Really. I'm looking forward to the lunch." I've picked a Polish restaurant, "Paul's Lunch," a family place operating out of the basement of an old brownstone on Junction. It doesn't look like much because it isn't much. There's an odd collection of card tables and folding chairs crammed into a space no bigger than the church we've just left. As far as fine dining goes, the ambience at Paul's is just about that of the kids' table during Thanksgiving dinner. The food, however, is exquisite. Homemade pierogies, borscht, kiszka, sour rye soup: it seems a fitting tribute to our departed friend. Davros shocked me last night by offering to foot the bill for whoever shows up. I didn't turn him down. At first I didn't understand the motive behind his offer. Davros rarely does anything without a good reason, and he was no friend of Betty's. Then I realized that Dav was stepping up because Betty mattered to *me*, and for him, that's enough. I accepted his generosity. Maybe the Grinch's heart is growing.

I don't have much to say the rest of the way to the crematorium, nor does Davros. For the most part we ride in silence. The workers at that place help us unload, and the entire transaction takes only a few minutes. The task seems mundane, really, like I do this kind of thing every day. At the same time it's a bit surreal. Transporting the dead; somebody has to do it.

Then we're back on the freeway, making that fifteen-minute run to the restaurant.

"I need to tell you something," Davros starts. "I haven't been completely honest with you." *Like that should come as a shock.* I'm not sure that there was *ever* a time in which he was completely honest with me. Not that he'd lie, not *outright*, but it's not uncommon for him to engage in sins of omission. I'm wondering what it is this time.

"About?" There could be any number of lies. I could come up with a wide variety of guesses, and finally decide to let him say it directly and avoid playing twenty questions.

"Susan."

"What about Susan?" She wasn't on my list.

"She's not yours."

"Define *not mine.*" I don't think I like where this conversation is headed, turning my head in his direction. I'm not liking the sound of this at all. I almost jerk the car out of my lane in surprise. A trucker (passing me on the right) blares his horn. We get off the freeway at the next exit, West Grand Boulevard. I'm tempted to pull over, but I don't see any place that looks safe, so I keep driving and dodging potholes. "What exactly do you mean by 'not mine'?"

221

"Not yours as in *not your kid.* I made it up.*"*

If this is one of Dav's jokes, he's missing the mark big time. "That's not at all funny, Davros." I get a sick feeling in the pit of my stomach, and then the sickness begins morphing into outrage. Some things you just don't kid about.

"I'm not trying to be funny. She's not yours. I just *told* you she was because I thought it would do you some good."

I pull over at a spot where the road widens slightly. There's a little see-through cage for people to stand under and a signpost for the bus stop. There's no one waiting in the tiny plexiglass hut, and the busses don't run often, anyhow. We could probably sit here for a week before anyone noticed. I drop the truck in park and look him dead in the eye. I'm angry, and that's an understatement.

"You thought it would *do me some good,* telling me I have a full-grown child that in fact is not mine?" My voice is rising, beginning to break as I try to hold back my rage. "How do I know you're telling the truth *now?*" But he is; I can tell just by looking at him. "How exactly did you think this would, as you put it, *do me some good*? Exactly *what good* did you think you might accomplish?" I'm tempted to punch him in the face. It would feel good, at least on my end of things.

"When you showed up at the store, you seemed lost. You needed to lay down some roots, and I thought this would get you started, provide an anchor. Look at the bright side: it worked."

Absolutely un-fricking-believable. The man really is a piece of work. I slip the truck back into gear and continue driving, turning right at Michigan and working my way toward Paul's. Having my hands on the wheel might keep me from killing him. "You were doing me a favor," I say, shaking my head in disbelief. *Where do I find these people?*

"Exactly."

"Helping me out." *How did I not see this coming? He's the king of bullshit. Why would I have trusted him in the first place? I'm an idiot.*

222

"No need to thank me." Dav's looking out his window. Maybe he's contemplating whether to open the door, jump, and roll the next time I'm forced to slow down. He probably won't though: Dav's the one with a gun. There's no reason for him to be afraid of me.

A few minutes later I turn left on Junction, and we're almost there. The truck glides to a stop at the curb directly across the street from our destination. "Did it ever occur to you," I'm choosing my words carefully, trying not to say anything that I might regret later, "that perhaps the truth of this matter would eventually come to light?" *How could it not?* I'm thinking.

"Eventually," Davros admits. "I mean, sooner or later, I suppose."

"And what *precisely* did you think would occur when that day arrived?"

"We'd grab lunch," he grins.

CHAPTER TWENTY-FIVE

Elephant Hunting

Eighteen. That's how many people show up for a free meal at Paul's Lunch. Eighteen total, including six individuals that I barely know (the choir from the New Radiance Church of Eternal Life, plus Pastor June and Pastor Al), Davros and myself, Booker and Andy, Pete and Mark from the building, plus Katie and Leo from the third floor. That makes fourteen. We also break bread with Watchdog Mike and what might be his dealer, although that's being judgmental on my part and the strung-out chick with the unwashed hair might just as easily be his girlfriend or his sister. Maybe they're just friends. Maybe she's his life coach. We're up to sixteen. Last but not least, I find myself blessed with the presence of both Susan and Janey. I was hoping she wouldn't come (Janey, I mean), hoping she'd have more important things to do back at her restaurant or building a real estate empire throughout Midtown (I still prefer "The Corridor"), but sometimes you get what you get. I get lunch with the ex. It is not romantic, not in the least. Although, in all fairness, dining with Janey sitting there keeps me from killing Davros: she'd make a stellar witness for the prosecution.

After lunch things become a quick study in attrition. The choir is first to leave, not that I blame them: they have little in common with those that personally *knew* Betty. They've done their service and then some. The way I see it, a good lunch is the least we could provide. By "we" I mean Davros, whose generous offer to pay for lunch I now intend to fully exploit. Throughout the meal I heartily urged the others to eat their limit and then some. Mike and his dealer/girlfriend/sister/life coach are next out the door. Pete and Mark abandon me with some mention of an afternoon appointment. I can't blame any of them: I'd desert, too, if I thought I could get away with it. Andy leaves soon thereafter, under the pretense that there are some building repairs that require his attention. I've never noticed such urgency in our property manager prior to today.

Before long I find myself at a long table composed of two smaller tables pushed together, sitting with Pastors June and Al, Davros, Susan and Janey. The small talk has faded to a minimum and we're each looking for any excuse to go home. For some reason it reminds me of Russian Roulette: six bullets, but only five will survive. Who will be the last man standing? I'm praying it doesn't come down to Janey and myself.

"Thank you for the luncheon. It was really generous of you to invite us. Al and I have to get back to the church, get ready for this evening's service," Pastor June offers as she rises to leave.

"I can't thank you enough," I tell her. "I'll call you next week when things are settled. Again, thanks. It was a perfect send-off. You hit the right notes."

"No problem. Al and I are here to serve, whenever the opportunity arises. Any chance we'll see you at the church tomorrow morning?"

Davros snorts, like the iced tea that he's drinking might have bubbled up through his sinus cavity. I shoot him a dirty look, which fails to go undetected by June, Al, Susan, or Janey. I'm still pissed about the lie, and he's not helping any with his snorting. The only person who doesn't take note of my glare is the man for whom it was intended. Dav sucks another four ounces of tea through his straw like we're on a beachfront vacation at an all-inclusive resort in Cozumel. The man is oblivious.

"Church?" The pastor reminds me.

"Probably not," I tell June, and she nods her head in understanding.

"Maybe next week, then," she says with confidence.

"I'll see you next week, without a doubt," I confirm. "Probably not on Sunday."

"I know you will." Trusting, not challenging. "Call us if you need anything," she tells me. "God bless you all," June says to the rest of the group, and with that she and her husband quietly walk out the door. They're good people, June and Al. Now we are four, or five if you count the elephant in the room. I'm sipping a cup of coffee, black. Janey and Susan are both drinking herbal tea. Davros is still pulling sweet tea through his straw and acting like he's next to leave: it's obvious that he's getting restless. His feet scuffle on the floor, he shifts position in his seat, he asks for the check. I'm not about to let him off that easily.

"Why don't you have another glass of tea, Dav?" I beg. He's not much by way of comfort, but he's all I've got. Plus, I still owe him one.

"I need to get going. I've got a store to run."

"Stick around, we could use the company." I'm trying to threaten him with my eyes, but either he doesn't take the hint or he doesn't care. The man is nearly impossible to intimidate.

"No, I need to get back to the shop. I just hired a new clerk and he's clueless."

"Skinny guy in the black jeans?"

"New guy, a student," he answers.

New guy can't be that clueless if you let him run the store by himself on a Saturday, I'm thinking. "The kid can last a little while longer. Come on, just a little bit longer. Twenty minutes and I'll be ready to go myself." I don't want Dav to leave me cornered by my past. Janey hasn't said a word since the two pastors left. She hasn't said a word directly to me or to Davros since the moment we arrived. The others, sure, she carried on quiet conversations with a few of them. I can only guess what those conversations were about. Certainly not about Betty, the recently departed who she never knew. I spotted Janey chatting briefly with Watchdog Mike, which surprised me, and with two members of the choir that she seemed to recognize from I-don't-know-where. Mostly she sat back quietly and observed. Anyone else would think that Janey was being polite: it's just as likely that she was accumulating ammunition. The woman has always been a collector of knowledge. Though it is true that Susan might provide a buffer should things turn ugly between us, I doubt she'd be much of one. Picking sides in a street fight, I'd take Janey every time.

"Ten minutes, then I've got to go," Davros concedes.

"Thanks." I mean it. I'm grateful. I could use the immoral support.

A waitress is clearing the last of the dishes from our table, leaving us with just our beverage cups. The clock reads ten-after-two. We're the only customers remaining in the doldrums of the afternoon. There's a discussion I don't want to have, but eventually I'll have to face my demons and embrace the inevitable. Davros has dropped two hundred-dollar bills on the table and told the waitress to keep the change. This seems like as good a time as any to go elephant hunting.

"Jane," I start, "could I have a moment with you, alone?"

"There is nothing you can say to me that you can't say in front of my daughter." She stares at me with that smug self-assuredness I've come to expect. The woman is all bravado. On the other hand, I realize, it might just be her defense mechanisms kicking in. It might just be my impression. This could be a facade, her way of appearing brave when she's really quaking inside. Somehow I doubt it.

"Two minutes, *please?"* I implore. *Why am I begging to have this conversation? It isn't something I relish.*

She does concede, though not verbally. Jane reluctantly slides her chair out from under the table and walks over toward the door, well out of earshot from Dav and Susan. I follow her. "Two minutes," her first and final offer, take it or leave it. I decide I'll take it.

I describe as quickly and concisely as I can that Davros had led me to believe that Susan was my daughter. I explain how *that* was the reason I'd agreed to rent a place around the corner from Susan, and that was a large part of the reason I'd accepted a job with Booker that starts on Monday morning. I wanted to do the right thing, however late this might seem. I tell Janey that I wasn't trying to come between her and her daughter, I was just trying to get to know Susan while the opportunity was still present. I sure as heck haven't been trying to date the kid. I bring up the ride back from the crematorium, and how Dav had finally come clean that he'd led me to believe that Susan was my daughter, made the whole thing up in order to get me to stick around. I apologize again for the confusion and brace for the slap across the face that anyone could see is headed my way. Only it isn't.

Instead Janey laughs. She laughs the kind of deep, bent-over belly laugh that I haven't heard in years, haven't heard in decades, really. Certainly not from her. Her entire body wrenches with laughter. She's laughing so hard that tears come to her eyes. She's gasping for breath, and she grabs the edge of the nearest table for support while she laughs some more. It's infectious, and I, too, find myself losing it. I'm laughing and crying with her, although I'm not entirely sure why. Davros and Susan don't know what to make of us. They sit shocked on the far side of the room. Janey and I, we're both damn near hysterical.

"And you thought that *you* were her father?" she manages to choke out the words between fits of laughter.

At this I sober up a bit. The way she says '*you*' makes it seem like a wholly asinine concept, that Susan couldn't *possibly* be mine. It hurts. *Why should it be that amusing?* I'm wondering. She comes across as insulting. Very insulting, when you get right down to it. I'm still laughing with her, but I'm not quite sure why. "I thought it was possible, yeah," I tell her, regaining my composure. "Why wouldn't it be?"

"Too funny!" She's settling down a bit, catching her breath, but still clearly enjoying the moment.

Now my feelings are hurt. "Why *too* funny? It's not completely preposterous, right? I'm remembering that one time, down on the island, we were parked near the lagoon. Right before we broke up. It is possible."

She dries her eyes with the clean corner of a tablecloth. "Trust me; it's *not* possible, not remotely. I should know." She pauses, laughter dying down. "Your timing is off, or at least your *memory* is off. Her father is most certainly her father. We were just forced to rush our wedding a bit. Check your dates, Einstein."

I can't say I'm not offended. I'd been enjoying my role as a new dad come late to the party. Suddenly I feel as if I'm nineteen and getting dumped all over again. "Davros said it *is* possible," I whine, and realize how hollow that rings. I know this is not true. I can *feel* it's not true. Davros was playing me, one more in a long string of stories he's spun. His stories, his "truths" such that they are, often have veiled motives. I took the bait and I got hooked. He's even admitting as much. *Janey,* of all people, should know.

"Oh, you poor, misguided boy," she responds, taking my face between her palms and kissing me atop my forehead. "You make me smile." Those are words I never again expected to hear come from her lips. Just as quickly, she returns to the table, leaving me to wonder what has just happened.

CHAPTER TWENTY-SIX

After the Fire

At first I was angry. I was angry at Davros for lying to me, angry at myself for being so gullible, and angry at Janey for, well, *for just being Janey.* Anger is a missile without aim, random and often fatal. That didn't last long, however. Staying mad is just too damn taxing, for one thing. It takes an enormous amount of energy, and there are only so many hours in a day, so many days in a week, so many weeks in a lifetime. After a few days of smoldering rage, Davros took me aside and told me to cut that shit out. My friend was correct; I wasn't doing anyone any good. I moved on to sulking, and that, too, quickly wore thin. At some point, a man has to decide to commit to something. This seemed a strange idea for me to embrace, but I hugged it for all it was worth.

The hard part for me was deciding *what* exactly I was committing *to,* because the primary thing that had been holding me here, that false belief that Susan was my daughter, no longer existed. So what was the point, really? If she's not my daughter, why subject myself to living in a city that's teetering on the brink? My initial reaction was that I should leave. Left, right, up, down: events in this place could easily go in any direction. Is Detroit a city on the rebound, or is it a dead fish slowly circling the drain? Chaos or renaissance: either way I'd be dragged along for the ride. Who would sign up for that? Was this *home*, or just another stop on the gypsy wagon train? All of these were questions in need of answers.

What nailed it down for me was Bruce: the dog seemed happy, and I reasoned that it wouldn't be fair for me to further upend his world with another sudden change. That sounds silly, I'm sure. It's certainly indicative of one man's odd sense of morality. I'm reshaping my life, putting down roots and choosing a job and an apartment based largely on the perceived satisfaction level of a dog. Not even *my* dog, mind you, but *a* dog, an *inherited* dog, at that. While Bruce might technically belong to me, we're still finding our way, slowly building trust. We depend on each other in a loosely-structured way. He needs food and walks, I need companionship. The relationship works. We hang out. More often than not I forego his given name and call him "Roomie," because that's what this feels like. Maybe I'm fooling myself here: it's possible that Bruce is just my excuse. Life is, after all, but a process.

Mary was not happy when I handed over the relics. This was at Patrick's house, where we all got together for Thanksgiving dinner. The holiday had snuck up on me. It felt more than a little strange, sitting down for a "family" meal for the first time in decades. It didn't help that our parents were no longer around to witness the spectacle, or that two of my four siblings (God rest their souls) were long dead. Most of these people that remain in my life, my brother, his lovely wife and kids, my sister and her husband, they are real to me, but only real in the sense that the Internal Revenue Service is "real"; I've come to expect certain things from them, come to expect certain actions and reactions. I know that they will always be there waiting if I'm desperate, but in the end, there isn't a whole lot of warmth to our relationships. Perhaps that will come with time.

I told my sister about the Hound of Ulster and about what I'd learned from the good folks at the university. At first she accused me of a bait-and-switch, thinking maybe I'd absconded with our ancestors' precious artifacts and handed her a five-and-ten store imitation. Then she accused me of making the entire story up (I don't think I could if I tried). Fortunately the Associate Dean of Linguistic Something or Other had provided a letter explaining his authentication process and some additional supporting documentation. Mary didn't really read through it all, merely skimming the surface. The papers looked official enough. They came on university letterhead. They used big words. In the end that was enough for her, and she reluctantly accepted my "gift" of her inheritance.

Everyone present could see the disappointment on her face, the realization that a bunch of ancient dog bones were not going to win her any worldwide accolades or great fortune. There would be no giant payday, no audience with the newly elected pope in her near future. You would think that this might have given me some satisfaction, some vindication for all the abuse she'd heaped on me over the years, but it didn't. I should have taken joy in Mary's sorrow. Instead I felt sorry for her, though I didn't exactly share her loss: I'd not expected much from the beginning. Mary did perk up noticeably when I suggested that she donate the lot to the University of Galway, which would provide her with a modest tax deduction and, more importantly, a certificate of contribution that she could frame and hang prominently somewhere in her home. It was a peace offering on my part, a consolation prize. Her friends would be impressed, and bragging rights were what she was really after in the first place. I even promised to help her arrange the transaction.

Dinner was excellent We shared a large turkey with oyster stuffing, mashed potatoes with gravy, and cranberries (the real things, not that red gelatinous crap that people pour from a can and slice with a fork). There was fresh corn and green bean casserole, sweet potato casserole with marshmallow topping, another casserole that I never did identify, pecan pie and pumpkin pie and apple pie and more dishes than any one man could possibly sample. I ate too much, and then I ate some more. Everyone was stuffed. Patrick's wife was more than gracious, because the whole thing had to be a little odd for her, too, having all these estranged in-laws at her house for a traditional family feast: we might as well have been aliens. She was "putting on the dog," as we Irish like to say; bringing out the good china and making a fancy show of things. She did this solely because she loves my brother, though I'm sure that there are worse motivations for kindness. Patrick's kids called me "Uncle," even though I'm a stranger to them, and that honorary has begun to grow on me. A little. We'll see if it sticks.

I didn't stay late because I had to work the next morning. That's what happens when you're the new guy, the low man on the totem pole. You get to hold down the fort on the day after Thanksgiving, not that I'm complaining. Any steady job is a good job in this town, and who am I to look a gift horse in the mouth? The pay is decent if unspectacular, and I'll be eligible for medical benefits within sixty days. I'm better off than ninety-percent of this town: everything in life is relative. I owe him one, my "roomie."

Booker was off on a long weekend somewhere. I hadn't been seeing as much of him, not lately, anyway. Once Betty's funeral was taken care of I'd only needed about five minutes to realize that her apartment was infinitely nicer and moderately larger than the one that Booker and I were sharing. I took over Betty's place, making that long move down the hall. I let Booker keep my joint, which was great by him. I even let him keep the couch and lamp. He kept most of my meager possessions. It was easier than moving everything, and his stuff had recently gone up in flames. He needed a break. I miss him. We see each other at work (rarely), and we pass each other in the hall (every few days or so). We even get together and have a drink every week or so, when it works into both of our schedules. Still, it's not quite the same. Who'd have guessed that I'd mourn the loss of my accidental roommate? And yet I do.

From what I've learned, he seems to have broken things off with Giselle, or (more likely) she grew tired of him and broke things off. Booker's not saying which and I haven't pressed him. Why rub salt in fresh wounds? This should come as a surprise to no one. That relationship, at least from Booker's end of things, was far too good to be true. He was out of his league and then some. I spoke with him briefly right before he left for the holiday, and I get the impression there's a new woman in his world. He recovers quickly. As long as her name isn't "Monica," he'll come out okay.

The month of December disappeared in the blink of an eye.

There was the little issue of Betty's worldly possessions and what I should do with them. By law they are rightfully mine. Her will, hastily written and informal though it was, left everything to me. Still, it didn't seem right. I hardly knew her. Once the first of the month rolled around, my landlord cut me a check for Betty's security deposit and applied my own security deposit to the new digs. I immediately called Lisa Wojtkowiak of New Britain, Connecticut, and explained the situation. There was nothing of Betty's that Lisa wanted, no artifact or family memento of significance to her. Her aunt was an anomaly, a vestige from some past that she'd never personally known. I could relate. She told me to do "whatever I thought was fair." I could keep it all, she really didn't mind. One week later I mailed Lisa a check for the security deposit, plus one thousand dollars of my own money for Betty's old but serviceable household furnishings, along with a small glass snow-globe I'd found on the windowsill in Betty's kitchen. I thought Lisa might like it. The souvenir sphere contained a miniature brass hammer on a mound of fake granite, adorned with a brass plate lauding "New Britain, the Hardware City!" Like Betty herself, it was a remnant from the past. It wasn't much, but seemed to be situated in the general vicinity of "fair."

You would think it's strange, living amongst the belongings of my recently departed neighbor. I've made a few changes, taken down the floral curtains and put up mini blinds, that sort of thing. On the whole, though, I've kept the place the same. If I had an interior decorator, he would tell me that the place is done wholly in the style of early-70's neo-traditional Polish lady. There's an adage that all things come back into fashion sooner or later, but I suspect the world of fashion will skip directly over that particular era. That's all well and good. There's something oddly comforting about living amidst her stuff, like a warm embrace from a former aunt. Bruce is happy. And hell, I've even got my own television now.

Davros and I are talking again. I haven't yet killed him. I've thought about it, Lord knows I've thought about it (frequently, as a matter of fact). But whenever I get truly riled up, get that pure Irish anger boiling through my veins, I realize that the deception was my own fault. What did I expect? Davros is Davros, and he always has been. Can a leopard change his spots? I suppose so, if he uses enough bleach, but the odds would suggest otherwise. I've always known who my friend is, and I've always accepted him for *what* he is. He is a bullshitter. I knew what he was capable of, and I didn't come into this city a doe-eyed virgin. I walked right into the punch. It's almost always a question of balance in any relationship, whether the good outweighs the bad. While Davros outdid himself with this particular lie, the scales still tip in his favor. He and I have stuck by one another this long and we'll continue to do so, 'til death do us part, for better or for worse and all that rot. We remain friends.

Yesterday, in fact, I bought a leather jacket from him, a late Christmas present to myself. It's a sturdy one. I've decided that if I'm going to live in a northern city, I'll need a warm coat. Thick black steer hide, American made; it's the kind of jacket most stores can no longer afford to sell. People would rather purchase something imported, something that looks good but costs next to nothing. You get what you pay for. The price on the tag read six-hundred dollars, but Davros gave me a "special" deal at five-fifty. "For you, my friend...." You know how that goes. I still think his price was steep, but I've learned not to argue with a leopard.

My relationship with Susan has cooled. Not soured, not exactly, but it has certainly cooled. After that little scene at the restaurant, we each retreated to our own worlds, Janey, Susan, Davros and I. Work, school, family. I still bump into Susan occasionally, going out the door or coming in from wherever it is that she has been. We chat, in that friendly-neighbor sort of way. But once we'd discovered that she wasn't *ever* my daughter, the whole thing seemed to have lost any sense of urgency. It came apart at the seams. I became just another guy who lives on the floor below her, a guy who'd once dated her mom. Chalk one up for the "creepy" factor in that equation. So our drifting apart, our going our natural ways, it seems inevitable. Not that we can't remain friends, because people make all sorts of acquaintances from all age groups and all walks of life. Still, when you get right down to it, what do we have in common? She's just a kid.

I've been to City Fusion exactly once since the funeral. Janey was not in (it was her day off) and I have no complaint. It would have done me no good to see her. I think our relationship might have defrosted with that conversation at Paul's Lunch, defrosted just the tiniest bit, but I can't imagine that it will ever grow much beyond cordial. There have been too many years passed between now and then, too many important moments creating chasms from when our lives once touched. There's no time for crossing oceans, no time for chasing ghosts. She has a husband, children, a business to run. She volunteers (how does she have time to volunteer?). I'm sure she has her own group of friends and interests, stretching wide and deep; at least, wider and deeper than the fragmented pieces which I'm trying to place together.

One thing that has taken me by surprise is my newly evolving friendship with Watchdog Mike. I'd thought he was just some stoner dude that liked to sit on the front stoop and watch the world pass him by. Instead, it turns out that he's a deep thinker with extremely passionate views on a variety of subjects. Some of them are off the wall, but most are fairly solid. He holds a master's degree from MIT, if you can believe it. Mike works, he even built his own consulting business that has some fairly major clients. He's a member of the prestigious downtown athletic club, although I've yet to see him work out. He contributes generously to the soup kitchen and a couple of other charities. Mike is not currently dating but he could probably have his pick of women throughout the city if he ever decided that it was where he wished to apply his efforts. Watchdog makes over six figures and I can't for the life of me figure out why he's still living here, standing sentinel over Selden Avenue.

The Watchdog and I share a love of chess, although "love" should not be confused with competence on my part. Every Thursday night he comes up to my place and beats the daylights out of me on the game board. Mike has routed me every time excepting one, and I'm fairly certain that he let me win that one. Though my game is getting better, I enjoy our conversation and the single malt scotch more than the chess itself.

Superintendent Andy finally got Booker's old place glued back together. He cleared out the smoke damage, hung new drywall where once there was plaster and installed entirely new kitchen cabinets and appliances. Booker is staying put in my old apartment. He says he's had enough change for one year and remains content where he is. A new tenant is moving into his old place next door to me: a single woman, it would appear, about my age or maybe a little younger. She doesn't technically take possession until tomorrow (which would be the first, the beginning of a new month and the start of a new year), but Andy let this new renter move some of her furnishings in over the Christmas break. I saw the woman carrying a laundry basket full of miscellanea up the stairs as I was heading out the door yesterday. I waved and said "hello." She smiled and said "hello back at you." I've got to admit, she is kind of cute. I'm slowly beginning to let myself think beyond today, beyond tomorrow even. I'm learning to accept that this world might as yet contain some undefined possibilities and surprises. I am learning to hope without expectation. Maybe that's the true definition of faith.

"You're coming to the party tonight, right?" Leo is on his way up to the third floor, passing me as I make my way down the stairs. He and his wife are having a little get-together for friends and neighbors, and I've said I'd come.

"Absolutely," I tell him. "Wouldn't miss it for the world. What time?" I'm quickly becoming absorbed into the fabric of this building, this community, this city.

"Nine or so. Whatever works for you."

I look at my watch and it's four o'clock now. "Is there anything I can bring?"

"No, we've got it covered. Kate's made tons of food and we've got drinks, both hard and soft. There should be about fifteen of us. Susan will be there, Booker and his girlfriend. I even invited that new chick that's moving in next door to you. Bring your wit and your smile," he adds (almost as an afterthought), and bounds up the stairs. Here is yet another unexpected friend I've found amongst the strays and the loosely tethered, the wandering and the solitary, the eccentric and the artistic, the unclaimed persons and the flotsam of this fine city.

Nine p.m. is only a few hours away, but first there are two things that I need to accomplish.

CHAPTER TWENTY-SEVEN

From the Ashes

"I didn't expect to see you today," Pastor June tells me.

I hadn't said anything about stopping by, but during the course of the day I'd decided that I needed to see her anyhow. "I have a small favor to ask."

"Ask and ye shall receive. Within reason," she adds as a caveat. "Don't you have somewhere better to be on New Year's Eve?" The woman knows me.

"Not likely," I respond. I'm being honest. "Someplace to be, but not better. I'm supposed to show up at a party later, but there's no place better than here. Friends in the building invited me," I explain.

"Well, good for you! Have a seat. I'm not going to bother to ask if you're sticking around for this evening's service. Don't feel bad, I know you won't. Let me get Al: he's in the back. He'll be glad to see you."

Who'd have guessed? I remember the faces of most of the clergy I've known, dating back to a childhood at Our Lady of Sorrows. A clear majority of those pastoral folk were *rarely* glad to see me. I was the kid with too many questions, the one who thought he had "all the answers," the child that was, and I quote here from Father Murphy and at least two of his successors, "too big for his britches." I was beyond salvation, a reclamation project without hope. I raised questions that the priests were unable or unwilling to answer, and the fact that I raised those questions only inflamed their frustrations. Who needs some little-shit heathen monkeying up the works? In the eyes of the clergy (such that I knew them) I was the hand of Satan, come to tempt and pollute the minds of my peers. They were *never* happy to see me. The fact that a pastor, *any* pastor, is 'glad to see me' comes as a bit of a shock. "He doesn't need to come out front if he's busy," I suggest shyly.

"Nonsense. He's your friend. Al will be excited to see you," and she disappears into the back room.

There's that 'f-word' again: "*friend*." I get up and pace the room, because that is what I do best. *Friends:* I seem to be accumulating them faster than ever, and I have no idea how. It certainly isn't intentional. This is what 'growing roots' means, I suppose. We're all gaining appendages, desired or not. I walk from one end of the small room to the other, making my way through the tiny chapel and back four times before June reappears with her husband by her side.

"My friend," Al exclaims, and shakes my hand firmly with that bear paw grip of his. "Always good to see you."

I'm still not a believer; I don't attend services or anything like that. But I have, however, gotten into the habit of stopping by every now and then, just to shoot the breeze with the pastors. They don't seem to mind. "Thanks, Al."

"June said you need a favor?" His voice trails up at the end, a question rather than a statement.

"If it's not too much trouble."

"Anything we can do," he tells me.

"I've got Betty's ashes with me." I don't need to explain further.

"You need a blessing?"

"Please. Whatever you'd normally say in these circumstances."

"No problem," Al tells me.

"Do you want us to come with you?" The offer is from June.

"Thanks, but this is something I'd like to take care of on my own. I just thought you might, you know, say a prayer. For *her*," I add, making it clear by my tone that this is for Betty's benefit, not mine. I'm not sure how much truth there is to that: Betty's dead, after all. Who is a funeral really for? Betty's ticket is punched. If there's someone upstairs tallying up the scorecards, there's not much I can say or do that will change the numbers in her favor. Funerals are for the survivors. "Just a small prayer."

237

"Uh-huh," she nods knowingly.

"Absolutely," they add in unison.

Thus we all hold hands, forming a small circle while four pounds of burned and pulverized calcium phosphate and a handful of minor minerals (Betty's cremains) rest in a stainless urn between us. Pastor June recites a short prayer, something from Psalms if I remember correctly. Then Pastor Al says a few words from his heart. One more brief prayer from June. Another quick word from Al. I keep my head down and my tongue silent. Five minutes in all. Once the prayers and the preaching are done we all say "amen" and we let go.

"It's no trouble at all if you want us to ride along," June tells me. "Just to keep you company, if nothing else."

"No, but thanks. I appreciate it, I really do. But for whatever reason, Betty chose me to handle things, and I guess this is between the two of us. That probably doesn't make a ton of sense. We didn't know each other all that well. It's just the way it is."

"Oh, it makes plenty of sense," June tells me as she squeezes my forearm and her eyes smile. "She saw something in you. You're a good man." There is another thing I'd never heard from Father Murphy and his ilk.

"Don't let the wind catch you," Al warns. "I've seen it happen before. Hard to keep from bursting out laughing when that shit happens, even for a preacher," and he and I share a smile at the thought. For certain, it would be one of those things that's downright hysterical when it happens to *other* people. It would make a great video, watching some poor schmuck catch a face full of ashes.

"Thank you again for what you did here," June tells me as we walk out the door. "There's no way we could have afforded that. It's beautiful."

"It was the least I could do."

I've got the heavy urn in my hand. I look up to the sky as we cross the threshold to the sidewalk outside, making sure that the new sign is still there, confirming that the scrappers haven't gotten to it yet. Two steps back toward the curb and I can better admire the handiwork. *Jesus Died For Our Sins*, it

FROM THE ASHES

reads, red neon tubing over a black Art Deco cross. I took some liberties with the design. I was working from memory, and that's always a recipe for disaster. It's close enough, anyway, and the message is the same, or *nearly* the same. It is probably improved over the original, although I'll leave that up to the theologians of this city. I changed the original *'Your Sins'* to *'Our Sins.'* Jesus Died For *Our* Sins. A little less finger pointing and a little more collective accountability, if you will. June and Al think it looks great, and I agree. Below that, in the same style and the same red neon tubing running nearly the width of the storefront, *New Radiance Church of Life Eternal.*

Don't ask what that piece set me back. Davros has a friend in the sign business who cut me a "special deal" because it was for such a good cause. There is a significant chance that this "special deal" means the "friend" applied an additional surcharge, one "sins of association with Davros" fee. If so, it was still worth it. There's quality workmanship here. I'll be making payments for the next twelve months, and that's okay. Al and June helped me in my hour of need: this seems like such a small token in comparison, a gift to the keepers of the flame.

We say our goodbyes, and then I'm driving up Jefferson Avenue, fifteen minutes to the island. The radio is tuned to a local all-news station. Most of the chatter (while not necessarily uplifting) is benign. A new mayor for the new year. There've been no more fires at Heidelberg in the last month. No arrests have been made, no suspects identified. Officials are unsure if this signifies an end to the arsons or merely a temporary lull in the action. Either way, I'll take it (small victories, remember). The city itself (now deep into bankruptcy proceedings and under the auspices of an Emergency Financial Manager) has cleared the path for construction of a new hockey arena and entertainment district, not far from where I live. A handful of citizens will be displaced, and a few businessmen have complained that the government has run roughshod over them in order to acquire the land. The powers-that-be claim that this is a small price to pay for progress. We'll see. This isn't a new song and dance, what passes for "progress."

The DIA may have to sell off artwork to pay for underfunded pensions. A new bridge to Canada is slowly gaining approval, the end to one more long-term pissing match. More construction news: Wayne County has finally admitted that building a new jail in the core of downtown wasn't such a swift idea after all. There have been a hundred-and-fifty million dollars or so already flushed down the drain, and the County is desperately trying to sell

239

the half-built property for whatever they can get, probably less than half of that. Corruption or incompetence: who can tell? Certainly not this guy. There were no murders reported in the city over the past twenty-four hours, no accidents on the Lodge Freeway at this time. A polar vortex (this is a new one to me, as best as I can figure it would be a cyclone of cold air) will be sweeping into the Midwest shortly after the first of the year. Temperatures will drop to fifteen or twenty below zero. That includes Detroit, the radio man reminds me, in case I've somehow forgotten what part of the country I'm in. Again, what passes for good news is so often relative.

This final bit catches my ear because, up until now, I've been totally unaware of a planned takeover: the City of Detroit has agreed to lease Belle Isle to the State of Michigan for a term of thirty years. At first the radio man makes it sound nefarious. I'm almost to the bridge when I learn that the island will be managed as a State Park. People are angry that they will have to pay to get onto the island, and citizens are fearful that the state government has plans to, and I quote, "steal the city's jewels." Apparently those angry and fearful people haven't visited lately. Not that the island isn't a jewel, but it has needed polishing for a very long time. Heaven knows that the status quo isn't working. A push of the radio's power button cuts the man off, and I revel in the silence.

I swing a right onto the MacArthur Bridge and make my way to The Strand, that main road straddling the perimeter of Belle Isle, Hog Island, Île Aux Cochons. There are no other cars on the island. The Strand itself is covered by a thick dusting of fresh white powder, and the tire tracks behind me are the only tracks visible. Dirty gray piles of sludge line the curb where the snowplow has been on some previous day. A harsh New Year's wind whips more fine snow from the jagged ice lining the river's edge and pushes it along the shoreline. There's an even heftier coating of white on the unpaved areas, six or eight inches in most places and more where the wind has forced it into sculpted marshmallow drifts. It's a lonely place. The winter sun ebbs low in the sky and filters through a milky haze as another snow squall works its way up from the Gulf of Mexico. Three to four inches of new snow are expected before midnight.

The truck putters along methodically. A slick road surface and the buffeting forces of the wind howling up the river channel force me to keep my speed low. The truck shakes. I pass the Scott Fountain, the Dossin Great Lakes Museum, the now-frozen model yacht basin. A mangy coyote strolls up from the river's edge and stops dead center in the road, forcing me to gently tap on the brakes. He stares with curiosity at the approaching truck, one or two seconds, not much longer, before losing interest and leisurely continuing on his way. He has no fear. The coyote disappears amidst a brush pile on the lagoon side of the road. I remember how the original settlers thought this place to be a safe haven for their livestock and poultry. How times have changed. Nature reclaims everything, it turns out. It might take a while, in some instances two centuries or more, but eventually nature will always win. We are fools to believe otherwise.

When I finally get to the South Fishing Pier it's deserted, and for a moment I'm worried that I won't find a place to park. The shoulders of the road have yet to be plowed. Crusted ice mounds along the edge of The Strand, making it unlikely that I'd be able to pull off to the side safely, let alone manage to crawl back onto the pavement later. I look around, but there's no parking lot. Sure, the Coast Guard station up ahead has one, but that's fenced in and closed to the public. The rest of us (in this case, the rest of us is *me*) are on our own. Park at your own risk. Better yet, don't park at all.

I sit at idle for a few minutes, mulling over the options before deciding to take my chances. The truck can sit right where it is, blocking the eastbound lane. What kind of an idiot would be driving here on New Year's Eve, anyhow? The risk is slim, and should some fool come along in the next fifteen, twenty minutes, he can just pull around my truck. *Or hit it*, I muse. I prefer the former. Hitting it would be bad. I shut the motor off, get out, and lock the door just in case.

Cremains are heavier than you'd think. Not as heavy as hauling a body, obviously, but there's something substantial about the package they hand you at the crematorium. It reminded me of my days at the hot dog stand, the weight of Betty the equivalent of one order of friend, to go. Throw in a stainless urn and I'm packing about ten pounds of death and metal in my hands. The snow out here is knee deep, as no one has thought to shovel the pier. Who would, and what would be their incentive? The Detroit River is three-quarters frozen, and I can think of few good reasons to be here: even the freighters have given up on her. I make my way out to the end of the structure, and already any exposed skin is burnt raw by the cold and the wind. It's a painstaking journey through the deep drifts. The new leather coat, my good, expensive new leather coat, is adequate, but barely so.

Shivers run down my spine. Gloves and a hat would have been a good idea, too: my face and ears are showing early signs of frost nip.

In the distance looms the city's horizon, the Renaissance Center (or whatever alias those glass towers are now known by), and the Ambassador Bridge arcing across the river. Monoliths of ice rise up from the water. The first granules of airborne sleet, precursors of a storm yet to come, lick my face. I need to hustle or I'll freeze out here. This is about Betty: I didn't know the woman well, but every life deserves respect, closure. A proper burial is the least I can do. Still, it seems odd that mere months earlier I hadn't even known her, and in fact had no intention of settling in my old home town. One kind stranger guided my decision to stay. She did this in no small part through her unexpected death and irrational bequeathal of Bruce. Did the old woman know what she was doing? At times it seems that way. Betty, Davros, Booker, Watchdog Mike, and of course my "roomie" Bruce; each and every one of them part of the reason I'm here. We're gradually building a community of former strays and misfits, a menagerie of once unclaimed persons. It feels good to belong.

The wind seems stronger at the far edge of the pier. For a moment I fumble with the urn's lid. I struggle to pull it free, but it won't budge. Applying more force gets me nowhere. My hands sting with the cold. I curse and strain some more before realizing that the lid screws off. *Like a thermos, genius.* I should say a prayer. I know that I should say a prayer, that it wouldn't be right to pitch Betty to the skies without some acknowledgement, some small words ushering her toward whatever lies beyond. There's one problem: I don't know that there is a God, a deity, whatever you want to call it. I don't know that there is life after life. How should I pray? I no longer speak the language. I did, once, but it's been far too long. And yet I've learned to hedge my bets. I'm reminded of something I'd learned back in college.

Pascal's Wager, it is called: the idea that either God exists, or He does not. Given the possibility that God *could* exist, at least in theory, and given the alleged costs and benefits associated with paying homage to such a deity, the rational person should live and act as though someone is listening and watching. The smart money says double down on God. That's his theory, anyhow. If God *doesn't* exist, and yet you act as though He does, what have you truly lost? Time and effort. Trivial outlays compared to that potential eternal jackpot. There are some flaws with this argument, some presuppositions that I disagree with strongly, but New Year's Eve on the North Fishing Pier is neither the time nor the place for a philosophical debate. Betty deserves a prayer, and she's going to get one.

It's cold, damn cold. My cheeks, my ears and my nose burn from the cold. The air temperature has dropped to around ten degrees Fahrenheit, down about five degrees since I first got here and dropping still. Snow is rolling in sideways and hard from the west. I stand exposed. Crystalline beads pelt painfully against every inch of my unprotected skin. A prayer for Betty is a small risk to take, a cheap lotto ticket for her soul, my opportunity to get off this pier and into a warm truck: it's all of these things, and yet I cannot seem to find the words.

"Hail Mary," I start, and realize how stupid that sounds. I'm not even praying to the Big Man himself, but rather pleading with middle management. If Betty's getting a prayer, I should at least take it straight to the source. God or nothing. I switch tactics, "Our Father, who art in heaven..." before stopping myself again. The words ring hollow. Shouldn't a prayer of this magnitude contain some honest conversation, or at the very least an honest monologue? Recitation of something I learned in grade school will hardly fit the bill. If a man can't tell God what's on his mind *here*, standing alone on a pier with nothing but a jar of ashes in one hand and a raging snowstorm in his face, when *might* he be honest? The sun is fading fast, inching below the horizon and quietly becoming smothered by the encroaching squall.

I need to make a decision, and I need to make one now. In another ten minutes I won't be able to see my own arm. My mind scrambles desperately for the right words: if only I could send out a search party. I watch a piece of cardboard blowing past, part of a refrigerator box tumbling down the frozen surface of the water. The cardboard rips back and forth with the wind, left then right, drifting with what appears to be no clear purpose or direction. Yet upon closer inspection I realize that this is not true at all: two minutes of undivided attention reveals that the box is actually following the river's channel. The box has no mind of its own; it follows a destiny beyond its control. I can only wonder if that's true for each of us: is life driven by fate or free will? It's now that inspiration strikes.

"May the road rise up to meet you," I begin, a thread from my poor Irish upbringing suddenly finding purchase on a wanderer's tongue (I know, Betty was Polish, but I also know that Betty wouldn't mind. My sister would be proud: it turns out that I *did* learn something as a child, despite her very best efforts). The urn is raised overhead, elevated high into the tempest as I continue: "May the wind be always at your back. May the sun shine warm upon your face." I'm fighting with the storm, the zephyr buffeting my arms from side to side. Betty deserves a prayer, and by God, she's getting one hell of a prayer. A world-class prayer. Her prayer will be heard, shouted loud and clear into the encroaching fray. My voice lets it be known that this is not so much a plea as a dare, a challenge for Someone to show his cards, time for the all-powerful and all-forgiving to step up to the plate and come through on a promise. Betty might not have been a religious woman, but I believe she was a good woman. She brought people together, held up her end of the bargain. Is there someone listening on the other end? Was the promise of salvation real? Louder I roar: "May the rains fall soft upon your fields, and until we meet again, may the Lord hold you in the palm of His hand." It turns out that I can roll with the best of them, the Father Murphys and Father O'Brians and Father Feenys of this world. I've no idea if it did any good.

I prepare to pour Betty into the gale, let her drift upstream, waft off towards Windsor and whatever lies beyond. Let *her* be that piece of cardboard in the wind. Let Betty follow the hidden path beneath the surface. The thermos is tilted, angled at forty-five degrees and slowly dropping, my eyes filling with ice and stray tears. A tempest is howling across the pier and that funeral cylinder almost passes the tipping point when one last thought comes to mind, a variation on an old toast I'd often rehearsed at the true altars of my forefathers, the local pub. "Tis better to live above with the saints we love," I pronounce solemnly, "than to live below with the saints we know. Drink up, my friend." I flip the urn and let her fly.

AUTHOR'S NOTES

Unclaimed Persons marks a wide diversion from the my two previous novels, *Sparrow River* and *The Hatchery*. This is the story of a world in transition. More importantly, this is the story of a soul in transition. It's about change, and about how one person absorbs and reacts to that change. It's not meant to be an encyclopedic history of the city itself, nor is it a catalogue of all that needs repair. Smatterings of these issues are raised in the novel, those which were necessary to capture the mood of a place in time. The decline (some would say abandonment) of Detroit and the reasons for that decline are well documented and debated elsewhere, and any good bookstore can help you if you wish to do the research. I expect that in a few years the city as it is described here, for better or for worse, will no longer exist. The metamorphosis has already begun. Let us hope for "better."

This is a work of fiction. I do not have a long-forgotten daughter, nor do I live in the Cass Corridor. I do not (at least to my knowledge) have any ex-girlfriends that wish I would move to another town (although you shouldn't bet against it). I do, on the other hand, have an incredible wife (one who tolerates my overactive imagination) and a love of storytelling.

Some of the places mentioned in this novel are real. Some are amalgams, combinations of things that I've seen in different places. Most of the key places in the story are pure fabrications. They are "types," if you will. Should you recognize something that seems familiar, I've done my job well.

As always, this book represents a combination of love and sweat. Much of that sweat comes from others, key people without whom the entire project would fall apart. First and foremost I wish to credit my editorial staff (Paula and Deanna), who fix what needs fixing. I owe much to my first readers, who caught a few of my quirks and helped me to write a better story. I'm also indebted to one particular person in Graphic Arts and Internet Technologies; Teemu, you should ask for more money. Thanks as always to Charles, who leads me to the obvious. Last but not least I'd like to thank the V.P. of Marketing and Distribution (Cindy), who helps bring home the bacon.

About the Author

Kevin J Garrity was born in 1964 in the city of Detroit, the eighth of nine children. Throughout his high school and college years, he performed as a musician of some local renown. After studies at Wayne State University he moved to Traverse City, Seattle, back to Detroit, Chicago, and then to Grayling. Kevin currently resides in southeastern Michigan with his wife Deanna and two sons. He's an avid hunter and fisherman. His critically acclaimed Walt Pitowski mysteries (*Sparrow River* and *The Hatchery)* reflect a great love of the outdoors and all things wild.

In this, his third novel, he breaks new ground. The landscape of *Unclaimed Persons* draws liberally from images (real and imagined) of a Detroit that no longer exists, all during a time of great turmoil and change. The novel's primary character, a prodigal son with a sketchy past, attempts to make sense of those changes and what they might mean within the context of his own nomadic life.